Selena's Song

BOOK ONE OF THE SIREN SERIES

By Alisa K. Michaels

❧ A YA Novel ❧

This is a work of fiction. Names, characters, businesses, places, events, locales, and incidents are either the products of the author's imagination or used in a fictitious manner. Any resemblance to actual persons, living or dead, or actual events or places is purely coincidental.

ISBN: 978-1-959715-03-0

Library of Congress Control Number: 2022949300

Published by Belen Books, LLC
7901 4th St. N, Ste 300, St. Petersburg, FL. 33702 USA
Belenbookspublishing.com

Edited by Paul L. Hight & Beverly R. Waalewyn
Cover by Belen Media Group

Printed in the United States of America

For Nennie

"Music expresses that which cannot be put into words and that which cannot remain silent."

–Victor Hugo

Selena's Song

BOOK ONE OF THE SIREN SERIES

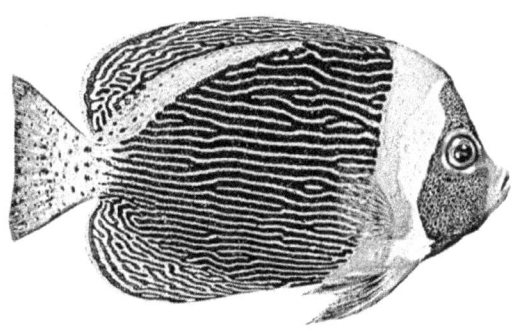

PREFACE

Before I ever saw the sea, I longed for it…ached for it…like a mother's ache to hold her newborn baby in her arms. It is this ache that guides me now through a world where I feel alone, disconnected, alienated. Then I hear it, through the din of human voices I hear the sweet, melodious tune that calls to my soul; promising to set my spirit free, allowing my heart to love once more. It is a call so intense…so primal…that I want to cover my ears in order to shield them from the longing that it creates within me.

"Don't be afraid," she sings.

"I am not afraid," I reply defiantly.

"Follow me…into the sea…in the ocean's waves we'll play."

Cautiously, I step into the water; shattering its glass-like surface. A shrill cry of a passing seagull wakes me from my trance, causing panic to replace courage. Part of me wants to turn around and sprint back to the safety of the beach, but the rebel in me takes hold, urging me onward.

Looking around, I realize I am alone; a crazy teenager wading out toward the open sea in some sort of suicidal daze, but before I can change my mind, the undertow grabs hold of my legs and begins to pull me out towards the sapphire depths. Fear engulfs me, washing over my body like a wave washes upon the shore. Unable to fight against its wishes, I close my eyes and allow my body to sink below the surface. The watery embrace devours me as I feel my lungs fill with salty liquid, but somehow, I am not afraid. I am at peace for the first time in months.

Slowly, almost seductively, this liquid world begins to fade as I drift into the abyss, but in the distance, swimming toward me, is a shape. As it gets closer, I realize it is a woman with long, curly red locks; locks as crimson as the sun's unapologetic first light ushering in each new day, and as she gets closer, I can see her beautiful aquamarine eyes…

CHAPTER ONE

Dark menacing clouds are coming in from the east, covering the sky like a smothering blanket. The horizon, once painted a soft Caribbean blue, is now matted with sullen shades of gray. Squawking seagulls, which not long before were diving for dinner a few yards offshore, have now flown back toward the shoreline and the protection it offers. While I, on the other hand, find it almost impossible to move.

In the distance, I hear that song again: soft, alluring, intriguing. It beckons my entire being and I fight with every ounce of strength against its will. I fight so hard that my legs begin to shake causing me to fall onto the rocky ground.

"Come to me my dearest child…. follow me into the sea," it calls again. *"Don't be afraid…Don't be afraid…we are always near…"*

Suddenly, my body jerks awake, lingering memories sending chills down my spine. Still lost in the dream, I lie on the bed almost catatonic. Exhausted eyes filled with confusion try desperately to focus on a thin stream of moonlight, which illuminates a spot on the freshly painted Tiffany blue walls of my new bedroom. Eerily, the song from my dream still lingers; weighing on my soul like a heavy, woolen fabric.

"We are always near," it speaks again, this time from just outside the bedroom window.

Another chill climbs my spinal column as my mind acknowledges the sweat drenched nightshirt against my fevered skin. It clings to me like a piece of *Saran Wrap* clings to a metal bowl.

"Great!" I mumble cynically, quickly stripping off the sopping clothes; still trying to separate reality from the dream that came before.

To my relief, I become accustom to the surrounding darkness as I lay on my back naked; too lazy to hunt through boxes still scattered throughout the space. Two weeks without a good night's sleep would aggravate anyone. My heartbeat accelerates as exhaustion morphs into annoyance. *Damn it!* Not only is this reoccurring nightmare interrupting my rest, but it keeps intruding on my make-out sessions with Dean Winchester from the television series *Supernatural.*

How unfortunate is that?

Glancing over at the digital clock on the bedside table, I realize it is only half-past midnight. Another unpleasant thought begins to plague my mind: school starts tomorrow, and puffy eyes will not make a good first impression.

I will probably look like a raccoon in the morning.

"Terrific!" I mutter throwing still drenched arms over my head.

Just terrific!

As I lay counting the divots on the ceiling, several gusts of moist Caribbean air rushes inside through the long row of open louvered windows, disturbing the sheer white curtains adorning either side; the movement tries to provoke my attention. Rhythmically, the material begins to sway under its invisible fingers like a cobra under the spell of a snake charmer's flute.

Stealthily, the unseen entity filters through those gaps across the room, skimming the rumpled bed where I lay contemplating the swiftly approaching dawn. On padded paws, the breeze creeps over the black and white floral comforter beneath my nude form, tracing each clammy curve. Modesty quickly whispers chastisement in my ear and I reach for my robe; shielding myself from the glare of each visiting moonbeam.

Obviously, time moves slowly when the weight of the world is on your shoulders, or so it seems. Two weeks ago, my family and I moved from Ohio to Isla Flora, a small island in the Caribbean thirty miles off the coast of the United States Virgin Islands. For anyone else, I suppose, living on a beautiful tropical island would be a dream come true, but for me it is hell.

I loved my life in Ohio. I loved my friends. This place offers nothing.

Like a distant memory, I recall my sixteenth birthday celebrated a month early in order to be with my friends. The extravagant gala was meant to cheer me up, but instead it just made me sadder…more lost. I do not think anything can console me now. Lately, the only thing that gives me any type of solace is listening to the sea.

Fortunately, I manage to fall back asleep around two, but awaken at sunrise much like a reverse vampire if such a thing really existed. Sitting up in bed, I listen for sounds of my family. Other than the pounding of the waves against the rocks hundreds of feet below, the house is still; holding its breath, awaiting the new day as well as new possibilities.

With sluggish fingers, I manage to tie my robe which still cocoons my bare form, grab my towel, and make my way to the bathroom my brother and I share. The lock on the bathroom door is broken, so I push a heavy box of toiletries against it to hold it shut. As I disrobe, I notice purplish bruises between my toes and fingers. Bruises in my experience, are usually found on shins, legs, arms, and other more obvious appendages, but never in these areas. Curiously, I examine them, trying to figure out how they got there and wondering what kind of acrobatics could have caused me to hurt myself in such strange places. Then I touch the skin on the sides of my neck which also feels sore, as if afflicted with a mild sunburn.

This is crazy!

I have been stuck indoors since we got to this forsaken island, so the possibility of getting sunburned is non-existent; however, the sensitivity of my skin tells another story. Puzzled, and still groggy from the night's sleeplessness, I turn the shower on to its coldest setting and step under the massaging stream. Cool water comforts me as it hits my flesh; regrettably, the song still lingers, haunting my thoughts with its unnerving melody.

"Don't be afraid," I sing quietly, remembering the tune. "Come with me into the sea…come with me…don't be afraid…"

A rapid knocking at the door startles me.

"Lena! I have to use the bathroom!" My little brother, Ando, yells from outside of the door. "I'm gonna tell Mommy you won't get out of the shower!"

With an annoyed jerk of the shower knob, I turn off the water, wrap my towel around me, and rush past him as he leans against the wall outside the now wide-open door.

"Tattletale," I tease with a half-hearted chuckle.

"Mommy!" he shouts at the top of his lungs. "Lena called me a tattletale!"

Back in my room, I rummage through the boxes for underwear and socks. It only takes a few minutes to get dressed now that I am forced to wear these prison garbs. Whoever invented school uniforms should be cow-tied, covered in honey and left sitting on a red ant mound.

Yeah! That's the ticket! Honey covered and munched on by ravenous ants that have not eaten for weeks!

I chuckle maniacally as a picture forms in my mind.

"Selena!" my mother calls from downstairs. "You'll be late for your first day of school. *Hurry!*"

"I'll be down in a minute!" I yell back, taking one last overly critical glance in the mirror.

A sixteen-year-old face returns my disappointment. Actually, my features are not too bad, if I do say so myself; high cheekbones, round face, flawless honey-colored complexion, and full lips, all framed by shoulder-length, blue-black tendril-like locks. All inherited from my mother's side of the family or so I am told.

The only thing I would change is my eyes. Sometimes they unnerve me. They are an intense shade of aquamarine, so bright they almost glow. It also does not help that they are encompassed by thick, ebony lashes that seem fabricated. Truthfully, my lashes are so thick it looks as though I went to a beauty salon and got permanent mascara and eye-liner applied. Teenage angst aside, I would look even better if I did not have to wear such a hideous school uniform.

Another bout of self-doubt hits me as I look at my ensemble one more time. All joking aside, it really does suck: boring blue plaid knee-length skirt, institutional white polo shirt with the school emblem sewn on, plain white ankle-socks and unembellished black sneakers. At least in Columbus I attended public school where I got to wear regular clothes. Now, I am stuck wearing this costume. Riled up, I stick my tongue out at my reflection. When I can no longer stand the sight of it, I finally pull my hair into a low ponytail and add a thin, luminous layer of cherry-flavored lip gloss to my naturally pink lips.

Quickly, I scan the room for my backpack; unadorned walls, generic plastic mini-blinds, and a wobbly outdated ceiling fan add to my growing hostility. The only familiar element in the room is the contemporary light oak bedroom set bought in Columbus. My parents let me pick it out several years ago when my brother was born. They did not want me to feel jealous because Ando was now the center of attention, so they transformed my bedroom into a spectacular underwater seascape complete with a hand-painted mural of frolicking dolphins, mermaids, and tropical fish. It was my own private marine sanctuary filled with memories of slumber parties and indoor adventures during the cold season which seemed to last most of the year. Mom says she is going to recreate it in this room as soon as things are more settled. So far, the only thing she has been able to do is paint the walls.

After a brief search, I spot my backpack hiding beneath a pile of dirty laundry. Relieved, I fish it out from under the slightly smelly stack, throw it over one shoulder, and take one last look in the full-length mirror. In true Selena fashion, I nervously practice my smiles; full smile, half smile, quarter smile, then just a grin.

"Hi, I'm Selena Thermopolis." I clear my throat and try again. "Hi! I'm Selena." Next, I try a deeper inflection: "I'm Selena…Selena Thermopolis."

I frown.

This is hopeless.

Against my will, my vision blurs from the onslaught of tears. Angrily, I wipe them away as I head downstairs to face my mother. I hope she does not want to discuss how great this place is, again. I do not think I can handle that right now. However, truth be told, if I was not so upset with my parents, I would admit that the house is absolutely breathtaking.

Mom's father, Grandpa Theodore, was a Greek architect who designed and built the house in the 1950s. It was constructed into the side of a cliff overlooking the Caribbean Sea, so if one looks over the balcony railing, they would see the jagged teeth-like rocks being assaulted by the waves.

The interior of the two-story, three bedroom and two-bathroom house has lofty cathedral ceilings with skylights that allow the sky to become the ceiling. Solid, hand-carved cypress crown moldings and doors complement every room, and there is a large extended balcony that runs around the entire back of the house, which provides a spectacular view of the Caribbean.

Facing out towards the sea is a wall of floor to ceiling windows that can be opened to enjoy the salt-perfumed air. At night, I like to open them and listen to the melodic tunes the waves play as they beat against the rocky shore. There are even steps carved into the cliff leading down to the rocks below; however, Ando and I are forbidden to go down there.

As a bonus, this house is only a ten-minute walk to Coconut Palm Beach; one of the most stunning beaches on the planet. We have not been able to check it out yet even though we arrived on the island two weeks ago. Mom promises to take me and my brother soon. The idea of living on a rock out in the middle of the ocean was not high on my priority list, but there is only so much protest a jobless teen can do without risking grounding or loss of allowance.

"Why do I have to go to a private Catholic school?" I ask Mom again as I slowly descend the staircase.

"Because it's the best school on the island," she replies matter-of-factly, adjusting the sleeves on her pajamas. "Not only will you have a top-notch education, but it has a diverse student population."

I roll my eyes in silent protest before stating, "I know...I know...you've mentioned that several times before."

Ignoring my snarky retort, Mom continues, "Also, Isla Flora is one of the most beautiful islands in the world," she beams, "and the weather is amazing. The coldest it ever gets here is seventy-five degrees.

"I had such fun here when I was growing up," she graces me with a perfect smile. "I know you and Ando will too. You are going to love it here, Selena. I can feel it. Please give it a chance."

"I don't know if it's beautiful or not," I reply as my mother shoos an extra-large Daddy-Longlegs spider out of the house. "We've been trapped inside for days unpacking boxes, tackling softball-sized dust bunnies, and other undesirable creatures."

Glancing around the room, I see another spider building a web above the cabinet nearest the window indifferent to our close vicinity.

"Think of it as an adventure," she adds with a smile. "Soon this place will be spick-and-span. It will be incredible and filled with natural lighting and—"

"Okay... okay," I pout, cutting her off. "I get it. It's wonderful."

"Selena—"

11

"What about David?" I interject. "While we're doing all this '*stuff*', he's been attending boring orientation meetings for his new job so we hardly ever see him. I thought the whole point of moving here was to be a closer family."

"We will be, I promise," she answers indifferently as she continues looking around the unorganized room for something.

My stepfather, Dr. David Marquez, is the new lead marine biologist at an underwater sea-aquarium called Ocean World. That is why we moved here. Jobs in David's field are hard to come by these days and the economy in Columbus was not the best, so we packed up our stuff and moved to my maternal grandparents' house.

"It's a great opportunity," Mom keeps saying. I think she is trying to convince herself as well.

"I suppose," I huff.

Mom ignores me, continuing to mumble to herself, stopping only to say, "Could you please go and sit with your brother at the dining table?"

"Sure."

Entering the formal dining room, I see my little brother Fernando (Ando for short), sitting at the table shoveling spoonfuls of cereal into his mouth. He smiles when he sees me.

"I saved you some Crackleberry Crisps, Lena."

Knowing that he is at the *'girl hating'* stage, I lean over and kiss his cheek; causing him to make a disgusted face as he wipes away the sticky lip gloss imprint I leave behind.

"Eww!" he squeals. "That's gross!"

Pleased with myself, I plop down on the chair across from him.

"Are you ready for school?" I ask already knowing the answer.

Ando points to the blue and red *Spiderman* backpack on the floor beside him.

"Daddy helped me pack my backpack last night. It's waterproof," he gloats. "He got it at the dive store at Ocean World."

"David is home?" I probe with surprise, and at his leisure, Ando takes a sip of orange juice before answering.

"Daddy came home late last night. He brought presents!"

Overjoyed, he shows me the new shark's tooth pendent on his necklace. Another broad smile reveals a space where a tooth should be. Wanting to keep him in a good mood, I decide not to bother him about it.

From behind, Mom clears her throat to get our attention.

"I hear talking when I should be hearing crunching," she reminds, carrying a medium-sized box marked *'Bathroom Stuff,'* upstairs.

Finding no appetite, I still feel compelled to pour some cereal into a bowl with a little milk and a few slices of banana. The first bite is always the worst...exceedingly sweet. Ando, on the other hand, raises the bowl to his lips and drains the last of the strawberry-flavored milk. Right on cue, Mom reappears in the doorway, dressed in blue jeans, black t-shirt, white sneakers, and her favorite silver necklace adorned with an antique charm given to her by her mother. One day, she says, it will be mine to pass on to my daughter.

"You look like you're both ready for school," Mom says with a toothy smile.

Sullenly, I roll my eyes at her.

"I look like a dork," I mumble to the bowl.

"Maybe—" she examines me from head to toe, "—but a lovely dork nonetheless," she adds playfully, making me grin.

"I've actually started dreaming about this ridiculous uniform. I dream about burning it...the flames would be awe-inspiring...like the sky right before dawn."

A mischievous smile creeps across my lips. I would actually do it if I thought I could get away with it. Now, she laughs loudly, and with much enthusiasm, causing Ando to join in. Soon, we are all having a good time.

Everyone says that I am the spitting image of my mother, all except for the small scar on her right cheek, the fifteen pounds she gained during her pregnancy with Ando and a four-inch height discrepancy in her favor. I am not disappointed. I am happy being 5'5". Mom, on the other hand, wears flats so she does not look like *The Jolly Green Giant*.

Back in the day, Mom worked as a model before she met my stepfather. These days, she works as a freelance photographer and artist for advertising agencies, magazines, and other various print mediums. It sounds like a glamorous job, but in reality, it is a lot of work setting up all of that equipment. Believe me, I have been drafted several times to help out at 'shoots', and after a few hours in the heat—or dealing with weight-challenged models arguing over the last rice cake—it is no day at the spa.

"We have to leave in ten minutes or we'll be late," Mom informs. "Have you seen your dad yet?"

"Nope," I continue eating my now partially soggy cereal.

"You can't avoid him forever," she reminds.

With a wave of a hand, she motions towards the study.

"Ando," she prompts. "Go brush your teeth again. They're pink."

He giggles. The sound is adorable.

"Okay!"

Obediently, he runs upstairs, leaving Mom and me in uncomfortable silence.

"The last time we spoke, we had a horrible argument," I recap, casting my gaze to my sneakers. "I said some really awful things."

Mom sits down across from me and takes my hands in hers. The faint scent of tuna and *Cool Water* perfume tickles my nose. It is a scent I find comforting and disturbing at the same time.

"What did you say that was so horrible?" she sighs, bracing for the worst.

Overflowing with guilt, I squeeze her hands tightly.

"I reminded him that he is not my real father and…" I pause, feeling sick to my stomach.

Slowly, my mother presses her fingertips to her temples as if trying to control an oncoming headache.

"And what else?" Mom probes, her mind racing.

"I-I told him that I didn't want him to adopt me," I sheepishly confess.

At my admission, my mother's face turns ghastly white and her eyes appear to darken to a menacing shade of blue.

"Selena!" she gasps. "How could you say that to him? You know we've already started the process. The move just prolonged it for a bit."

"Dead or not, I still have a father." I shrug, not knowing what else to do to vindicate my rude behavior.

"You know that your real father was in the military and was killed in action before you were born," she reminds shakily. "David is your stepfather and a damn good one at that!"

Consumed with guilt, I gaze into my cereal bowl at the now completely soggy pink flakes.

"Tell me, what possessed you to be so cruel?" she insists.

"I was mad that we had to leave Columbus for his stupid job," I whisper, too upset to look at her.

"Oh, Selena," she moans, pinching the bridge of her nose.

"Why couldn't we stay in Ohio?" I ask, avoiding her sad expression.

"We need to be near the water," she answers brusquely, not masking her irritation with me.

"There's lots of water in Ohio," I counter.

"The company Dad worked for went out of business, remember? Plus, it's way too cold there." She pushes an escaped curl behind my ear. "Dad worked hard for this position. He got this job over forty other applicants. Do you know how lucky we are to be here?"

"No one asked me if I wanted to move," I stress, knowing she is right.

With stiff legs, she stands, pushes the chair neatly under the table, and walks back to the kitchen in silence. The clanking of dishes being loaded into the dishwasher is her only reply. Taking a deep, fortifying breath, I hesitantly trod toward the study to find David, holding my breath all the way.

♪♪♪

The door is slightly ajar and I peek in. Inside, my stepfather unpacks marine mammal anatomy textbooks from one of the many boxes cluttering the dark hardwood floor; the timeworn floorboards creak, causing him to look up.

"Hey!" he addresses me with a twinkle in his eyes. "Come on in. Help your old man with these heavy volumes."

I enter slowly, becoming even more uncomfortable than before. Honestly, I have always thought my stepdad was amazing. Brilliant and handsome, a lethal combination of dark brown hair speckled with grey at the temples, smiling hazel eyes, and Latin good looks; perfect in every way except for the onset of pre-shaven stubbles. Side stepping the elephant in the room, David hands me one of the boxes then goes back to stacking his leather-bound treasures.

"I'm sorry," I whisper truthfully.

Puzzled, he looks up, then clarity sets in.

"Don't worry about it," he reassures. "We both said things we didn't mean."

"I do consider you my father, blood-related or not," I fiddle with a piece of tape precariously hanging off one side of the box. "You're the only person I'd want as my father. Sometimes, I wish you were my real dad."

David stops unpacking and sits cross-legged on the newly polished hardwood floor. He motions for me to sit beside him, and without hesitation, I push the box out of the way, taking my place to his left on the extremely hard surface.

"You've been my daughter since you were four years old," he beams. "And for twelve years, I have tried to be the best husband, father, and provider that I can possibly be.

"Usually, everyone gets to voice their opinions about decisions that will impact the family, but sometimes your mom and I have to make the tough choices; especially when it comes to finances.

"I know you loved it in Ohio, but this is the perfect place for us right now."

Knowing that it is true, my eyes well and a lone tear rolls down my cheek.

"I know but—"

"I'm making great money now," he continues, ignoring my interruption. "And your mother is happier than she's been in a long time.

"We inherited this house from your grandparents, so we no longer have a mortgage payment.

"Ando is easy to please, as long as he's got his Spiderman stuff and Saturday morning cartoons. You're the only one I don't know how to satisfy."

"I'm happy," I respond, forcing a smile. "See?"

"Thanks for lying to me," he smirks, giving me a wink.

Feeling much lighter, I stand up as gracefully as possible, which, for me, is a feat in itself. I have been known to trip over air and run into invisible walls. Most times, my bruises have bruises. Mom says I will grow out of it, but I have my doubts.

"Here, this is for you." David reaches into his front shirt pocket and pulls out a small black jewelry box. "I saw it in the gift store window at work and immediately thought of you."

Elated, my hands begin to shake with excitement. Zealously, I take it from him, trying not to drop it, then slowly ease off the lid to reveal the surprise inside. Nestled in the soft pad of cotton is a single, perfectly formed, black pearl pendent. With a deafening squeal, I lunge at my stepfather, almost knocking him off balance, encircling him in a tight bear hug.

"I guess this means you like it?" he gasps for breath.

"I love it!" I exclaim, immediately unhooking my gold necklace then sliding the pearl onto its new resting place.

Thoughtfully, David helps me with the clasp.

"Thank you!"

I hug him again, this time more gently.

"Have an open mind about this place," David pleads. "When I first left my hometown of Anchorage up in Alaska for Ohio, I hated it there. I mean *really* hated being there.

"I missed the sound of the ocean outside my apartment window and the crying of the seagulls as they dove into the water. I even missed the smell of fish guts as the fishermen cleaned their daily catch."

"Wow!" I playfully mock, making a revolted expression. "Missing the smell of fish guts is pretty pathetic."

Unoffended, David lightheartedly nudges my arm.

"Not too long after, I met your mother in Columbus and a whole new life opened up for me," he reveals with a grin. "So give this place a chance, okay? Do it for me. I really want you to like it here."

"I'll try," I promise. "I really will."

CHAPTER TWO

The hallways of St. Peter and Paul's Catholic School are empty except for the occasional misplaced student. Mom, Ando, and I reach the front office a few minutes after the first bell rings to start the school day. A short, chubby, gray-haired East-Indian lady welcomes us as we enter.

"Good morning," she greets, giving us a beautiful smile. "How can I help you this morning?"

"I'm Mrs. Marina Marquez and this is my daughter Selena and my son, Fernando. Sorry we're a little late. Today is their first day at this school. Sister Anne told us to pickup Selena's schedule—"

"Oh! Yes, Selena Thermopolis and Fernando Marquez!" the woman interjects.

Politely, she shakes Mom's hand, then Ando's, and finally mine.

"It's very nice to meet you both," she beams. "I'm Mrs. Velu, the school secretary."

More at ease, our mother releases a held breath.

"It's nice to meet you," Mom finally relaxes completely. "I'm sorry we're late," she restates, quickly glancing around the cozily furnished office area.

"Don't worry, Mrs. Marquez," the older woman smiles warmly as she comforts. "We'll take good care of them."

Then she touches my mother's shoulder reassuringly.

"Just a reminder, school finishes at two-thirty," Mrs. Velu continues. "They'll see you then."

Still off of her game, Mom hugs us, then leaves without turning back.

Without warning, Ando grabs my hand. Sensing his apprehension, Mrs. Velu smiles at him like he is the only person in the room.

"Fernando—"

"He likes to be called Ando," I gently correct.

The school secretary smiles again.

"Of course, Ando; I will take you to your new classroom and introduce you to your teacher, Mrs. Anderson."

Mrs. Velu walks around the counter and offers Ando her hand, which he accepts.

"Mrs. Anderson is the best kindergarten teacher at the school. She's very sweet, and pretty too," she adds.

With that said, Ando smiles and releases my hand.

"Bye, Lena!" he waves, excited to get to class.

"And for you, young lady," Mrs. Velu says in that same pleasant voice. "We have a guide for you today. He went to the principal's office to get your schedule, but he'll be back in a few minutes."

Wasting no more time, she and Ando walk toward the door and suddenly, I dread being left alone in the quiet space.

"Just wait here," she implores over her shoulder. "If you have any problems or concerns, don't hesitate to come see me."

"Thank you," I reply as they disappear behind the door.

♪♪♪

A few minutes pass as I amuse myself reading the poems one of the first-grade classes has on display. A couple of poems are well written, clear, and concise, with excellent handwriting… for first graders.

"They have talent, don't they?" a pleasant male voice startles me.

A little too quickly, I turn to answer, almost tripping over my intertwined feet and come face to face with the most gorgeous male specimen I have ever seen. The clean-cut teen, just shy of six feet tall, with straight black hair, green eyes, and a thin, athletic build, stands before me with a huge grin.

Good gracious! My mind goes blank as it ogles the exquisite teenager standing before me. *He is absolutely tasty!*

Dumbfounded, I try to speak, but for some reason I cannot form any words. Instead, I stand like a moron with my mouth open, staring like a deer in headlights.

"This one is my favorite," he says, pointing to the poem about a goat.

"Yes, the goat poem is… v-very…very…g-good," I stutter, realizing my cheeks are on fire.

Shyly, he smiles, showing two rows of perfect teeth, with dimples you could crawl into and lose yourself completely.

"I'm Andrew… Andrew Barnett," he formally introduces himself.

"I'm…"

Good grief! I can't remember my own name!

"Selena Thermopolis, right?" he confirms as he hands me a neatly folded piece of paper.

"That's right!" I babble. It is coming back to me now. "I'm Selena Thermopolis, new student, idiot extraordinaire."

"Selena…that's a very uncommon name," he pacifies, amused by my obvious nervousness,

"Uh huh," I mumble.

"Is that a family name?" he expresses good-naturedly.

"My mom has always been obsessed with Greek mythology," I reply, slightly embarrassed. "She named me after their moon goddess."

Thoughtfully, he comforts, "I think it's a great name, unlike boring Andrew."

His comment makes me blush against my will.

"I think Andrew is a nice name too," I reply with a genuine smile.

This time he blushes.

"Follow me," he entreats, leading me out of the office into the now crowded hallway.

Curiously, I unfold the paper, revealing my six-class daily schedule.

"I have Calculus first period," I announce over the din.

"I know," he answers confidently. "We have the same schedule except for P. E. Boys and girls are separated for that class. I don't know why. Seems kinda ridiculous to me."

Expertly, he maneuvers me through the stream of oncoming students with a firm grip on my elbow.

"You must be really smart to have this kind of class load."

"I am," I poke matter-of-factly, smiling. This time, he laughs a wholehearted laugh that makes me laugh too.

"Our first subject is in room two-twelve: Calculus with Mrs. Brown. Try not to sit in the front row," Andrew warns. "She spits when she speaks."

A minute or two of bobbing and weaving through the congested hallways, we arrive at a rather unassuming gray door with a hand-painted sign that reads:

Mrs. Beverly Brown - Math Department

Very gallantly, Andrew holds the door open for me, then quickly finds a seat in the back of the room. Everyone is staring at me. I immediately feel the heat rise into my face once again. Mrs. Brown is standing at the blackboard, ready to begin today's lesson. She is a pleasant looking middle-aged woman with thick, black horned-rimmed glasses and a beauty mark above her right eye. She smiles warmly and motions for me to approach.

"You must be Selena Thermopolis." The teacher shakes my hand and then addresses the room. "Students, I'd like you to welcome Selena to our class. Please, help her with whatever she needs."

"I'd like to help her out!" an unusually muscular teenager shouts. "Help her out of those clothes!"

A wave of laughter follows. If I was not embarrassed before, I am definitely embarrassed now.

"Richard!" annoyance fills Mrs. Brown's voice. "One more word and you will be picking up trash in the cafeteria for a week!"

From the nearby cabinet, she hands me a Calculus text book, a class syllabus, and a supply list needed for the remainder of the school year.

"Thank you," I whisper shyly, wanting very badly to leave the front of the classroom.

"If you need any help at all getting settled, just let me know," Mrs. Brown tries to put me at ease; unfortunately, I feel even more nervous now than I had last night.

"Yeah, baby!" Richard flirts again. "Let me know if there is *anything* I can do to make you feel welcomed, too!"

Mrs. Brown rolls her eyes.

"See me after class, Richard," she says calmly.

"Ahh, man," he groans, causing the other students to snicker.

"Thank you, Mrs. Brown," I whisper, even quieter than before. "I will."

"Selena, you can take that seat behind Nicole Wong."

A hand rises out of the sea of blue and white uniforms; it reminds me of a mast on a ship. As I approach the hand, I see the sixteen-year-old that it belongs to. The young woman reminds me of R&B singer Alicia Keys with her mocha complexion, long black hair, high-chiseled cheekbones, and full lips, but with almond-shaped, doe-brown, Asian eyes.

"Hi," Nicole greets cordially.

"Hi," I reply, breathing a sigh of relief. "Thank goodness I don't have to sit near that muscle-bound Neanderthal."

I glance over at Richard, who is making disgusting gestures with his pelvis.

Nicole shakes her head.

"Richard can be a little hard to take, but he's harmless," she reassures. "I've known him since the first grade. He'll grow on you."

Somehow, I don't find that comforting.

Nicole snickers then adds, "Look on the bright side. At least you didn't have to sit in the front row next to Mrs. Brown."

"Yeah...I was told it's like being in the splash zone at Ocean World."

Unable to stop ourselves, we both giggle.

♪♪♪

To my surprise, class goes by quickly and before I know it, I am walking with Andrew *'The Hunk'* Barnett to second period. On our way there, he informs me about the safe food items in the cafeteria, where to find the clean restrooms, and the best places to sit during pep-rallies.

"The burgers, fries, and chicken fingers are always good," he states assuredly. "The beef stroganoff tastes like salmon and has been known to send some of the younger kids to the clinic. Oh and never, *ever*, under any circumstances, eat the tuna surprise, well unless you like diarrhea. Mr. Simms—the new guidance counselor—ate it last week and had to be taken to the hospital to get his stomach pumped."

I grimace.

"No beef stroganoff or tuna surprise; *check!*"

"The cleanest bathrooms are in the library," he continues. "Sister Mary Camilla—the school librarian—is a germophobe, so the janitor cleans those restrooms at least three times a day. Also, the ones on the fifth floor across from the detention room are always spotless. They make the students who get in trouble clean those as part of their punishment.

"I feel sorry for Richard!" he surmises with a devilish laugh. "You know: the class clown in Calculus who was giving you a hard time?"

"Yeah! That guy," my face begins to feel warm again. "I'm glad he'll be scrubbing toilets."

"Don't blame him for having good taste," my guide compliments, looking straight ahead.

Not knowing how to respond, I pretend not to have heard his last comment.

"You were telling me about the restrooms?"

"Yes, the ones in the church are really clean too," he educates.

"Clean bathrooms are located in the library, fifth floor across from detention, and the church; check!"

Andrew nods and gives a thumbs-up.

"Finally, pep-rallies are fun, but you have to know where to sit."

"Enlighten me, oh wise one," I bow with false reverence.

"Always sit at the top or middle sections of the bleachers—"

"Why?" I ask with furrowed brows.

"Because the teaching staff usually pulls students sitting on the bottom rows of the bleachers to participate in school pride games." Andrew suddenly leans in close, so close I can smell the heady fragrance of his unique scent, and whispers, "Believe me, that's worse than detention."

Holy moly! He smells incredible!

It is a combination of soap, some type of body spray, and natural male muskiness.

"Never sit at the bottom section of the bleachers; *check!*"

I salute playfully causing him to grin, and he concludes with: "If you remember all of that, you truly are a genius."

"Thanks for the four-one-one." I look down at my shoes nervously.

"No problem," he winks. "That's my job."

I am just about to thank him for his much-needed information when we hear someone calling.

"Andrew!" A cute blonde waves him over.

My guide looks over at her and nods in acknowledgement, his cheeks turning a pastel pink.

Clearing his throat, he informs, "The Chorus room is the third door on the left. There's a picture of a music staff on the door. You can't miss it!"

The handsome teen runs toward the girl with his perfectly quaffed hair staying in place as he moves among the stream of students. Shockingly, he looks just as good at leaving as he does coming.

♪♪♪

I find the Chorus room without any difficulty. Inside, Miss Khan sits at a large oak desk writing in her daily planner. The twenty-something year old woman looks more like an East-Indian movie star rather than a music teacher. Her onyx hair cascades past her waist, each lock as black as a raven's wings, so dark in fact they appear deep purple, and her medium complexion is smooth and without a single blemish.

Wearing a silly grin, I stand next to her desk eagerly awaiting instructions, but instead of looking up, she continues frantically scribbling on the page. Tired of standing, I clear my throat to get her attention and at last she looks up and smiles, revealing two rows of impeccable, bright-white teeth.

"Please forgive me," the teacher apologizes, then stands to greet me properly. "I'm Miss Khan, so nice to have you in my class. Chorus is usually the subject no one takes unless all of the other electives are full."

Surprisingly, her honesty is appreciated. I smile, clasping my hands together to keep from *Eeee*-ing.

"Have you ever had Chorus before?"

"No, but I've always wanted to sing," I admit, shaking my head. "I figure this way, it will count toward keeping my GPA high, so no, this is my first time."

"I'm sure you'll do well," she grins, putting me more at ease.

Miss Khan is about to introduce me to the class, when Andrew and the blonde girl enter the room.

"Mr. Barnett, Miss Jacobs, you are both tardy and will receive detentions the next time you are late. Do I make myself clear?"

"Sorry, Miss Khan," Andrew apologizes. "It won't happen again."

His female companion just makes a face and goes to her seat in the soprano section.

Without missing a beat, Miss Khan hands me a piece of sheet music.

"This is the current music selection we're going to be learning," she informs. "It is an aria by new age composer, *Yanni*. I'll make a copy of last week's introduction lecture so you will be caught up."

"That would be great." I exhale a held breath.

"I'm sorry, Selena," the music teacher adds. "I forgot to ask, but what range are you?"

"What is *'range'*?" I whisper, puzzled by the question.

Miss Khan smiles before answering.

"Soprano, which is a higher range or alto, which is lower."

All eyes are on me, including Andrew's.

"I have no idea which one I am," I answer timidly.

"Say your name for me," she requests.

Respectfully, I do as she wishes, and the room goes quiet; so quiet that I can hear the ceiling tiles settling.

Miss Khan seems a little bewildered, but she smiles and asks again, "Could you say it once more?"

"Selena Thermopolis," I repeat, a little bit louder.

"Well, this is a first," she states, sounding a little surprised. "I think you can sing both soprano and alto and maybe even bass."

"Is that unusual?" I ask, not understanding the weight of the comment.

"Yes, it is. I think I'm a little jealous," she jokes.

"Don't be jealous," I giggle. "You haven't heard me sing yet."

The teacher laughs as she looks around, trying to figure out where to put me.

"We are short on sopranos, so I'll put you in that section."

Quickly, I find an empty seat next to the girl Andrew was talking to before class.

Andrew waves to me from his seat in the bass section; his green eyes look even brighter under the fluorescent lights. Sheepishly, I wave back, surprised by the attention.

"I'm Selena," I offer my hand to the girl, who looks at me with her nose turned up in disgust, then turns to face the skinny brunette to her left.

There is a tap on my shoulder.

"Don't worry about her," a tall, red-headed, freckled face girl with glasses in the row behind me whispers in my ear. "Amy thinks her stuff doesn't stink. The majority of us know it does."

Not wanting to disturb the class, I suppress a snicker.

"Thanks for the advice," I answer, pleased to have found another potential friend.

The sound of loud tapping on the wood podium brings us back to the lesson.

"Okay, class, let's get started," our teacher increases in volume, trying to get our attention. "We are continuing our lesson on the Greek composer, *Yanni*, specifically, his *Aria*.

"As you will remember from last week's lecture, the inspiration for this piece is loosely based on an opera completed in eighteen-eighty-three by French composer *Leo Delibes'* titled *Lakme*."

Miss Khan explains, taking a deep breath.

"The opera is set in India during the British occupation; however, unlike traditional operas, *Yanni* does not use actual words in the song. Instead, he uses vocal expressions or sounds made with singing voices. Some of the sounds may seem like real words, but they are not… at least, not intentionally."

Astonishingly, all the students seem interested. Some are discussing it amongst each other, while others wear huge, excited grins. My excitement manifests as sweaty palms, which is quite normal for me.

"I want you all to listen and pay close attention to the inflection and tone of the piece," Miss Khan pleads, as she inserts the shiny metallic disk into the CD player and adjusts the volume. "Listen to the feeling. Try to connect with the joy of the performance. Feel the passion that each singer adds to the section. Then we'll try singing the first few stanzas."

In an invisible torrent, the music enters the room through four large overhead speakers suspended from the ceiling, each located in the corners of the space. As I continue to listen, satin-smooth voices begin filling my soul with their flawless harmony; their voices floating downward, over the risers of students, and begin to encircle me, wrapping around every inch of my form. An electric surge engulfs me, from the tips of my toes to the top of my head. Then, as if by magic, all of my worries disappear and contentment takes its place, cradling me in its arms. I have never felt so much undiluted elation.

Instinctively, my eyes close, trying to store each sound to memory. I feel my body begin to sway in time to the music; a swell of emotion builds inside until I can no longer contain my desire. Inside my head, I hear my voice join in…the sound leaves me as it rises toward the heavens in a glorious orchestra of consonants and dissonant. It builds and builds, nearly lifting me from my seat, then softens and returns to the empty place inside of me.

Sadly, the happiness fades away as the music dies.

It takes all of my determination to open my eyes to witness everyone in class staring at me; eyes wide with disbelief. Startled by their bewildered gawks, I inadvertently take a step back, forgetting that I am on risers, but instead of smashing into the redhead behind me, I bump into a muscular chest. Slowly, I look around. It is then that I realize that several male bodies are pressed against me, surrounding me; suffocating me with their body heat.

What the freaking hell?! I push them away as I try to catch my breath.

A few seconds pass before the entire class erupts with thunderous applause. Miss Khan is smiling, her hands clapping as fast as a hummingbird's wings as it hovers over the nectar-filled petals of a flower. Andrew, along with every guy in class, is staring at me; wide goofy grins cover their features.

"I guess I've found the soloist for this piece!" Miss Khan proclaims.

The other students are still applauding and before long the classroom door opens and a group of nuns, teachers, students, even the school janitor enters, all of them searching for the source of the commotion. To my dismay, they also join the masses, adding another burst of applause. The only person not impressed is Amy, who if looks could kill, I would be dog meat by now.

To my relief, the bell rings, and needing to escape, I grab my backpack and rush toward the door, hoping to avoid any questions. Andrew runs to catch up, a grin plastered on his face.

"I've never heard anyone sing like that!" He beams uncontrollably, his pace quickening to meet my stride.

"Pretty bad, huh?" I jest, hastening my step.

Widening his gaze, he stares at me in disbelief.

"You have the voice of an angel," Andrew smiles and his dimples appear. "How long have you been able to do that?"

"Do what? Sing?" I blush, and increase my speed to almost a gallop. "That was my first time."

With skepticism, he shakes his head.

"You've never sung?"

"Nope," I huff.

"You're kidding," he blinks, robotically.

"No... never... not once," I ramble, trying to get away.

"That's hard to believe," he continues, rubbing the nape of his neck.

"Well, believe it!" I snap, feeling apprehensive. "I wouldn't lie to you over something as stupid as this."

Suddenly, he comes to a complete stop.

"You are very impressive," he flatters sincerely.

I stop too, taken aback by his praise.

"Why?" I counter. "I'm not the only girl who can sing."

"But you are the only girl I've ever known who can sing both soprano *and* alto parts simultaneously!"

"That's impossible!" I bark. "It's not humanly possible."

The handsome teen scratches his head while gathering his thoughts.

"When you were singing, I noticed that you somehow echoed the sounds in a lower octave, then all of a sudden you switched to a higher one, then you were singing both parts together."

"I did not!" my voice grows louder, catching the attention of a passing priest. We both wave as he continues walking.

"You did," Andrew insists.

"You are out of your mind," I glare at him like he has lost his grip on reality.

Then, without warning, he shouts.

"Mike!" Andrew waves another student from our Chorus class over to where we stand debating. "This is Selena Thermopolis. Selena, this is my best friend, Michael Taylor, Jr."

The first thing you notice about Michael Taylor, Jr. is that he is tall, extremely tall; at least 6'2" and could easily play Forward on any basketball team in the NBA. The second thing about Michael is his smile: friendly and comforting, which makes you feel like you are the only person in the room. Finally, you notice the smoothness of his skin, milk chocolaty goodness and even with all of that, it does not hurt that he has got that sweet *'boy-next-door'* face.

"Hi, Michael," I smile and blush at the same time.

"Call me Mike," he grins, showing his dimples. "Only my mom calls me Michael."

"It's nice to meet you, Mike."

Quite unnerving, Mike stares at me like I am his last meal before going to the gas chamber. Andrew notices and punches him in the arm as the three of us begin walking toward the science building.

"What did you think of Selena's song?" Andrew nudges his friend.

Mike looks at me, pupils dilated, eyes glazed over.

"It was the most intense, most incredible sound I've ever heard. I felt like I was drowning for a moment."

"That's exactly how I felt," Andrew chimes in as he calls over the tall red-head who sits behind me in Chorus. "Jenny!"

"Hey, party people." Jenny saunters over, joining our procession. Sassily, she winks at Mike, who stares ahead, trying to ignore her.

"What did you think of Selena's song?" Andrew probes.

Jenny glances at me admiringly.

"It was awesome!" she informs with all sincerity. "I wish I could sound as good as you."

"Thanks!" I nudge her playfully.

Suddenly Andrew stops, causing a ten-student pile-up.

"When Selena sang, did you feel like a wave of water was washing over your body and kind of suffocating you?"

"Yeah, but in a good, sort of sexy way," Mike adds reassuringly, making Jenny and I extremely uncomfortable.

"No," she glares at them with eyebrows arched like *Mr. Spock*. "I didn't feel the sensation of drowning or any other type of strange side effect. However—" she places both hands on her hips, "—I didn't appreciate those moronic guys in class who pushed me off of the risers in order to stand next to her!"

"Really?" both guys reply in unison.

Jenny shakes her head.

"What were you and Mike smoking before class?" she mocks while reaching into her pocket for a tissue to wipe the condensation from her lenses.

"C'mon, Red," Mike pushes Jenny playfully, making her stumble. "Her singing was ah-maze-ing!"

Completely defeated, the young woman rolls her eyes in protest.

"It was beautiful and all, but that was it," she informs then officially introduces herself: "I'm Jennifer Marie Baggins, but everyone calls me Jenny."

"Obviously, you know who I am," I laugh, trying to make light of all of the fuss being made.

Several feet behind us, Andrew and Mike follow, discussing football or some other sport with a ball, while Jenny and I chat on the way to third period: Earth Space Science Honors with Mr. Klein. In the minute and a half that it takes us to walk across campus to the science labs, Jenny gives me the skinny about the goings-on and the who's-who of St. Peter and Paul's Catholic School. She is amazing, like a teenage Perez Hilton, but without the five-o'clock-shadow.

"...and that's how the boys' track team got suspended," Jenny finally takes a deep breath.

Speechless, I stare at her, unable to blink.

"How do you know all of this?" I gasp.

"When you're not drop-dead gorgeous like you or insanely popular like those characters behind us—" she motions to Mike and Andrew, "—people tend to overlook you which means they let down their guard, forget you're around, and spill all of their juicy secrets."

She wiggles her eyebrows like *Groucho Marks*.

"I see," I manage to snort, amused at her perceptiveness.

"In the future, I'm going to be a journalist," she announces in a more serious tone.

"I can honestly see you doing that job," I confirm with a nod, causing her to chuckle.

"Right now, I'm the assistant editor of the school newspaper, The Covenant," she continues. "Last month, I did a cutting-edge Exposé on the toxic tuna surprise ingredients."

Impressed, my eyes open wide.

"That is definitely an article worth reading," I agree, making a mental note. "Thanks!"

"You're welcome," she giggles.

"By the way, you aren't average looking," I state truthfully. "If I was a guy, I'd notice you."

"You would?" Jenny places her hands playfully over her heart; enunciating each word dramatically. "You don't know what that means to me. You have given me hope."

"You're such a drama queen," I guffaw, practically choking on my own spit.

"Yes, I am, but you'll learn to love it," Jenny curtsies.

"I already do," I add, even though I do not believe the theory she has about the lunch ladies secretly plotting to kill all of the students.

♪♪♪

The four of us reach our next class with only seconds to spare before the tardy bell rings. Nicole is already sitting at her desk at the back of the classroom. She waves and I happily wave back.

Proficiently, Mr. Klein introduces himself, gives me all of the appropriate items for the class, and assigns me a seat toward the front of the room near his desk. Unfortunately, my new desk is adjacent to Richard's, my heckler from Calc.

"Oh, no," I groan, keeping my head down.

"Hello again, gorgeous," Richard leers mischievously.

"Super! You're in this class too," I blurt, and something tells me not to make eye contact.

Wishing I could disappear, I look back at Nicole and Jenny, who both look genuinely concerned for my welfare. I mouth the words '*Help me!*' but they can do nothing to rescue me from my current predicament. It is then I come to the conclusion that I am cursed.

Ten minutes or so into the class period, Richard gets bored flirting with me and begins concentrating on his work, thank goodness! A feeling of relief comes over me as the uneventful Earth Space session comes to an end. Exactly on time, the shrill sound of the bell relieves us and the pupils begin to pour into the halls.

Giggling and chatting, Jenny, Nicole, and I make our way through the hallway, up two flights of stairs and into the noisy student-filled cafeteria. Right away, we find an empty table at the back of the large open room filled with picnic-style lunch tables with attached benches.

As though we have not eaten in days, we lay out our lunches in front of us. Ravenously, Nicole and Jenny begin eating their room-temperature sandwiches and lukewarm drinks. I, on the other hand, sit quietly, trying to hold back the nausea coming over me.

"Aren't you hungry?" Nicole asks while opening her brown thermos.

"No, not really," I answer, willing my stomach to behave. "I think it's all the excitement of starting a new school."

"Here, eat these." Nicole hands me a small plastic sandwich bag out of her lunchbox containing fish-shaped crackers. "It will settle your stomach."

"Thanks," I whimper before popping a few of the uniquely shaped crackers into my mouth. Immediately, my stomach stops turning. "I do feel better."

"Works like a charm," Nicole smiles, returning to her food.

Jenny, on the other hand, is less interested in my stomachache and more concerned with my knowledge of the cafeteria. Her facial features become stern as the lesson begins.

"At the front of the room is the lunch line; there you can pick out hot items like soups and casseroles, you know, stuff like that. Remember, stay away from the tuna surprise. Off to the side of the main lunch line is the cold station; you can get salads, wraps, fruits, and drinks there."

Nicole stops eating long enough to chime in.

"Every Thursday, the cafeteria ladies make an awesome strawberry walnut salad with raspberry vinaigrette that is to die for."

Jenny sighs and continues her lesson, slightly irritated by Nicole's interruption. Nicole, unaffected by her friend, resumes eating her sandwich, ignoring Jenny's obvious disapproval.

"At the back of the cafeteria is the dessert station," Jenny continues. "Father O'Connor used to be a professional pastry chef back in Ireland, and he makes the best pies and ice cream you will ever put in your mouth."

"I promise to share this information with all of the new students that follow," I profess with a chuckle while simultaneously placing my hand over my heart.

It surprises me that Jenny's lecture is so clear and precise, everything laid out thoughtfully; she could have passed for a red-headed social influencer.

Then I notice it, several times during Jenny's talk, boys from class keep coming to our table trying to make small talk with me. Unable to stand it any longer, Jenny threatens to throw her chocolate milk at them if they do not leave us alone. Like disappointed puppies, they make their way back to their own tables; every once in a while, looking over at me, debating whether to try another approach, also assessing Jenny's willingness to follow through with her threat.

"Do you always have such a strange effect on the opposite sex?" Jenny queries suspiciously, her blue eyes narrowing playfully.

"Definitely not!" I huff. "I'm usually the one that no one remembers."

"That's hard to believe," Andrew sits down across from me.

"Really...I like being low key, ya know?" I admit unashamed.

"I can't imagine anyone not noticing you, especially with those incredible eyes..." Andrew's voice trails off as though his mind is somewhere miles away. Heat begins to spread across my features and my vision becomes a bit blurry.

"Okay, Barnett," Jenny punches his arm. "You are making her feel uncomfortable. Don't make me report you on sexual harassment charges."

"Sorry," he replies, continuing to stare into my eyes.

Thankfully, the remaining time is spent describing my life as pre-Isla Flora. With animated hand gestures, I talk about my house and school in Columbus and how much I miss it there. Proudly, I talk about my mother, the ex-model turned photographer/artist. I also hold nothing back about David's new job and the inconvenience it has caused in my life.

"Your stepfather is a marine biologist?" Nicole beams, taking the last bite of her *Steak-Umm* and ketchup sandwich.

"I think that's incredible!" Andrew confesses. "That's the field I want to major in at college. I've always been fascinated by the sea. Do you think your dad needs any help at Ocean World?"

"I have no idea," I respond, shrugging my shoulders. "He's been busy since we moved here, but he seems to really love it."

"I wish my parents had glamorous jobs," Nicole informs. "My father's a butcher and my mom makes cheese. They own a little grocery store in town."

"Your mother makes cheese?" I try not to snicker.

Nicole blushes.

"Yeah, she makes gourmet goat cheese."

"I think that's great! I love cheese!" I exclaim, impressed.

"Me too!" Jenny slurps down the remaining liquid in her carton of chocolate milk. "Mrs. Wong makes delicious cheeses!"

"Selena, do you have any brothers or sisters?" Nicole asks, gathering her trash.

"I have a little brother named Ando," I reveal with a huge grin. "He's in kindergarten. What about you?"

"I am the youngest of three; I have older twin brothers who think they are the boss of me," Nicole makes a face.

"They are really hot!" Jenny exclaims as Nicole pushes her away.

"That's why I never invite you over anymore!" Nicole reprimands. "You're so hormonal."

Ignoring their outburst, I continue.

"Are they students here?"

"No," she shakes her head. "They went off island to attend college—"

Unfortunately, the bell to end lunch cuts Nicole off, abruptly ending our conversation. Standing to head back to class, I realize that all the girls in the cafeteria are engaged in conversations, but all the boys from Chorus, including Andrew, have been watching me for the entire lunch break. Spookily, Andrew continues to stare at me without saying a word; he has not even touched his food, which, according to both Jenny and Nicole, has never happened before.

♪♪♪

Thankfully, the rest of the day goes by quickly and before I know it, my first day at this new school is almost over. On schedule, the bell rings and everyone begins to disperse to their last class. Andrew walks with me to advanced English, again not saying a word as the strange incident in Chorus still plagues me.

Maybe it was just a onetime fluke?

You know, the novelty of being a new student at a new school and everything, or maybe…

"Selena!" Mike's voice startles me. Unashamed, he waves from across the school's concrete courtyard. Suddenly, I feel more eyes upon me and notice the handsome teenager is accompanied by a small entourage of similarly aged boys. Unnervingly, their gazes are fixed on me; still glazed over and disturbingly wild. No longer do they exude the teen spirit of carefree young men. Instead, they resemble a pack of hungry hyenas on the prowl. Unsure of what to do next, I wave back, afraid of the consequences if I choose to ignore them.

Like robots, they take a step so to cross the courtyard, but I raise my hand like a police officer halting traffic and they immediately stay where they are, even Mike stays put. Andrew, on the other hand, is looking ahead at Amy, who is leaning against the wall talking with several of her friends, but every once in a while, he glances in my direction, all the while smiling shyly. Amy notices this and motions for him to join her, but he continues to walk with me. Not wanting him to feel as though he is obligated to stay with me, I decide to give him a way out.

"If you need to talk with her, I can find my own way," I inform, trying to sound uninterested.

"It's okay," Andrew's grip tightens on the strap of his backpack. "I don't have time for her games right now."

"Are you having relationship issues?" I pry. "Buy her some flowers. She'll forgive you."

Confused, Andrew looks at me as if my head is on fire.

"I'm not going out with Amy," annoyance fills his comment.

Against my will, my face heats and I know I look completely discombobulated.

"I'm sorry…I just thought…it just looked like…" I ramble out of control.

Someone just shoot me now before I stick my foot in my mouth again!

"Forget about it," he dismisses my mistake as he opens the door to our classroom and holds it as I enter.

The English teacher, Sister Mary Alice, greets me amiably, gives me the customary materials needed for class along with the standard spiel, and asks Andrew to escort me to the empty desk in front of him. He smiles, then quietly leads me to it and waits for me to sit down. As I sit, I can feel him giving me the once over, but I refuse to look in his direction. When it becomes too much to take, I turn and shoot him an irritated stare. However, instead of turning away, he simply grins and sighs.

Ugg!

"Andrew, Selena," the thin nun signals for us to pay attention. "This isn't social hour."

Embarrassed for both of us, I glance down, pretending not to have heard the teacher's snide reprimand, but the young man does not seem to be bothered. Instead, he continues to study me as I open my textbook, then retrieve my pencil and notebook.

Sister Mary Alice clears her throat to get his attention once more.

"Mr. Barnett," the nun rolls her expressive hazel eyes.

This time, Andrew turns away, returning to our lesson instructions on the whiteboard.

"S-sorry," his cheeks redden.

The woman chortles.

"Let's begin."

♪♪♪

The class flies by. Before long, I have said goodbye to Andrew, visited my new locker to switch out some books, and I am picking up Ando outside of his classroom. His teacher seems very friendly and tells me all about his first day.

"Your brother is such a sweetheart," the beautiful woman commends, making my brother beam.

I can tell he has a crush on her when Mrs. Anderson hugs him and he blushes.

"He is the most helpful student I have ever had," she compliments. "Thank you, Ando."

With even rosier cheeks, he grins.

"Goodbye!" he waves as we begin walking away. "See you tomorrow!"

As we make our way to the front of the school, we converse about the day's events.

"I see that your first day went well," I chuckle, making his face heat again.

"It did," he boasts, grinning. "Mrs. Anderson is nice."

Being mischievous, I ask, "I thought you said that girls are yucky?"

In true Ando form, he gives me an unamused expression.

"She's not a girl," he emphasizes, boldly. "She's a teacher."

I smile at his ability to separate the two.

"How was your first day, Lena?" he asks, changing the subject.

"Where do I begin…?" I reply, tapping my bottom lip.

As best as I can, I review all that had happened during the school day, starting with meeting Andrew in the front office all the way through when I picked him up from class. Of course, Chorus was my main focus. My brother just listens intently while I rattle things off.

"Wow!" he mumbles as he switches his lunchbox to the other hand. "The most exciting thing that happened to me was making a macaroni necklace during art class."

"I don't know what to do," I blab. "I wanted to be incognito, ya know?"

He nods his understanding, then takes my hand. Having his little paw in my mitt comforts me. It always has.

"Don't worry, Lena," Ando pacifies. "It will be better tomorrow."

Of course, I grin at his positivity.

"Do you really think so?"

Gently, he squeezes my hand, and somehow, I believe him.

"You have a very old soul," I grin, remembering that he is only five.

He has been this way since I can remember. Even as an infant, he always seemed to be deep in thought, like he was contemplating the nature of the universe. Unlike me, a late bloomer, my brother did almost everything early. He spoke in complete sentences at the age of six months and could read kindergarten level books at two. I, on the other hand, did not utter my first word until almost a year old and could barely read in kindergarten.

As we continue our leisurely stroll to the student pickup area, Ando tells me about everything that happened in class and I do mean *everything*. He begins with a funny story about a little boy named Tommy who likes to eat paste, and finishes with him helping a little girl with freckles — whose name he could not recall at the moment — tie her shoelaces.

Before we realize it, we have arrived at our destination outside of the school's gates. The street is still cluttered with parents getting their children. Unfortunately, the strong fumes escaping from the idling vehicles make my nose and eyes itch. Hopefully, Mom is already in the pickup line.

"That was a thoughtful thing for you to do, baby bro," I praise, mussing his hair like I often do, knowing that he dislikes it.

Keenly, we both scan the row of cars for our mom.

"Do you see her?" I ask, tiptoeing and straining my neck.

Ando shakes his head.

"No, I don't," he answers with a disappointed frown.

"I'm sure she'll be here soon," I respond, trying to stay positive as I check the time on my watch.

Regrettably, we wait outside for Mom longer than expected. At a few minutes past three, Ando and I are still waiting in the smothering Isla Flora heat. Sweaty and grumpy, Ando wipes his brow with the back of his hand and wipes it on his uniform pants.

"When is Mommy going to get here?" he moans, shading his eyes from the glaring sun.

I take another glimpse at my watch again; it has been two minutes since the last time I have checked. Bored, Ando decides to pull leaves off of a nearby pink hibiscus bush, their vibrant green leaves crackle as they land on the scorching sidewalk.

"Where is Mommy?" he asks for the umpteenth time, his forehead dripping.

"I don't know!" I answer more harshly than intended. "She'll be here soon. Don't worry, okay?"

"Did she forget to pick us up?" he pouts as he plucks one of the bright hibiscus flowers from the bush.

"No, she wouldn't forget to pick us up." I reply, shaking my head.

"Hey!" Andrew calls from several feet away. "What are you still doing here?"

Unable to help myself, I grin like the Cheshire Cat in *Alice in Wonderland*.

"I could ask you the same question," I smirk trying to contain my excitement.

"I have swim practice after school," he replies with a broad smile. "But Coach Evans had a doctor's appointment. So practice was cancelled. I went to the library to return some overdue books."

Slowly, he turns to study Ando who has now started throwing leaves into the street.

"Who is this?" the teen subtly grills with a great deal of curiosity.

Immediately, my sibling puffs up his chest like a male gorilla protecting his female.

"I'm Ando," my brother speaks up.

"Is that short for Andover?" the tenacious teen teases.

"No, it's short for Fernando," Ando giggles.

Then, as if they have known each other for years, they slap hands.

"It's nice to meet you," Andrew states, then turns to me. "Your ride is late?"

"Seems like it. Our mom should have been here already," I respond, voice filled with distress. "She probably just lost track of time."

"That's too bad," he whistles. "It's sweltering out here."

I nod in agreement.

"Where are you heading?" I pry, intrusively.

"My mom is the editor of a local publishing house further up Main Street," he reveals. "I usually walk there after practice. It's not far."

As we make small talk, Mom's white RAV4 turns the corner.

"There she is!" I exclaim as relief rushes over me.

"I'm so sorry," my mom apologizes through the open window. "I got lost trying to find the cable television office."

Without being asked, and in true gentleman fashion, Andrew opens the back passenger side door for Ando, and then opens the front passenger door for me. Patiently, he waits until I buckle my seatbelt, then closes the door as Mom waits for an introduction.

"Andrew, this is my mom, Mrs. Marquez," I present, uneasily. "Mom, this is Andrew Barnett, my student guide for today."

Naturally, my mother gives a wry little smile, an all-knowing glimmer in her eyes.

"Nice to meet you, Mrs. Marquez," Andrew gives a friendly nod.

"Thank you for helping Selena," Mom counters with her best smile.

"No worries," Andrew blushes.

"How was my daughter's first day?" Mom pokes, glancing over at my reddened cheeks.

"Selena blew the whole Chorus class away today," the teenager babbles. "She has the most incredible voice; it was the most beautiful singing I have ever heard."

Suddenly, Mom's expression changes.

"Singing?" her eyes narrow. "Chorus class?"

"Chorus is my elective," I mutter, not understanding what the big deal is.

Suddenly, in a rush, she hastily ends the conversation.

"Thanks for showing Selena around—" she fake smiles, nervously tapping her bottom lip. "We've got to go."

"Nice to meet you, Mrs. Marquez," he grins.

"I'll see you tomorrow, Andrew," I announce, hoping Mom will take the hint and drive away before she inadvertently embarrasses me.

Thank goodness she does.

As we pull away from the curve, Andrew waves goodbye then begins walking up the street, backwards; backpack flung carelessly over one shoulder, top two buttons of his white polo unbuttoned partially, revealing the smooth tanned chest beneath.

"He's very cute...polite too!" Mom slaps my knee teasingly. "Do you like him?"

Embarrassed, I smirk, but say nothing else.

To my relief, the drive home is quiet except for a Greek music CD playing in the background. Something in the song sounds familiar. Mom was born in Greece, but moved to Isla Flora when she was still young. In fact, my mother's entire family was originally from the Mediterranean, but my maternal grandfather, Grandpa Theo, fell in love with Isla Flora while he was working on a housing subdivision in the early fifties. According to my mother, he was also quite a historian. After he died, a few years ago, she inherited the house, which was rented out until about a month ago when David accepted his new job.

"So, what *exactly* happened in Chorus class?" Mom interrogates out of the blue.

Breathlessly, I begin telling her about my crazy first day just like I did with Ando. She listens carefully, never once interrupting until I have spilled every ounce of data that plagues my cerebral cortex.

Taking a deep breath, I finish with: "Surprisingly, I made lots of new friends, especially guys who heard me. According to Andrew—"

"Andrew, the cute tour guide?" Mom teases.

"Yes," I blush. "He said my voice was like a tidal wave that lifted him off of the ground and filled him entirely."

I bat my long lashes like a well-skilled fan dancer and then continue, "Some of them said that the song had left them aching, like being hit too hard in the stomach and having the wind knocked out of you and they followed me around the rest of the day. One freshman even trailed me into the girl's washroom!"

"Are you serious?!" Mom gasps.

My face heats more as I give an overly exaggerated nod.

"All of them wanted me to perform for them again," I explain, still trying to sort it all out. "Weird, right?"

"Absolutely," Mom agrees with a scowl.

"A group of them actually stopped me, begging and pleading for me to serenade them," I laugh. "But Nicole and Jenny shooed them away. By the end of the day, I'm sure they felt like my personal bodyguards."

"What about the girls?" Mom's eyes narrow curiously. "Did they have anything to say about your performance?"

"No, not really," I giggle with relief. "Jenny said it was beautiful, but that was about it."

"Hmm," my mother makes only that one sound as she continues to take it all in.

I take a deep breath before adding: "Nicole and Jenny are in some of my classes; they were very nice to me and so were Andrew and Mike—"

"It's sort of cool feeling so powerful, huh?" she interrupts.

I shrug, downplaying the thrill I felt being the center of attention.

"It was alright, I guess."

"Really?" Mom states nervously, then says offhandedly: "Well, don't get too used to it. Things will probably be back to normal by tomorrow."

"What do you mean?" I blurt, startled by her flippant reply.

"Oh... nothing, probably just first day excitement over the new girl," she plays it off too. "Boys are like that, but Andrew seems truly fond of you."

"Maybe," I turn toward the window, signaling that I am finished discussing this uneasy subject.

"I didn't know you were interested in singing," Mom counters, unwilling to drop the subject.

"I'm not," I stretch the truth. "It was the only elective that wasn't full."

"I'll go to the office tomorrow morning and get someone to change it."

"Whu-why?" I stammer, unable to understand why she opposes my choice in classes.

Oddly, she stares at me, but does not respond.

"I like the class," I finally admit with a sigh. "The teacher, Miss Khan, is really nice, and she knows so much about music."

"Selena— "

"Jenny and Mike are in that class too…so is Andrew…well, Andrew is in all of my classes except physical education…" I ramble on as my mouth tries to catch up to my brain; Mom's eyebrows hitch as she continues to stare. "I don't want to leave the class. Please, don't make me."

Obviously frustrated with me, her grip on the steering wheel tightens.

Feeling the same, I take a much-needed breath, then ask, "Why don't you want me in that particular class?"

For a long moment, she mulls over my question before responding.

"It's not that I don't want you in Chorus," she finally continues. "I just thought you'd want something more challenging."

"I want to stay in the class," I reply firmly.

To my surprise, Mom agrees.

CHAPTER THREE

Our new house is on the east side of the island, about a twenty-minute drive from town, depending on traffic. As we leave the bustling city, I lean my head against the cool glass and peer outside, admiring the surrounding hillside, which is lush and green and speckled with brightly painted houses. The air has that heady fragrance of hibiscus flowers and bromeliads, combined with tropical fruit trees and coconut palms; melded by the intense heat and humidity of the day. The unique combination is almost too overwhelming to stand.

In truth, everything about Isla Flora takes my breath away. From the exotic assortment of native islanders with their diverse skin tones, varying sizes and figures, who leisurely stroll along the small, but immaculately kept streets; each of them lending their distinctive customs to this living, breathing 'callaloo' pot.

It is on this small piece of earth, secluded from the rest of society's taboos, that these special people cohabitate and coexist. It is here where the mixing of races comes to its most perfect compilation.

"Look at that view," Mom points.

Ahead of us, deep purple mountains stretch their arms towards the heavens, while wistful salt-kissed breezes caress each verdantly colored tree branch, bush, and hillside. On overhead branches, iguanas lay outstretched, soaking up warm tropical rays as gossiping birds scan below for their next meal. However, the best thing about these picturesque surroundings is that it is encapsulated by the shimmering aquamarine of the Caribbean Sea. Today, the ocean is the exact shade of my eyes.

As our vehicle passes the main waterfront pier, I notice the local fishing boats bobbing upon the undulating waves as the crew separates their catch. Along that same stretch, open-aired trucks filled with freshly picked young coconuts packed over ice wait for native and tourist alike to stop for a taste of nirvana. I smile, knowing the flavor oh so well.

As usual, we turn off of the broad lanes of the waterfront onto the steep winding road leading toward the country, temporarily halted by colorfully dressed women carrying baskets filled with provisions from the outdoor market. Oblivious to our existence, they cross the road chatting on cell phones. Their scarlet, green and canary yellow outfits hypnotize onlookers as they mingle among paler-complexioned, more conservatively dressed tourists; smiling and nodding hello as they go. Mom was right; this is truly a utopia with a dynamic blend of modern conveniences married to old world traditions.

At last, Mom breaks the silence.

"Did you know that Isla Flora is only thirty miles long and twenty miles wide?"

With that fact, I perk up.

"No, I didn't know that," I respond sincerely, visualizing it in my mind.

As the next traffic light turns red, we stop beside a small, well-manicured park, where caramel-hued girls play freeze-tag with pigtails flying behind them like kite strings. In another corner of the park, uniformed boys play after school touch football; their intertwining laughter creates its own distinctive song. In the sea of players, I recognize one face in particular. It is Andrew. Without a care in the world, he runs around with his shirt disheveled and hair plastered to his forehead with sweat, voice louder than everyone else.

Exuberantly, Ando rolls down the back window and shouts as loud as he can.

"Andrew!"

Startled, Andrew looks around, spots our vehicle, and excitedly waves back.

"Andover!" he shouts, and his distraction gets him beamed in the head with the football.

Holding back a snort, I stare forward, pretending not to have seen him.

Boys!

♪♪♪

Our journey to the country is quiet except for Ando making fighting sounds as he makes his green plastic army men battle to the death. Dad's blue truck is already parked in the driveway beside an older white van with 'Harold's Handy Work' painted in rainbow colors on the sides. Mom parks along the far side of the house near the red flamboyant tree; it is a spectacular tree covered with bright red-orange blossoms. Mom says that the flowers bloom in mid-summer and create fiery splashes of color all over the island.

"Be careful, honey!" Mom waves to David, who is helping to patch a hole in the roof. He waves back, unable to answer because of the roofing nails held securely between his teeth.

"Daddy!" Ando yells. "All the kids liked my new backpack!"

David gives him a thumbs-up. I wave also, but continue into the house with Mom and Ando.

Immediately, Mom goes to the kitchen, washes her hands, and begins gathering ingredients from the pantry: tuna, noodles, cream of mushroom soup, and an assortment of pre-diced vegetables. I also wash my hands and start opening the metal cans, smiling to myself as I remember the warnings of the school's tuna surprise.

"Why were you so late today?" I ask, practicing my interrogation skills.

Mom looks up briefly as she hunts for a large casserole dish.

"I went to the beach this morning after I took you all to school, just to look around, and before I knew it, it was afternoon."

Of course, I believe her, but she has a strange glimmer in her eyes, like she is still on the beach.

"Was it pretty?"

This time, Mom closes her eyes and lets out a long sigh.

"It was incredible," she confesses, and starts assembling the dish.

To pass the time, my brother and I help unpack more boxes and organize the kitchen pantry. Meticulously, I group similar items neatly on the shelves, even making sure to compile a shopping list of things that are still needed. Ando is in charge of the two lower shelves since he is the right height for the job; before long, the space is neat, tidy, and well-organized.

Dinner is ready shortly after that and the aroma of tuna casserole permeates the entire first floor; it smells *awful*. I have no idea why. Usually, I can eat an entire tuna casserole all by myself, but disgusted by the scent, I place a hand over my stomach as it begins to gurgle in protest.

Ando notices my sickened expression.

"What's the matter, Lena?" he asks, full of real concern.

"Nothing." I force a thin smile, not wanting my brother to worry. "Could you please go and get a tablecloth from the linen closet upstairs?"

Obediently, he follows my instructions, his little legs rushing to get the task done. As soon as he leaves the room, I immediately start gasping for air, not understanding why I suddenly feel ill. With trembling fingers, I touch my brow, which is dripping and feverish.

"Why am I so sweaty?" I mumble to myself, making a face.

Not wanting Ando to see me in this condition, I wash my face in the sink and dab it dry with a paper towel. Surprisingly, the cool water makes me feel a tad better. After all, if my sibling knew I was sick, he would rat me out to our parents like a two-dollar stoolie.

Then another thought comes to me: *Suppose I really am sick? Should I tell Mom?*

"No, I'll be alright," I whisper, shaking my head.

My brother's footsteps on the stairs warn of his approach.

"I've got it!" Ando announces as he comes back into the kitchen. "It was hidden under some towels."

Frowning, he glares at me.

"*What?!*" I snap, feeling like a bug under a microscope and my brother is the curious scientist conducting the experiment.

"You look funny," he announces, eyes glued to my face. "Are you sure you're okay?"

"I'm tired." I downplay how I really feel, adding a manufactured yawn to throw him off of my scent. "I just need a good night's sleep is all."

He nods in acknowledgement.

"Okay," he shrugs as he spreads the tablecloth over the kitchen table.

I love that brother of mine! More than I could have ever imagined possible.

Wanting to be helpful, he sets the dining table while I fill the drink glasses with water.

♪♪♪

As we all sit down to dinner, everyone except for me begins digging into the steaming dish. Ando is already shoveling the creamy substance into his mouth, almost burning his tongue in the process. Mom and David also seem to be enjoying it. Before long, they are on their second serving.

Hesitantly, I take my first bite of salad and even that tastes odd, like it is off somehow. From across the table, my mother studies me curiously, just as she had done in the car on the way home after hearing about my adventures at school.

"Selena, aren't you hungry?" David grills with concern. "Tuna casserole is one of your favorite meals."

"Yeah, Lena," Ando fills his mouth with another bite and I can actually hear the metal of the spoon grating against his teeth as it leaves his mouth, as well as his deafening chewing.

Dear Father! What's happening to me?

As if my hearing has been amplified, their voices come at me from all directions. Trying to avoid the agonizing clamor, I cover my ears tightly with my hands. Strangely, now I can hear my mother's voice in my mind as she ponders my 'condition'. Unable to shut the voices out, I turn away, but the glare from the kitchen lights hurt my eyes and even the muted noises outdoors seem louder than usual.

Contemplating a different approach, I close my eyes and wait for it to pass, and thankfully, it does.

Mom looks at me strangely, the gears in her mind turning.

"What's the matter?" she presses.

I begin to answer, but my stomach starts to churn.

"I don't feel so—"

Knowing what is coming next, I slapping a hand over my mouth, and run to the kitchen sink. A mouthful of acidic foam comes gushing out. Disgusted, I wipe my mouth with the dish towel as everyone at the small kitchenette stares.

Naturally, Mom jumps up and quickly walks over to me, her features grave.

"Are you okay?" she probes, looking deeply into my eyes as she rubs my back like she would do when I was younger.

Lightheaded, I shake my head, still holding my abdomen, the pain too overwhelming to bear.

"I'm not sure why my stomach is bothering me," I admit, feeling a rush of dizziness slam into me.

"How long have you been feeling ill?" My stepfather joins us at the sink.

"Off and on today," I willingly divulge, grasping the nearby counter in order to stay upright.

Ugg!

"Selena, why don't you go upstairs and take a shower," Mom insists. "I'll bring up some crackers and ginger ale."

Feeling dizzy, I nod, clutching my belly, and slowly head towards the stairs.

With cautious steps, I make my way to the upstairs bathroom, grabbing a clean towel from the linen closet along with my blue terrycloth bathrobe. My stomach feels as if it will jump out of my mouth. Too weak to care, I do not even bother to push the box against the door to keep it closed.

All of a sudden, icy stabbing pains lance through my body, chilling me to the bone. The sensation feels as if I am standing on an iceberg in Antarctica. Quickly, I strip down to bare skin as goosebumps appear all over my arms and legs. It is then I realize that the tiny bruises are still between my fingers and toes, but now instead of being purple, they are turning a bright shade of blue. Thank goodness the bruises are small, only the size of pinheads, so no one else should notice.

With shaking fingers, I turn the dial that controls the temperature to the hottest setting I can stand. The heated water feels good against my clammy skin, but something else is wrong. A strange tingling sensation begins in my fingers, then travels to my toes. Unexpectedly, they go numb and I feel the overwhelming need to scratch. Arms, legs, chest, scalp; nowhere on my skin is safe. Unable to stop it, a blood-curdling scream escapes me when the terrifying feeling of the room spinning starts.

Joining the fray, my stomach gurgles and spurts as bitter liquid rises into my throat. No longer in control of my body, I start to gag, fortunately this time nothing comes up. Leaning against the cold ceramic tiles of the shower is the only thing that seems to ease my suffering.

Outside, the ocean sounds so loud. Requiring more fresh air, I unlock the window and prop the glass open using a bottle of shampoo. A rush of seaweed perfumed breeze fills the room along with the pungent scent of salt.

Then I hear it.

Needing to focus, I close my eyes and strain to make out the voices of the waves as they call for me.

"Don't be afraid," they sing.

"I'm not afraid," I answer.

"Sing with us," the soft voices command.

Keeping my eyes closed, I tune everything else out. Impulsively and without any regard to how ludicrous this is, I open my mouth, releasing an orchestra of sounds. The sounds rise, then fall, then they rise again, building and swelling in volume like royal trumpets, then softening to barely a whisper. I sing until it engulfs me entirely, like ocean waves hammering over me, drowning me with contentment.

I stumble back to the present when an angry knock at the bathroom door brings me back to reality.

"Selena!" Mom calls, sternly.

"Yes?" I respond meekly, wondering if she heard my song.

"What's wrong?" Her tone is anxious and unnerved. "Why are you screaming?"

"I'm sorry," I apologize, glancing around, trying to steady myself. "I didn't know I was being so loud."

There is an uncomfortable pause before she answers.

"You've been in there a long time!"

Without further delay, she barges in and notices that the window is wide open. Angrily, she slams it closed; her features are a combination of anxiety and another emotion that I cannot quite figure out. All I know is that whatever it is has her off of her game.

"I want you to keep the windows closed at night!" she commands. "Do you understand me?!"

Still recuperating from the sudden sickliness, I glare at her with heavy eyes still unable to focus. With great effort, I nod my understanding. Answering for itself, my body begins to sway just as another more gut-wrenching bout of nausea slams into me followed by a shroud of pleasant darkness as the world goes black.

♪♪♪

I do not know how long I had been unconscious, but I wake surrounded by Mom, Dad, and Ando. Gradually, my mind clears and I realize I am in my room in bed wearing my favorite pajamas, but I cannot remember how I got into them. As we all sit in silence, a strong gust of wind rattles the loose windowpane; outside, the voice of the sea calls again.

My mother scowls, making me think she can hear it too.

"Are you okay?" David inquires, appearing very worried, Ando hugs me, and Mom blankly stares at me.

"Stop staring at me!" I bark. "I'm probably just lightheaded because I haven't eaten anything since lunch."

"Would you like me to make some soup?" Mom asks.

"No, thank you," I hear the voices calling to me again. Mom scans the area as if she hears it too, but I cannot be certain. David and Ando are only concentrating on me.

"Could I please be alone for a few minutes?" I huff indignantly. "All of this family togetherness is stifling me! Just give me a few minutes!"

David nods and gives me a quick kiss on the forehead.

"Feel better, sweetheart," he requests, taking my brother by the hand and leading him away.

Mom tries to feel my forehead, but I pull away before she can touch me. Her eyes narrow at my reaction, but the way I feel right now, I do not care.

"If you need anything, anything at all, call for me, okay?"

I nod halfheartedly, wishing she would leave.

"I'll check on you in a while," she reassures with a weak smile.

As soon as they leave, I open the window, allowing another gust of seaweed-scented air to fill the room. At first, it is silent, almost tomb-like, and several of the longest minutes of my life pass before the now familiar voices return.

"Don't be afraid," they sing.

"I'm not afraid," I answer.

And like we are old friends; it wraps its cool invisible fingers around me and for the first time in weeks I feel at ease.

For the first time in my life, I feel at home

.

CHAPTER FOUR

Saturday morning, I am one gigantic, walking mess of swollen eyes and a heavy tongue, accompanied by a headache the size of Texas.

"You look terrible," Ando informs on our way to the beach where David's job is located.

Jokingly, I stick my tongue out, making him giggle uncontrollably.

"I've been having these weird dreams," I announce to no one in particular as Mom pulls into the parking lot, needing to share my torment.

"What kind of *weird* dreams?" Mom counters as she searches for an empty parking space, obviously interested.

Briefly, I pause, recalling the events, wanting my description to be accurate.

"It's late at night and I'm walking on a deserted beach. The sky is illuminated with thousands of twinkling stars. Suddenly, the weather changes; ominous clouds begin rolling in, and a soft voice sings: *Don't be afraid…Follow me…into the sea…in the ocean's waves, we'll play*."

Drained, I halt the memory for only a moment to rub my eyes as they begin to burn from another sleepless night.

"Sometimes the dreams change a little," I continue at last. "But usually, I'm on the shoreline below our house."

My mother's posture straightens like she is bracing for bad news.

"Is there anything else?" She looks ahead, hands now gripping the steering wheel tighter.

"The time of day sometimes changes, but the gist of it is always the same," I admit meekly.

"Have you been keeping your windows closed at night?" Mom's expression is stern.

Confusion creeps over my features.

"Why does that matter?" I fold my arms across my chest.

"Are you keeping your windows closed?!" she barks.

"Yes," I lie, not wanting to be lectured or possibly grounded.

That answer seems to pacify her and her smile reappears.

"Let's put these ugly dreams behind us and find Dad," she states exuberantly.

Grr! Her mood swings are giving me whiplash!

As promised, David is waiting for us in the Ocean World parking lot. Mom quickly parks the SUV and we all pile out. Anxious to have our behind-the-scenes tour, Ando runs towards David, who scoops his small body into his arms.

"Is this where you work?" Ando beams, his eyes wide.

"Yes, it is," my stepfather answers proudly. "You want to take a look around?"

Ando nods quickly.

"C'mon you guys!" David yells across the parking lot, hurrying us along.

Quickening her pace, Mom reaches David first and kisses him hello. I lag behind feeling queasier. Perhaps the strong scent of marine life, along with buckets of bait fish used for feeding, is overloading my sense of smell. Taking a piece of gum out of my pocket, I pop it into my mouth, hoping the sweetness will mask the surrounding smells.

"Are you still not feeling well?" David feels my forehead.

"No," I answer. "I think I'm feeling worse."

"Enough sick talk," Ando orders. "Let's go see the fish."

My stepfather concedes with a robust chuckle.

"Let me give you the tour," David grins, taking my brother by the hand.

Like V.I.P's, we enter the grounds through an unmarked gate guarded by one of the park's armed security officers. With a smile, the man checks David's identification badge, then has him sign some paperwork. Finally, he allows us inside.

"Have fun," the tall dark-skinned man says with a nod.

"We will!" Ando exclaims, giving him a thumbs-up.

The guard winks at him, then returns to his original *'don't-mess with-me'* attitude.

"Thanks a lot, Bobby!" David adds over his shoulder.

Filled with much deserved pride, my stepdad leads the way down a ramp to a long concrete pathway circling the administration building. We end up at another entrance where he flashes his ID and is waved through by another guard. I am surprised at all of the security measures.

"Why is there so much security?" I prod, filled with interest. "Isn't this just a marine science center?"

"It is, but we are also a research facility that specializes in state-of-the-art marine equipment," David explains. "Believe it or not, there are a lot of rival companies who would love to take a peek at our labs."

His enthusiasm makes us all smile.

As we continue walking, we spot another guard. Several feet away from the officer's desk is a thick steel door with an ID reader.

"Is this your family, Dr. Marquez?" the cheerful woman questions with a welcoming smile.

My parent chuckles as he swipes his badge, places his thumb into the scanner, and waits.

"Yes, it is, Margie," he grins from ear to ear. "I've promised them a personal tour today."

Margie waves as we wait for David's credentials to be verified by the computer system.

Finally, we hear the salutation of a pleasant artificial voice: *"Good morning, Dr. Marquez…Verification complete…Please enter."*

Instantly, the light on the door turns from red to green, and David opens it for us. Inside is dimly lit, and the air is comfortably conditioned. Around the room's perimeter are transparent tanks with a variety of sea creatures, including eels, barracudas, starfish, sea anemones, stingrays, baby nurse sharks, even jellyfish. Several technicians wearing white lab coats are observing the marine life and logging their data into tablet-computers. One looks up, smiles, and then walks over to us. Excitedly, she shakes Mom's hand, who smiles at the friendly gesture.

"You must be Marina," the woman says. "Your husband talks about you and the children so much that I feel like I already know you."

Mom looks at her ID badge for a name.

"I'm sorry, sometimes my mouth gets ahead of my brain and my brain takes a while to catch up," she blushes. "I'm Dr. Dorinda Khan, but feel free to call me Dorinda. I hate all that formal crap."

Dorinda realizes her inappropriate word choice and leans down to speak directly to Ando.

"I'm sorry. I shouldn't have said c-r-a-p," she spells the word crap, making us laugh. We all snicker, especially my brother.

"*Khan*," I repeat. "My Chorus teacher's name is Miss Khan," I disclose.

"That is my daughter, Indra," Dorinda says proudly. "She's a wonderful teacher. I'm sure you'll learn a lot about music as well as yourself," she adds cryptically.

"Okay…"

"Don't tell me…you are Selena," Dr. Khan continues.

I nod.

"Did you know Selena was the Moon Goddess in Greek mythology?"

"I do know that," I say proudly. "How do you know?"

"I know a lot of things," she winks. "Plus, I've always been intrigued by myths of any kind."

"Me too!" Mom smiles.

Next, the doctor turns to Ando.

"Did you know that Fernando is a Spanish name meaning 'adventurer'?"

"I like adventures!" Ando beams.

Lastly, Dorinda turns to Mom.

"Of course, I can't forget your name, Marina. It's Latin for 'from the sea', my favorite place."

Mom grins and gives her a tight hug, which is totally out of character. Typically, it takes a while for my mother to bond with new people. We tease her all the time about her being a social hermit, but today she surprises us all.

"Dorinda has been showing me the ropes," David tells. "I don't know how I would have made it without her this past week. It has been a blessing that she decided to transfer to Ocean World from its sister park in India."

"I like not being the new kid on the block anymore," Dorinda jokes, gently elbowing my dad in the ribcage.

Quickly, we say our goodbyes as my stepdad waves for us to follow him into another section of the room.

"Let's continue," he says, beginning to walk.

"I look forward to seeing you again, Dorinda," Mom waves at our newest friend.

Wasting no more time, David leads us to a spiral staircase leading into the main observatories. Spreading out, we leisurely stroll around the glass encased room looking out into the vastness of the Caribbean Sea. In true pessimistic form, I imagine that the seawater which is hugging at the glass panes is searching for one weak spot to enter and kill us all.

David melodramatically clears his throat to get our attention.

"This facility is the only one of its kind in the Caribbean," he educates. "This particular underwater observatory tower is approximately two-hundred feet offshore and descends almost forty feet beneath the water's surface."

"Are the fish contained with some type of netting or...?" Mom touches the glass with the tips of her fingers; her features sadden.

He shakes his head.

"There are no barriers keeping them here," he emphatically informs. "They come and go freely, so the variety of species changes often."

"That's amazing, Daddy!" Ando claps his excitement.

"Yesterday a huge school of silversides paid us a visit," he adds. "There must have been at least a few hundred of them."

Other onlookers gather around us in order to hear David; some of them even snap pictures of him like he is a celebrity. In true David-form, he simply ignores the cameras and continues delivering his information.

"Last night, I saw a couple of reef sharks and today an enormous sea turtle came by with a mouth full of seaweed," my stepfather pauses to gather his thoughts. "I think they are more curious of us than we are of them."

"They are," my mother mumbles.

As we continue watching the glass, a queen angel fish passes the window, turns around, and stops directly in front of Mom. Noticing the graceful creature, she smiles, then makes a strange clicking sound with her tongue. To my surprise, the fish moves closer to the glass, studying us.

"What's that sound you're making?" I ask.

"What sound?" Mom stares blankly ahead.

Wondering why she is denying it, I continue to stare.

"It sounded like a metronome, or a clock or something ticking," I recall, getting my dander up.

I try to mimic the sound, and to my amusement, the fish turns toward me and gives me a tiny...*smile?* Ando's excited squealing brings me back to the moment, but bored with my weird noises, the fish swims away. My brother is now jumping in place and clapping his hands together, reminding me of one of those toy monkeys that play the cymbals.

"I want to do that! Teach me how to do that sound, Mommy!"

Ando begins clicking and clacking his tongue and, before we realize it, there are several other types of fish gathered near the glass where we are standing. Sadly, they all seem to lose interest at the same time and swim off into the azure expanse.

Mom uses this moment to her advantage.

"Who wants ice cream?" she exclaims.

"I do!" My brother licks his lips, forgetting the weird occurrence.

It is then, out of my peripheral vision, I realize that David is staring at all three of us with a bewildered expression.

"Did you hear the fish talking to me, Daddy?" Ando beams, temporarily forgetting about the ice cream.

"I didn't hear anything," David admits.

"Show us more, honey," Mom artfully distracts them both.

Her husband frowns; knowing my mother's distraction tactic all too well.

"Let's go see the deep reef tank before we get those cones," he suggests, smile returning.

"Let's go!" Ando agrees, pulling me along and I push the thought of our awaiting desserts down and refocus on the exhibit.

♪♪♪

The deep reef tank is crowded with tourists as far as the eye can see. Some of them are wearing the same-colored t-shirts to let everyone know they are part of the same group. Unsupervised children are busy tapping on the observatory glass, which seems to be annoying the sharks. I am starting to get a little annoyed by their actions as well.

"Should they be tapping on the glass like that?" I question my stepdad.

"Absolutely not," he practically growls his irritation.

On a mission, he walks over to another Ocean World employee and whispers in her ear. Shortly after, the heavy-set woman's voice blares over the intercom system.

"Ladies and gentlemen, please restrain children from tapping on the glass. Sharks, as you know, are extremely sensitive to sounds and may become agitated. Thank you for your cooperation and please enjoy the rest of your day here at Ocean World."

Some parents immediately grab their children and move them from near the tank. Others, however, stand nearby, continuing other conversations, completely oblivious to the announcement. Getting upset, I shake my head with contempt. I guess some parents just do not care what their children do.

Lost in thought, David scrutinizes the tank. Almost immediately, he notices several reef sharks circling at the top, their body language stressed. One overly aggressive reef shark keeps getting closer to the onlookers; his movements became more and more frantic as people in the crowd bump the glass or flash fluorescent bulbs in front of his face.

Nearby, a little girl eating an ice cream cone climbs the stairs up to the main platform surrounding the tank and stands close to the edge, looking down into the clear water. Her sandy blonde ponytails sway every time she bends further down. Unfortunately, her grandparents do not seem to notice that she has wandered away, but David, concerned with the child's safety, does.

"Excuse me, Sir," he approaches an elderly gentleman who was standing beside her. "Could you please move your little girl? She shouldn't be so close to the tank. It's a restricted area."

"What's your problem, buddy?" the old man barks; his thick accent is hard to understand. "I'm on vacation and had to pay over a hundred dollars to get my grandchildren in here, so you need to go clean a tank or something."

Unintimidated, David refuses to back down.

"I understand, Sir," he tries reasoning with the man. "I'm just looking out for your little girl's safety."

As he argues with the tourist, there is a blood-curdling scream from the platform, and the crowd turns in time to see the child tumble into the shark tank. Obviously terrified, she desperately tries to tread water, but she hopelessly begins slipping beneath the surface. Fearlessly and without any regard for his own safety, David snatches off his shoes and dives into the tank filled with frenzied reef sharks.

Horrified at the sight, Mom's face turns ashen as she fights her way through the mob-like crowd to the platform. Without hesitation, she throws her purse down, kicks off her flip-flops, and dives in after them. The surrounding crowd rushes toward the observation area to witness the scene. Panic-stricken, Ando and I charge the glass and stare in disbelief. David has hold of the girl who locks her thin, suntanned arms around his neck like a vise. Instinctively, Mom helps him carry the screaming child closer to the edge of the tank, but the sharks have already begun to circle.

"I'll distract them while you get her out!" Mom clamors frantically.

"No, you take her and I'll keep them busy!" he insists.

"David, I'm not debating this now!"

With that said, she swims toward the far side of the tank yelling, splashing, and making as much noise as possible, but the sharks pay her no mind as they continue to stalk. Boldly, one of the larger sharks bumps David with his snout. Terrified, the girl screams even louder. By this time, several more workers have arrived with bang-sticks and life preservers. Immediately, they throw the preservers into the tank, but as soon as they do, the overexcited sharks savagely attack those.

My mother, oddly calm, scans her surroundings, then focuses on the man-made coral reef at the bottom of the tank. Like a seasoned free-diver, she plunges downward, and without hesitation slashes her arm on one of the jagged edges; slicing it cleanly open. Immediately, the surrounding water becomes a scarlet cloud, and everyone gasps.

"What is she doing?" I whisper to myself in disbelief.

Throughout the crowd, onlookers shout warnings as the sharks take notice and propel towards her, but Mom, on the other hand, appears unnaturally calm considering her current predicament. David, still holding the child, quickly swims to safety; completely unaware of his wife's dangerous diversion.

Straightaway, they are pulled from the water, and once safe, he desperately scans the tank for her.

"*Marina!*" he bellows, horror-stricken and waterlogged.

"She's down at the reef!" a burly man in the crowd wearing a Hawaiian-print shirt shouts.

Unfortunately, his warning comes too late because the sharks are already circling her. The one that assaulted David darts straight at her with its mouth open; cold black eyes fixed on its prey while the other sharks wait. Suddenly, I see Mom's lips begin to move and notice her tongue is making the same bizarre movements from earlier. Curiously, over the din of the excited crowd, I can hear a soft clicking sound, both purposeful, yet alien. Shockingly, the shark swims away, clearing a path between Mom and the platform where David fishes her out of the water. The crowd bursts into thunderous applause, woots and whistles.

"What were you thinking?" David grills while tightly embracing her. "You could have been killed!"

"I wasn't thinking," she admits, blushing and hugging him back.

Dad sighs deeply, his eyes welling.

"Don't ever...*ever* do that again!" he forbids, kissing her forehead.

His wife giggles.

"I promise."

♪♪♪

After the *'incident'*, David closes the attraction for the rest of the afternoon so the sharks can be observed, and some new safety barriers installed. Still recuperating, the four of us sit in David's office as they change into some dry clothes from the gift store. As if reading my mind, Dr. Khan appears holding a tray of hot chocolate and sandwiches from the employee cafeteria.

"Here you go," she says. "Eat this. You've earned a snack."

Dr. Khan winks at my parents.

"I didn't know you did superhero work on the side, Dr. Marquez," she teases.

My parents grin in unison at the woman's praise.

"Marina, I can definitely see why he can't say enough about you. I think I'm officially your newest fan."

Embarrassed, my mother blushes as she averts her eyes, trying to compose herself.

"It was nothing," Mom replies modestly; trying to downplay the rescue. "I saw the little girl fall, then David dove in, and before I knew what was happening, I was in the tank as well. Pretty stupid, if you ask me."

"Mommy," Ando chimes in, nibbling on a ham and cheese sandwich. "I didn't know you could swim like that!"

"Me either," I acknowledge proudly.

"You were like Aquaman!" he beams as he moves his arms in a swimming motion.

Mom chuckles.

"I was on the swim team in college," she answers too quickly, then takes another sip of the chocolate beverage. David looks down at the floor, unable to say anything as Dr. Khan picks up the empty tray and begins to leave.

"You should have been a professional swimmer because I've never seen anyone move that fast," Dad's coworker compliments.

"Yeah," I wholeheartedly agree. "Mom swims faster than any Olympic swimmer that I've ever seen."

"Okay," David unceremoniously rushes Dr. Khan out of the room. "Could you check on the sharks for me?"

With an understanding nod, she gives Mom a wink and waves goodbye as she departs.

"How is your hand?" My stepfather examines Mom's cut.

"It is fine," she replies, then kisses him on the lips. "You did a great job cleaning and bandaging it, thank you."

"I think you both earned the title of hero today," a short, Armani wearing man bursts into David's office. "I'm Stuart Jacobs, co-owner and general manager of Ocean World."

Brusquely, he shakes Mom's hand.

"You caused quite a hoopla jumping into that tank," he beams like a used car salesman. "Reporters and news crews are already outside asking for interviews."

"My wife's not interested in doing any interviews, Mr. Jacobs," David states flatly.

"I understand," the other man smirks. "She needs to go home and get a good night's rest, then tomorrow she'll be ready."

Wow! Is he serious?

Stuart is a pushy little man about 5'2", with large plump features and small beady eyes that remind me of a rat. At my height, I notice the large bald-spot he tries to hide with a comb-over. Truthfully, the only thing pleasing about him is his expensive suit. Not wanting to offend him, I decide to hold my tongue for David's sake. I would not want him to fire my dad because of my rudeness.

"Mr. Jacobs, my wife doesn't want any attention—" David begins.

"She may not have wanted it, but good gracious, she has got it!" Mr. Jacobs retorts, his face turning beet-red.

Trying to manage his temper, my stepfather clenches his teeth at his boss' bold comment, but does not reply.

"This is great publicity for the facility, Dr. Marquez. You and your beautiful wife saving that child could bring in much needed revenue…" his voice lowers to a threatening tone, "…and it would mean great job security for you."

David's hands clench into fists, alerting everyone in the room to take cover. He is known for a lot of things, but holding his tongue is not one of them. Knowing this, Mom quickly speaks up.

"I'd be happy to give an interview," Mom presents her most mesmerizing smile; taking control of the situation. "Give us a few minutes to freshen up and we'll be right out."

"Thank you, Mrs. Marquez," the man gives a nod. "I really appreciate this."

Silently, we all watch as Mr. Jacobs scurries away.

♪♪♪

A few minutes later, Mom and David stand on the platform of the shark tank trying to look natural for the cameras; ocean breezes tug at the hem of Mom's new blue floral sundress from the park gift store. The color enhances her magnificent aquamarine eyes, causing them to sparkle like jewels. Around her neck, the antique silver pendant also glistens under the lights of the surrounding cameras. David stands nervously beside her, sporting an emerald green t-shirt and tan cargo shorts, also from the gift store. They squint as camera-flashes go off like fireworks a few feet away from their faces.

"Tell me, Dr. Marquez," one male reporter bellows over the commotion. "What was the first thing that you thought about when you saw that little girl in the shark tank?"

All of the microphones turn towards David, who nervously clears his throat.

"I didn't really think, I just acted," he answers a bit robotically. "I imagined it being my own daughter and wanted to get her to safety."

My chest tightens at his response.

"What about you, Mrs. Marquez?" a different man asks.

Mom gives her best smile; after all, as an ex-model, she knows how to work a crowd.

"I saw my husband dive in, panicked, and did the same thing any mother would have done. I'm so proud of my husband...of my entire family...I'm happy we are all safe."

The reporters scramble to ask more questions, but David speaks up.

"Thank you all so much for your concern towards my wife and me, but it has been a long, tiring day, and we just want to take our children home and spend some quality time together."

"Of course, Dr. Marquez," the reporters agree.

"One last question for the children!" a female television reporter yells.

Mr. Jacobs looks at his employee, who then answers, "That's up to the children."

The cameras are now on me and Ando, and I hope nothing is stuck in my teeth. Enjoying being the center of attention, Ando smiles and waves to the cameras, which make the reporters laugh.

"What are your names?" the well-dressed anchor inquires.

Remaining placid, I clear my throat.

"I'm Selena, and this is my brother, Fernando."

"Ando," he corrects, causing the crowd to guffaw.

"Ando, how do you feel about how brave your parents were today?"

He smiles, showing the gap between his front teeth.

"I think they were really brave," he replies proudly.

The pack of reporters then turns to me.

"And you, Selena? What went through your mind?"

Watching my parents supporting each other when it matters the most, I realize that David will always protect us, always put us first and always love us. Finally, I understand. So, I simply say the first thing that comes to mind.

"My parents are the kind of people who always put others before themselves. I wouldn't have expected anything less from them."

I look at my parents in time to see a tear roll down my mother's cheek. Yes. We are truly a family, blood or not.

CHAPTER FIVE

"You are famous, girl!" Nicole squeals excitedly as she gives me a hug.

"What are you talking about?" I play it off, trying to escape her embrace.

"I saw you on the news last night," she cheekily grins.

"Oh!" I exclaim, wanting to forget that we were on all of the local news stations.

"You are a celebrity!" Nicole exclaims.

Shaking my head, I downplayed the incident by saying, "My mom and dad were being interviewed, and some reporter asked me and Ando our opinion."

As I explain, Jenny runs up and embraces me as well.

"Sign my polo!" the spicy redhead insists, handing me a pen.

"What for?" I laugh, pushing the plastic object away.

"So, I can sell it for millions of dollars on eBay," she teases, causing Nicole to slap her playfully.

"You looked great, by the way!" Nicole comments. "And your parents…how do you have such *hot* parents? My father looks like he's nine months pregnant and my mom resembles an eighties pop star."

"What's the matter with that?" I question with a long sigh, suppressing a giggle.

Nicole opens her eyes really wide and scrunches up her face.

"It's like being stuck in *The Twilight Zone,* that's what!"

We laugh at her facial expression more than we do her comment just before someone covers my eyes.

"Guess who?" the voice requests.

"Is it Jensen Ackles?" I poke, only half-jokingly.

"Nope."

"What about the singer, John Legend?"

"Guess again," the masculine voice chuckles.

"Wait! I know who it is," I respond casually. "It must be Dwayne *'The Rock'* Johnson."

At last, Mike uncovers my eyes, mock disappointment spreads across his features.

"You were meant to say, Mike Taylor, *'Love God'*."

"Forgive me, Mike Taylor, *'Love God'*," I mock, innocently kissing his cheek.

"That's much better," he gives us a boyish grin, showing his perfect teeth, which makes us all giggle.

"What are you guys laughing at?" Andrew pushes through the densely populated group of teens.

"They were just making fun of parents," Jenny informs.

"That's easy to do," Andrew licks his thumb then touches Jenny's lenses with it leaving a large imprint.

Disgusted, Jenny punches his arm.

"Thanks a lot, Andrew!" she pulls Nicole with her toward the girls' restroom. "Now I have to go clean this!"

"Why do I have to go with you?" Nicole complains as she is pulled away.

"Because we've been friends since the second grade and you love me," the redhead pouts.

"When did I ever say that I love you?" Nicole goads with a snicker. "I don't love you. I only put up with you because you make me laugh."

"Whatever!" Jenny bashes, ignoring her disapproval.

Quickly, they disappear into the restroom, leaving the rest of us standing aimlessly in the hallway.

"Mike, don't you have to see Coach before school starts?" Andrew reminds, trying unsuccessfully to get him to vamoose.

"Nah, man, I spoke—" Mike stops in mid-sentence as he notices his best friend's face. "Right, I forgot! Thanks for reminding me!"

Mike playfully pushes me out of the way, causing me to wobble into Andrew, who grabs my arm to keep me from falling.

"What was that all about?" I interrogate Andrew as I steady myself.

Innocently, he shrugs.

"That was a great response you gave to those reporters yesterday," Andrew praises, glancing down at his black sneakers. "Your pictures were in the papers."

"Great!" I respond sarcastically. "I didn't feel well this weekend. I probably looked like a week-old roadkill."

Without permission, Andrew reaches over and pushes a stray curl behind my ear.

"No, you didn't," he grins.

I notice his eyes crinkle at the sides when he smiles.

"You looked more like day-old road-kill," he jokes.

I smirk, but punch him on the arm just for kicks and giggles.

♪♪♪

All day kids kept coming up to me asking me questions about the accident at Ocean World. By the end of school, I wished I could transform into someone else, maybe a member of the British Royal Family, or at least someone with highly trained bodyguards. Thankfully, by the last bell, the boys have stopped following me around campus.

As usual, Ando and I resume our waiting ritual in front of the main school building, at the same place directly in front of the hibiscus bush. Most of the students have left campus, except for the few attending detention or the after-school clubs, and only a handful of the faculty still remain.

My musing is interrupted when my cell phone rings out of the blue, startling us.

"Hello," I answer without looking at the caller ID.

"Selena, it's Dad."

Thank goodness! At least one of our parents is concerned about our welfare.

"Hi, Dad! Do you know where Mom is?" I probe, scanning the street. "Ando and I are still at school."

"I'm not sure where she is, sweetheart," he answers gruffly. "I've been calling her cell phone all day, but she's not picking up."

"What should we do?" I inquire, feeling beads of perspiration running down the back of my neck.

"Stay where you are. I'm on my way," he replies through gritted teeth, which he seldom does. "If your mother gets there before I do, give me a call back, please. If not, I'll see you in twenty minutes or so, depending on traffic."

He hangs up abruptly without saying goodbye.

Needing to avoid the growing humidity, Ando and I go back inside the school. I remember that Andrew has swim practice, so we head to the school's lap pool located behind the gymnasium. As we turn the corner, we see the swim coach timing each member in order to select the starting swimmers for this weekend's meet.

"Move it, Barnett!" Coach bellows. "You are not going to win any matches going so slow! My grandmother can move faster than you and she's ninety years old. Move it! *Move it!*"

Ando and I scan the pool for Andrew and, of course, I see him first.

"Way to go, Andrew!" I yell without thinking.

At my outburst, everyone turns to look at us, including Coach Evans. Mortified, my face tightens, and I glance around nervously, hoping there is a bus to throw myself under. Andrew looks embarrassed also; his face begins to turn an awkward shade of red. Fortunately, other girls are cheering him on as well, which causes Coach Evans to order all of us to either sit down on the bleachers or remove ourselves from the premises.

"I'm very sorry, Coach...I didn't realize I was being so loud...I didn't mean to interrupt your practice," I apologize in a rushed jumble of words as everyone in the stands judges me.

Coach Evans releases a frustrated *'harrumph'* as he shakes his head in dismay.

"Don't worry about it, but if you want to stay—" he says, looking at the pair of us, "—you will have to be quiet."

"We'll be quiet," I promise, now suddenly aware that all of the swimmers on the team are also staring at us as well as Andrew. "You won't know we are here."

Coach's face softens as he stares at me, then at Ando.

"How strong are you, little man?"

114

Without hesitation, Ando makes a muscle.

"Hey, that's a big muscle!" Coach compliments with a jolly smile. "Why don't you help me get these swimmers into shape?"

Knowing that I am in charge, my brother turns to me with hope filled eyes.

"Can I, Lena?"

"Sure, just don't fall into the pool," I mischievously poke. "Mom and Dad aren't here to save you."

"Barnett!" Coach Evans yells. "Take a five-minute break!"

Compliantly, Andrew climbs out of the pool, wearing a black *Speedo* with the St. Peter and Paul's emblem on it, dripping wet, hair slicked back like the fur on a seal, his muscles rippling. I didn't know anyone could look that good in *Speedos*. Just like in the movies, he removes his goggles and grabs a towel from the pile nearby, looking good enough to —

"Nice job crashing practice," Andrew jokes. "Your Mom must be late again."

"Wow! Good looking and smart!" I tease back. "That's not a typical combination for a *pretty boy*. I guess the old saying about jocks might not be true, in some cases."

Getting even, he shakes his head, dowsing me with chlorine-scented droplets. As we continue chatting, my cell phone rings.

Woot! It's Mom!

"Mom, where are you?" I bark, trying not to sound frantic. "I thought something awful must have happened to you. Are you okay?"

"I'm just running a little late," she informs, out of breath.

One hand perches on my hip.

"Were you at the beach again?" I give her the third degree.

"No," Mom giggles bashfully. "One of the local magazine editors saw me on TV and offered me a job working in their art department."

"That's wonderful!" I exclaim loudly. "Congratulations!"

"Thanks, baby! I'm so sorry I didn't call, but I'll tell you all about it tonight," she gleefully announces. "I should be at the school in ten minutes."

"Mom, Dad has been trying to get a hold of you," I warn, not wanting her to be caught off guard.

"I just got off the phone with him," she admits. "Thank goodness he hadn't left work yet."

"Ando and I are at the school's pool watching the swim team practice," I also admit with a guilty little grin.

"Have fun!" she chuckles. "I'll call when I get there."

"See you soon, Mom."

Andrew smiles knowingly.

"Let me guess...your mom just interviewed for a job at the Isla Flora Journal?"

My mouth automatically opens with surprise.

"How did you know that?" I wonder aloud.

Again, he smiles.

"My mom is the editor of the magazine. We were watching the news last night when we saw your parents being interviewed. I mentioned that your mom is an artist. The rest is history."

Overjoyed, I throw my arms around him and squeeze.

"Thank you!" I beam from ear to ear, causing him to blush.

"What kind of reward do I get if I get her elected as governor?" he flirts, moving closer.

"I don't know," I smirk roguishly. "Get her elected as governor and we'll see."

♪♪♪

Ten minutes later, Mom picks us up rambling all the way home about her interview and new job. By the time we reach the house, she is totally breathless. It is terrific seeing her so excited. Even better, as we walk through the door, the scent of seafood welcomes us inside. To our surprise, Dad has already made dinner: broiled lobster tails, steamed broccoli, baked potatoes, and Mom's favorite coconut cream pie from the bakery down the street. Exuberantly, he hugs his wife, then me, finally Ando. I have never seen him this excited.

"What's all this?" Mom questions, grinning from ear to ear. "I was expecting takeout, not a royal feast."

Without much effort, Dad lifts her up.

"We are celebrating our new jobs, this beautiful house, and us being a family."

Lovingly, they kiss as Ando and I run upstairs to wash up for dinner.

♪♪♪

"Dad, you really outdid yourself!" I proclaim while licking the melted butter off of my fingers; dinner is delicious. David is an amazing cook; he can make old sneakers appetizing and I am thankful to be feeling like my old self.

"The food is incredible, Babe," Mom touches his hand affectionately.

"Thank you!" he grins. "I am glad everyone is enjoying it."

My stepfather stares at Ando, who has now begun to lick the lobster pieces off of his plate like a malnourished Pitbull.

Straightaway, Mom taps her son on the arm and gives him *'the look'*.

"Ando, you are not a dog," she scolds, wiping his glistening mouth with a clean napkin. "Stop that right now."

My brother immediately puts his plate down and begins using his fingers to pick up the remaining remnants of food. Both Mom and Dad shake their heads. What can they do? My brother is one of a kind.

"How's school?" David asks, removing his son from being the main attraction.

"School is great!" Ando grins, reaching for another piece of lobster. "My teacher is really nice and I have a best friend now. His name is Stanley, and he got a new puppy for his birthday last week."

"I'm glad you've made a friend, Ando," Dad smiles broadly. "What about you, Selena?"

"Lena likes Andrew!" the little snitch blurts before I can answer his question.

"*Ando!*" I scold; kicking his leg under the table and shooting him an icy stare.

"Ouch!" he hollers, rubbing his shin.

Dad looks at both of us, not at all surprised.

"You didn't tell me you like someone," my stepfather wiggles his eyebrows, making me want to sink into my chair.

"I don't like him," I lie, not wanting my parents asking too many questions about my love life, or the lack thereof, like they tend to do. "He's just a guy who was my student guide on my first day of school…that's all."

Sternly, I glare at my brother, silently warning him to keep his mouth shut.

"Just some guy, huh?" Dad grins, then takes a long drink of his lemonade. "Does he like you?"

"He is just a friend." I look sheepishly down at my plate. "Can we please change the subject?"

Hearing this, Ando looks up from his second serving of lobster long enough to add: "Andrew got Mommy the job. He told his mom that she is an artist."

"Andrew did that for me?" Mom smiles.

"Yes," I reply, smiling too. "He and his mom saw you on TV and he mentioned that you were looking for a job."

"That was very considerate of him," she gets a little misty. "I will thank him the next time I see him."

Happily, Mom stands and begins gathering the dirty dishes. Wanting to help, I follow her into the kitchen to load the dishwasher while Ando and Dad go into the study to finish Ando's homework. It is nice having Mom in a good mood and to myself for a change. Cheerfully, we chat as we clean the kitchen. She even tells me about getting the call from Ms. Barnett and all of the projects they have available for her. Honestly, I have not seen her so excited in a very long time. Her eyes have not stopped sparkling yet.

"Andrew seems like an amazing young man," Mom nudges me with her elbow as she walks by.

"I guess so," I answer, handing her one of the clean pots.

Instantly, her eyes focus on my hands, which are moist and glistening under the fluorescent lights of the kitchen.

121

"How long have you had those bruises between your fingers?" she grimaces.

"I noticed them a few nights ago," I answer to the best of my ability.

"Has anyone else seen them?" she frowns.

"No," I examine them again.

Mom sighs and then changes the subject.

"Have you made any other friends?"

"Actually, I hang around mostly with Nicole, Jenny, Mike, and Andrew. They are really nice; I feel like I've known them forever." I look into her aquamarine eyes and smile. "I think I am going to like it here."

She smiles back, but does not say anything else.

♪♪♪

After cleaning the kitchen, I take a shower, get dressed in an oversized football jersey, and begin working on my homework. The house seems so humid tonight. As quietly as possible, I open the window, hoping to get some fresh air, but there is no breeze tonight. The night is eerily still, like the foreboding stillness before an approaching storm. The image forces the hairs on my arms to stand up. Squinting into the darkness, I peer down to the rocky shoreline below; even the waves seem quieter than usual.

Missing its song, I listen for that sweet voice to greet me as it has every night since we moved into this house, but it never comes. Overhead, the moon is shining upon the sea, full and pregnant with mystery. I open the window a little wider and listen one last time. Just then, a movement near the front porch catches my attention. Stealthily, the shadow darts across the front lawn toward the side of the house, but it is gone before I can get a good look. Grabbing my robe and sneakers, I rush downstairs, praying to avoid any loose floorboards.

The front door is slightly open, which sets off silent warning bells in my head. Carefully, I open the door and softly close it behind me. Dad's snoring echoes through the house, then the night goes still again. I sigh, make the sign of the cross, and run in the same direction of the shadow.

Practicing my ninja-like surveillance skills, I begin tip-toeing when I reach the corner of the house. Not too far ahead, the shadow is descending the rocky steps to the dangerous coastline below. I am forbidden to go down, but suppose it is a prowler...or worse?

Turn back, my conscience whispers, but of course my curiosity has taken over.

Scared to death, my breathing is coming in short, terrified puffs.

Don't hyperventilate! My mind begs. *You'll pass out again and fall head-first down the steps!*

With my luck, my latent clumsiness would betray me just for the fun of it. Sometimes I think it really does have a mind of its own. This is not paranoia; I am positive it is out to get me!

Mom and Dad would raise you from the dead so they could kill you again. Good grief, Selena! Pull yourself together!

I take one more deep breath for good measure, and begin my careful descent down the slippery, moss-covered steps.

♪♪♪

It takes at least five minutes to reach the bottom. I am positive I could have gone faster, but the fear of plummeting to my death was a great motivator to go slow. There is a large rock near the cliff, probably placed in that position by the waves centuries ago. Not wanting to be discovered, I make a run for it and reach without incident.

Thankfully, the full moon above illuminates the coast in a supernatural greenish-gray hue; nothing like the soothing shades of daylight. Adding to my jumpiness, a strong gust of wind suddenly comes in from the east, cold and malevolent. Standing motionless, I feel a presence and realize that someone is watching me from close by.

"Come to us, Selena," a chorus of voices rises up from the sea. Determined to stay on dry land, I close my eyes and try to control the sudden urge to dive into the churning waters.

"I'm having an allergic reaction to the lobster, that's all this is," I pacify myself in a whisper. "David bought some spoiled seafood and now I'm having hallucinations."

"Come with us...into the sea...in the ocean's waves we will play!" the song beckons, louder and more compelling.

"Leave me alone!" I yell against the wind with all of my remaining strength, forgetting to be covert.

"You are ours," the voices chime stronger, louder. *"We are yours."*

"Please, leave me alone!" I plead, covering my ears with my hands.

"You are ours," they repeat.

"What do you want from me?" I mumble, hearing it inside of my head. "Why do you keep calling me?"

One voice separates from the others. It is stern and terrifying.

"The sea calls for a tribute, like the sea gods of ancient times. Or it will bring down more souls to Poseidon's kingdom. Beware...all who dare ignore this song."

Up ahead, the shadow appears again, hopping from rock to rock like a child playing hopscotch. I watch in amazement as it continues its effortless game, then slips out of sight again. Without notice, the wind picks up, causing the waves to pound angrily against the stubborn shore, as storm clouds begin to roll in, covering the distant gaze of the moon.

Terror shoots down my spinal column as my nightmares crawl their way up from the bowels of my unconscious into the realm of reality. This realization pushes down onto my chest, creating crippling spasms. It hurts too much to think, so much so that rationality shuts down, leaving me to survive on instinct alone. Purposely, I control each breath; fearful that I will be heard.

From the corner of my eye the shadow reemerges, bobbing and weaving around the jagged protruding rock formations of the Isla Flora shoreline. Without warning, it dives headfirst into the water, disappearing beneath the foamy surface. Panic-stricken, I scan the waves for any signs of life, but all I can see, all I can hear, is the roar of each furious wave.

Just wait, your answer is coming, a small scared voice deep inside me whispers. *Just wait.*

Help me! Someone please help me! A gruffer, and more convincing inner voice shouts its counter.

'The Brain' tells me to trust the latter, while *'The Flesh'* tells me to listen to the former; all the while, the rest of me does not know what to trust.

As if in response to my unspoken deliberation, soft music rises out of the sea. The slender shadow stops to listen, cocking its head from side to side, entranced by the sweetness of the tune. The crashing of the waves subsides and transforms into that familiar voice.

"Don't be afraid," the sea says over and over. *"Follow me… into the sea…in the ocean's waves we'll play."*

Then it changes unexpectedly; no longer a sweet child-like voice urging me to play, but instead a hoarse, raspy voice, longing to be heard. Compelled, I strain to hear it.

"Here we are...near we are...we sisters three..." over and over it sings until I think I am losing my mind. *"...long for you, ache for you...we sisters three!"*

In response, the waves hit the rocks violently, creating a salty mist that cascades over the shore. A cool spray hits my legs and a strange tingling sensation starts, like your limbs falling asleep. Quickly it begins to creep upward from my toes, into my feet and ankles, then finally into my legs. Within seconds, both legs are experiencing this sensation and are twitching uncontrollably. Without warning, they give way, sending my body tumbling onto the jagged ground. I call out in pain, but the pounding waves and howling wind drown my cries.

When I glance up, the shadow is closer. I hold my breath, suddenly frightened by its proximity. At last, the clouds begin to roll away, disappearing into the outstretching horizon and the moon is released from her cloudy prison; happy once again to watch over her earthbound children.

Sympathetic moonbeams drift quietly over the rocky terrain; their light gives chase to secrets. All the other shadows have fled to hidden crevices, all, but this one darkened figure. This shadow stands defiantly near the edge, enjoying the spray of each crashing wave. An eternity passes before it turns in my direction. My curiosity turns to surprise as Mom's face is revealed.

"What is she doing?" I whisper to myself.

Soundlessly, she strips down to the skin, leaving her clothes in a pile on the rocks. Carefully, she sits down; her legs hanging over, almost touching the water. Then slowly, she lowers herself in, avoiding any sharp corners.

I want to call out to her, but my mouth will not form the words. Instead, I hold my breath as her body disappears beneath the choppy surface. Feeling returns to my legs and I run toward the edge and look down into the water, but there is no trace of her.

Should I go and tell David? My mind races in desperation. *Or should I go in after her? Damn it! I can't think!*

Instead, I run back to the carved steps, desperate to have someone else share my misery, but before I can reach them, Mom resurfaces. Quickly, I throw myself onto the ground and crawl soldier-style back to my original hiding place behind the boulder. Ahead, she stands naked looking at the sea, making those strange clicking sounds with her tongue. After a moment, she kneels near the edge, listening to nothing.

Is she talking to the fish?

129

Then, without warning, she opens her mouth and releases the most heart-wrenching song I have ever heard. Enraptured, I listen closely, trying to hear the words, but I cannot quite make them out. It is then I realize there are no words (not real words anyway) only melodious, enchanting sounds.

Her lament is slow and sorrowful; it makes me want to throw my arms around her. Tears are streaming down my face, leaving a sparkling trail behind. Lost in her anguish, I listen closely, allowing my body to sway. My eyes close, and her song becomes a part of me; rising, falling, then rising again, both soft and melancholy, then high and cheerful; flowing deeper and deeper into my soul, until the song fades back into the sea.

♪♪♪

Slowly, I open my eyes; they are swollen, and I am having a hard time focusing. Behind, the sound of breathing alerts me that I have been caught. In time, my eyes focus and center, and there, standing like a Titan Goddess bathed in moonlight, is my mother. She dresses as I sit in quiet reflection as moonbeams cascade upon her perfect form. Her black curls resemble Medusa's snakes; tightly slithering and slinking smoothly against one another. She looks both beautiful and terrifying; her face is glowing, but filled with despair. She has not looked me in the eye the entire time.

Around us, the air is still again, too still, like the calm before the perfect storm. Finally, she sits beside me, legs outstretched and still damp from her swim. As always, she naturally smells of salt water and lilacs. Lost in her thoughts, her gaze is fixed on the slowly changing horizon as the dark purple canvas begins to transform into a pallet of lavender, crimson, and gold.

"Tell me what's going on," I beg, words shaky. "I'm scared...*please?*"

My mother takes a deep breath as I swipe the next onslaught of tears away.

"You're going to think I'm crazy," she replies.

"Then we'll be crazy together," I comfort, holding her hand.

"Do you remember Grandpa Theodore?" she questions, gazing up at the heavens.

"Yes, he'd visit us every summer. He had a strong Greek accent, and he made the best baklava I've ever tasted."

"Grandpa Theodore wasn't my father," Mom sighs.

"He was your stepfather?" I ask in an astonished gasp.

"Not exactly," she says. "What about Grandma? Do you remember her?"

I think back.

"You said she died before I was born," I reply with arched brows. "Was that a lie?"

"Not exactly," she repeats.

"Mom, what are you trying to say? Are you adopted?" She tries to answer, but I interrupt. "If you say 'not exactly' one more time, I'll scream!"

"Come with me," Mom requests, leading the way back up the steps to the house.

CHAPTER SIX

Dad is snoring peacefully on the couch when we enter. Gingerly, I close the door and follow her to my room. Upstairs, we stop briefly as she peeks inside Ando's room. Only the top of his black wavy hair can be seen peeking out from under the covers; resting beside him is Alfredo, the stuffed teddy bear that I bought him for his first birthday.

We make a quick detour to the dimly lit hallway closet, where Mom quietly searches for something. After several minutes, she reemerges with a meticulously carved wooden box. Carefully, she carries it to my room and closes the door behind her. The box is decorated with scenes of winged-women darting through clouds and mermaids sunning on rocks. As Mom opens the box, I run my hand over the carvings. To my surprise, the wood shines even in the darkness, and there is a strong woodsy smell that escapes as the lid is removed. The scent seems so familiar.

"What is it made of?" I whisper.

"It's Cypress," Mom says, inhaling deeply. All of Mom's favorite pieces of furniture must be made from Cypress, because the scent is all over our house.

Patiently, I wait as Mom removes an old leather journal from the box. It looks very worn, and the pages are yellowed and stained. Then I notice the cover of the journal is decorated with the same design as my mother's charm. Drawn to it, I touch it, feeling the smoothness of the leather against my fingertips.

"This is the same symbol on your necklace," I announce. "What does it mean?"

"It is the ancient symbol for Siren," she informs matter-of-factly.

"What's a *Siren*?" I question, still touching the strange symbol. "Is it like a police siren?"

She glares at me in bewilderment.

"Definitely *not* like a police siren," she smirks.

"You're going to need to elaborate," I shake my head.

Mom looks out of the window, disconcertedly; lost in thought as she tries to find an appropriate explanation.

"Well," she begins. "Sirens are ancient female sea creatures."

"Is it similar to a mermaid?" Cocking my head to the side, I confirm, running my fingers gingerly over the raised leather relief.

"Oh gosh, no!" she snaps indignantly. "Sirens aren't snooty or self-righteous like they are, and they certainly do not have tails!"

"I still don't understand," I blurt.

Mom opens the journal to the first page. There is a dedication on it which reads:

To Parthenope, Marina, and the sea for bringing meaning to my life. I will follow forever your Siren-Song.

—T.T.

The title of the journal is called *The Truth about Sirens by Dr. Theodore Thermopolis*; Theodore Thermopolis was my grandfather's name.

Now, I'm really confused.

"Grandpa Theo wrote this?" I try to wrap my mind around the idea.

"Yes," Mom answers without elaboration.

"I thought he was an architect?"

"He was, but he was also an expert on Greek Mythology. The Sirens were his specialty. He knew absolutely everything about them," she beams.

"What does this have to do with anything?"

At my remark, she takes a deep breath and then slowly releases it.

"Read this," she hands me the journal. "It's yours now."

I take it under protest, mumbling heavily under my breath. Obviously frustrated, Mom begins pacing back and forth like a lioness trapped in a cage. Holding my breath, I begin to read:

This is the history of the gods; before Adam and Eve...before man walked upright; mighty Zeus and his brethren walked the Earth and made the mountains shake and the oceans churn with their awe-inspiring power. It was in these days that

Melpomene the Muse bore to Tethys' son Akheloios

three sea nymphs named Parthenope, Leukosia and

Ligeia. The ancient world came to know them as

the Seirenes.

I stop reading and close the journal, more confused than before.

"Okay. So, what does this have to do with what I saw tonight?"

My mother takes another deep breath.

"Our entire history—both good and bad—is in these pages, and even though the words may sound unbelievable, you have to look into your heart. Then you'll know that every word is true."

She kisses my left cheek and then my right, smooths my tangled hair, then turns quietly on her heels and exits the room; never looking back.

Lost in my own thoughts and even more interested, I open the book again and continue reading:

I am Parthenope: sister, mother, wife, and

destroyer. Daughter of the air and the sea, protector

of the maiden Persephone...singer of

songs...harbinger of death; this is my gift for all

that come after. This is our Siren-Song.

I was born on an island off the coast of what is

now Italy. The island was a gift from the son of

Kronos, who loved my light-hearted songs. I named

this place Anthemoessa, meaning flowery, but

today it is known as Capri. As memory serves,

Anthemoessa was lovely, with towering Cypress

trees, majestic mountains, and air thick with

rosemary, oregano, and citrus. In the summertime,

the hillsides would be covered with honeybees and

butterflies all feeding on thousands of blooming

lavenders.

There I lived with my two sisters, Leukosia and

Ligeia. For centuries, we spent our days perfecting

songs taught to us by the birds and at night we

swam in the turquoise waters surrounding our

haven. On pleasant evenings, we would swim out to the enormous limestone masses surrounding the island and sing devotional praises to Zeus. But one day, a terrible mishap changed our lives forever.

Awestruck, I stop reading, assaulted by hundreds of strange thoughts now racing through my mind.

How can I believe this, any of this? The sheer impossibility of supernatural beings actually existing is preposterous. After all, I learned about Zeus and the gods and goddesses of Mt. Olympus in history class. They were stories created by humans to understand stuff like changes in the weather, misfortunes, and things that could not be explained.

Good grief! I'm rambling again!

With trembling fingers, I turn on my computer and wait as it takes a few minutes for the system to boot up. Automatically, the internet search engine appears and I type in 'Mythological Sirens'. Thousands of websites with information about Sirens appear. Rapidly, I scan the sites until one of them catches my attention. Anxiously, I click on a site created by a world-renowned Greek historian and anthropologist. The first page of the site reads:

> Sirens, according to Greek Mythology, were one of a group of sea nymphs who lured mariners with their angelic singing and seductive beauty to a watery demise on the rocks surrounding their island.

Feeling that pang of disbelief rising into my throat again, I stop reading; unable to comprehend the night's events or the turmoil now surrounding my family tree. Insanity must be rooted in our history, somewhere down the genetic line; a sister married a brother or some such nonsense for this to even be a topic of conversation.

♪♪♪

As expected, my night is filled with tossing, turning, and worrying. No matter how I replay all of the information, I cannot understand the events that are unfolding. Several times I go to the open window and listen for those beautiful voices, but the only sound that greets me are those of the pounding waves. Once, I even ventured down the dark, slippery carved steps to search the water for something, anything, but nothing was all that waited.

Sleep, however, came to me in pockets…pockets lined with disturbing visions of gods and goddesses, great battles, love won and love lost, and of the sea. Every time I closed my eyes, visions of wrathful deities, winged creatures, and crashing ships plagued my thoughts.

I awake even more tired than before; eyes puffy and sore from crying. My entire body is drained as if I was reliving every horrible incident in the sisters' history and my heart hurt for their loss. A loud beeping announces it is morning, six a.m. once more. Sunlight filters through the open windows, both warm and soothing; almost erasing the night's events.

Almost.

Outside, waves continue to pound against the rocky shoreline far below; their unique beat reminds me of its power. The wind blows again, adorned with the unique fragrance of salty seaweed and sweet island flora. The scent is intoxicating. Much akin to a bobbing pigeon, I tilt my head from side-to-side straining to hear that distant familiar melody. With eyes closed, I strain to hear its heartfelt call, but to my surprise, the voices from all the previous nights cannot be heard.

Relieved, I sigh.

CHAPTER SEVEN

Before the morning bell, I make my way to the school's library to search for more information on Sirens. Although the journal holds information about the 'creatures', it is difficult for me to take anything it contains seriously. Hopefully, I will find other more credible sources.

"Good morning, Sister Mary Camilla," I greet the school's librarian. "I was wondering if you had any books about Sirens?"

The plump, elderly nun smiles as she looks up the reference materials in the library database.

"Sirens, fascinating creatures," she states enthusiastically. "There're hundreds of lore about them, from every culture in the world. The legends are quite sad, though.

"Are you doing a paper on mythology?" Sister Mary Camilla asks as she continues to scroll down the page.

"No, ma'am, I'm just curious about what they are...I mean, were," I clarify as truthfully as possible. After all, I am not about to add lying to a nun to my clan's rather sketchy past. I do not want any more transgressions against me.

"Ah ha!" she exclaims happily. "We have some books you can look through."

Compliantly, I follow her to that section and gather all of the books I can carry, find a secluded table in the corner of the library, and open a leather-bound book in my stack. The first page reads:

> Greek Mythology describes the Sirens as dangerous bird-women who lived on a beautiful, flower-laden island surrounded by jagged cliffs and menacing rocky coastlines. These creatures lived for only one thing, to lure unsuspecting sailors who ventured near their home with their angelic voices to shipwreck on the rocky shoreline.

Crap! I think to myself as I close the book, disappointed that it did not give me any other pertinent material. Quickly, I glance through the other books when I come across a title that is listed on the *'Required Reading List for High School Seniors'*.

"Metamorphoses," I whisper the word as if it was somehow sacred.

Excited, I scan through the pages.

In Ovid's *Metamorphoses,* another account depicts the Sirens as companions of Persephone, who were blessed with wings by the goddess Demeter. Their only desire was to search for Persephone when she was abducted. According to Ovid, their song is continually calling for Persephone's return.

Other cultures describe the Sirens as mermaids once scorned by deceptive sailors, who used their supernatural gift of song to seduce then punish any disloyal man. In fact, the Spanish word for mermaid is *Sirena*. French, Polish, Italian, Romanian and Portuguese all have similar names for Sirens.

"What is the truth?" I whisper to myself.

Vicious bird-like creatures or beautiful seductresses, no one seems to know definitively. Regardless of the discrepancies among these tales, one fact remains the same: to follow a *'Siren's Song'* is to follow death.

♪♪♪

I feel worse and worse as the day goes by. Thoughts of the sea keep creeping over me…consuming me. During Calculus, I fall asleep for a few minutes and wake to the sound of my own screams. I not only embarrassed myself with the sudden

144

outburst, but I also caused Mrs. Brown to drop all of the quiz papers she was giving back onto the floor. Thankfully, she only gave me a disappointed glare as she gathered up the bundle of papers, and continues her task.

"You look really crappy," Nicole pronounces rather loudly over the lunchroom clamor.

"Thanks a lot!" I snap, resting my lunch tray on the table beside her and Jenny. "I appreciate the honesty."

Immediately, I apologize for my rude behavior.

"You must have had a rough night," Jenny proclaims with genuine concern.

"I didn't get much sleep," I admit on a yawn. "I kept having these awful nightmares,"

"That sucks," Jenny sympathizes. "I'm sorry."

"Thanks," my disposition softens along with my tense shoulders.

Quite unexpectedly, I feel someone pushing me toward the center of the wooden bench, and notice as Andrew and Mike join us. Their lunch trays filled with ice cream cups, slices of cheese pizza, chocolate milk, and peanut butter and jelly sandwiches.

"You two are pigs!" Nicole admonishes with a stunned sneer.

"Oink, oink," Jenny adds indignantly.

"Move over," Andrew requests playfully, but today I am not in the mood.

"I'm not feeling well," I huff, picking up my tray of uneaten spaghetti and meatballs and excusing myself from the table. Everyone looks at me strangely.

Gallant to a flaw, Andrew stands.

"I'll go with you," he offers sweetly.

"Stay and eat your lunch," I command as gently as possible. "I need some fresh air. I'm going to sit in the courtyard for a while."

♪♪♪

Outside, the day is sweltering. The unrelenting tropical heat creates sweat beads that insultingly roll down my neck, soaking my shirt collar. Fortunately, I am much too tired to care. Feeling a migraine forming, I close my eyes, hoping to catch a few winks before my next class, uncaring of the storm clouds beginning to roll in, gloomy and portentous. That now familiar sound floats upon the air, luring me back to the sea.

146

"Don't be afraid," whoever she is sings.

"I'm not afraid," I growl, followed by an uncontainable yawn.

"Follow me...into the sea...it's where you want to be...it's where you want to be," the singing fades.

Suddenly, someone grabs my arm, jerking me out of my nap. Fear engulfs me and I try with all of my might to pull away, but they are stronger than I am. Now, I am yelling, fighting desperately to break free.

"Let me go!" I scream, still in a haze. "I don't want to go! I don't belong to the sea! I don't belong to you!"

"Selena, wake up!" Andrew's deep voice orders me back. "You're dreaming! It's just a bad dream."

Burning eyes dart open to find his worry-lined face peering down at me.

"Andrew?" I whimper, realizing I am still in the courtyard. "I don't know what's happening to me."

Concern covers his flushed face.

"You look like crap," he gulps his anxiety when I shoot him a dirty look and he tries to correct his last comment. "Are you okay?"

Still shaky, I nod, wiping the sleep from my eyes.

"The first bell just rang," he notifies as students descend the staircases. "We've got to go to class."

"I must have fallen asleep," I inform, grabbing my backpack, still lost in a tired haze.

"It sounded like you were in pain." His voice crackles.

"Did it? I don't remember," I tell a little white lie.

"Why don't you go to the nurse's office?" he suggests. "They'll call your mom to get you."

"I can't do that," I respond with a muffled yawn. "She's working on a big project this week. I shouldn't bother her."

"Oh, right," he blushes. "I forgot."

"Thank you again for getting her the job," I give a small grin, changing the subject. "She couldn't stop talking about it. She also thinks you are very sweet for mentioning her to your mom."

"I didn't get her the job," Andrew fidgets nervously. "I just planted the thought in my mom's head, that's all. She must have excellent credentials. My mom is really impressed by her portfolio."

"Well, thank you anyway," this time I manage a thin smile.

Wearily, he stares at me, wanting to say something, but not.

"We have to get to fourth period," I remind, not wanting detention.

"Have I done something wrong?" he suddenly blurts.

"Huh?" I groggily reply, my mind still loitering in the dream world.

"I mean...I wanted to make sure everything is okay with...us," he clarifies as we begin walking.

"Listen, Andrew," I begin rather harshly. "I have so much stuff I'm dealing with right now—"

"Then you definitely need some relaxation," the teen suggests. "I want to ask you a question."

"Go ahead," I reply impatiently, climbing the stairs to the second floor.

He takes a deep breath and begins, "Selena, would you like to—"

Ding! Ding! Ding! The last bells warn.

Frustrated, Andrew sighs as we both race up the stairs.

♪♪♪

I daydream through all of my subjects; incapable of remembering anything except Andrew talking to me in the courtyard. Having him around seems to comfort me; makes me feel like a normal teenager and not some sort of potential fish-freak.

As usual, Ando and I stand in front of the school in our customary place, on the sidewalk in front of the sturdy hibiscus bush. Our mother, of course, is nowhere to be seen. This time, however, we are prepared for another long wait. We have an umbrella, two bottles of water, and a large bag of chocolate chip cookies. Quite animated, my brother eagerly tells me about his day at school when I realize he just asked me a question. As still as a statue, he stands staring at me as if I am an alien or a nine-headed hydra.

"Lena!" his small voice loudens. "You're not listening to me!"

"I am listening," I convince half-heartedly. "I promise."

"Then answer the question," he folds his arms across his chest.

"I'm tired and I don't feel like talking right now," my tone is clipped and harsh. "Ask me again later."

Slightly perturbed, he turns away and begins picking more leaves off of the bush.

"Hey little dude!" Andrew calls to my brother as he exits the wrought-iron gates.

Ignoring me, Ando runs toward him and gives him a high five.

"Hey big dude!"

"Is your mom late again?" Andrew probes, already knowing the answer.

"Yeah, but it's okay this time," my brother grins. "We brought cookies with us today."

Ando snatches the bag of cookies from me and offers some to Andrew, who takes a couple. Still not myself, I sit quietly, hoping he will go away. For some reason, every time I see a male today, a flood of hostility washes over me. I cannot explain why.

More than a little hesitant, Andrew walks over and taps me on the shoulder.

"Are you feeling any better?" he questions with genuine regard.

"Not really," I pout, turning away.

Unwilling to hold a conversation, I take my sunglasses out of my backpack and put them on. Andrew looks at Ando, who looks at me.

"What?" I grumble impolitely and they say nothing.

Ignoring my abrasiveness, Andrew takes a red and yellow hacky-sack out of his bag and he and Ando begin kicking it around. After a few minutes, he gives it to Ando and sits down on the sidewalk beside me.

"What is it?" I blurt, hating the scent of his cologne when normally it makes me swoon.

Nervously, he clears his throat.

"I know this is probably not the right time," he starts. "Especially with you not feeling well, but if I don't ask now, I never will."

Dramatically, he takes a full breath while twirling the drawstrings to his varsity hoodie around his index finger.

"I'll understand if you don't want to...you don't have to...why is this so difficult?" he rants. "There is absolutely nothing that obligates you to go anywhere with me...if you hate the idea, I'll understand... it won't ruin our friendship or anything. I mean—"

"Andrew!" I bark, disregarding my manners. "Get to the point."

Taking another breath, he continues.

"Okay, I know we just met a few weeks ago, but I feel like I've known you forever and I know that Mike likes you too—"

That last sentence catches my attention.

"You're rambling," I blush, my anger beginning to diminish. "Just say what you're trying to say: quite badly I may add."

"Will you go out with me?" Andrew utters below his breath. "I'd love if you come to this Saturday's swim meet. We can go to dinner afterward and maybe...a movie...in a group. Mike already asked Nicole and Jenny, so they'll go if you do."

"If my parents say it's alright," I smile, giddy over the idea of a night out. "I would love to go out with you."

Andrew finally exhales. Just then, my stepfather pulls up beside us; his expression changes when he sees this new boy. In full parental form, he rolls down the driver's side window, looks Andrew up and down, then narrows his eyes. Andrew's expression morphs into one similar to an animal startled by oncoming headlights.

"Hello, young man," David greets suspiciously, studying him from head to toe again. "What are you doing with my daughter?"

At this, all of the blood drains out of the teenager's face.

"I w-was j-just talking to Selena about—" Andrew stutters nervously as Dad begins to laugh.

"I'm just giving you a hard time," he grasps Andrew's hand firmly, and the teen breathes a sigh of relief. "I'm Dr. Marquez, Selena and Ando's father. You must be the young man my daughter is always talking about?"

Andrew turns beet-red and I suddenly want to throw myself off of a bridge.

"Dad, stop embarrassing me," I protest, turning a sickly green.

Needing to get away, I grab Ando by the arm and lead him to the car. Andrew opens the back door for him, then helps me with my door. David smiles at the respectful gesture.

"Dr. Marquez; I was wondering if it's possible for Selena to come to my swim meet this Saturday afternoon?"

His bravery surprises me.

"I don't see why not," David advocates. "I'll talk it over with my wife and Selena will relay the answer to you tomorrow."

"One more thing, Dr. Marquez," Andrew adds. "A group of us are going out for pizza and a movie after the meet, so I was wondering—if it's okay with you and Mrs. Marquez—if Selena could go with me, umm, I mean us?"

Wow! He's a worse rambler than me!

A thin film of perspiration appears on his tanned brow as he waits for a reply, all the while watching Ando play with his hacky sack in the back seat of Dad's Jeep.

"Ando could come too," he tacks on for good measure.

"We'll see," Dad replies and gives Andrew a promising smile.

Realizing we are about to leave, my brother tries to give Andrew back the hacky-sack, but the teen only gives him a wink.

"Hold on to it until Saturday for me."

"Okay," Ando grins.

Still looking a bit off-kilter, the courageous youth waves at me and then Ando as we pull away, leaving him standing alone with an almost nauseous expression. Casually, I look in the side-view mirror just in time to see him dancing like a maniac. I smile to myself; boys are so crazy.

"I thought Mom was picking us up," I say as my stepfather looks quietly ahead.

"So did I, but she called about an hour ago, saying that she wasn't able to make it on time." David seems pensive. "No surprise there. Every day there's something going on that keeps her busy." He scratches his head. "Has she said anything to you about what's happening?"

"No," I reply without hesitation; feeling the need to protect my mother from herself.

"I don't know how much more I can take of this," he mumbles, checking his rearview mirror before merging.

"Oh," I respond, not knowing what else to say.

♪♪♪

David makes a quick Fettuccini Alfredo with chicken and broccoli for dinner once we get home. The odor of it makes me gag. Trying not to toss my cookies, I sip my water, hoping it will help soothe my gurgling stomach. As we sit down at the dining table, Mom rushes into the house, slamming the door behind her, startling us.

"I am so sorry I'm late," she pants. "I had to finish doing some errands."

"*Errands?*" David repeats doubtfully. "What errands were you doing?"

Mom stares uneasily at him, shimmering aquamarine orbs darting back and forth between him and the front door, her exit to freedom.

"Just a few things for a presentation I'm doing next week…for a client from out of town."

"Why is your hair wet?" David glares at her directly in those mesmerizing eyes.

Floundering for a response, she hesitates, then touches her damp curls.

"The sprinklers were on at work, and I got caught in it," Mom glances at me for support, or possibly a diversion.

"Hmm," he scoffs and takes a big bite of his pasta.

"Dinner looks fantastic," my mother tries changing the subject. At last, she sits and helps herself to several scoops of dinner, but rather than purring at the delectable concoction, she seems revolted at having to consume it. "Did everyone have a good day?"

"Andrew, let me borrow his hacky-sack," Ando answers, still chewing a mouthful of noodles.

"That was really nice of him," Mom responds, still trying to take the first bite of her meal.

David notices her strange behavior, but says nothing.

"Are you going to tell Mom the big news?" he steers the conversation toward me.

"Tell Mom what big news?" Mom asks, finally taking a bite.

My stepfather makes a goofy face before informing, "Well...according to a reliable source, Andrew Barnett—the cutest, smartest boy in the eleventh grade—would like our permission to take out our lovely daughter and her charming younger brother."

It takes all of my self-control not to smile.

"You're hilarious, Dad," I manage as my face heats.

Mom, shockingly, shakes her head.

"Absolutely not!" she exclaims angrily, pushing the food around her plate with the tines of her fork.

Stunned at her outburst, we all stare at her, mouths gaping at the sudden and unexpected refusal. It takes a second or two to register what just happened. With shaking hands, I take a sip of water, trying to remain as calm as possible.

"Mom, you've met Andrew; you told me that he was a very nice boy, remember?" I remind, holding back the floodgates of tears threatening to break free. "Mike, Nicole, and Jenny will be there too."

"I think she should go," my stepdad supports, giving me a reassuring nod. "Plus, Ando will be there. He's better than a Doberman pinscher."

Ando gives him a thumbs-up and rips the crust off of a slice of garlic bread he is chewing.

"You are too young to date," my mother notifies, looking down at her plate.

"It's not a date," I reply as coolly as possible. "It's a group outing."

"I said no and that's final!" Mom replies sternly as she takes her plate to the kitchen and throws the remainder of her dinner in the trashcan.

David looks at her curiously.

"I thought you liked this dish?"

"I do," she mumbles. "I'm not feeling very well. I just need some air."

Without further debate, Mom goes outside, leaving us wondering what had just happened.

♪♪♪

Unable to choke down my dinner, I excuse myself from the table and go upstairs to finish my math homework. The window is still open, allowing a cool breeze to enter. On leaden feet, I trudge to the window, pausing briefly to breathe the night air. Below, the sea sends briny spray up to greet me. Tilting my head, I strain to hear that lovely song, but instead I hear my parents arguing.

"Why don't you want her to go to the swim meet?" David interrogates loudly.

"She's too young to date, that's why," the sound of Mom's shoes clacking against the wooden planks of the porch tells me that she is pacing. She always paces when she is upset.

"It's not like she's going out with just Andrew," her husband reminds. "She'll be with a whole group of people."

Suddenly, she stops.

"I said no."

"Marina, I don't understand why you are being so unreasonable?" I hear louder footsteps and realize that David has started to pace as well. "It is a controlled situation with new friends. I think we should let her go."

"Stop telling me what to do!" my mother growls. "I can be unreasonable if it suits me!"

"I can't believe we're arguing over something so trivial. Selena is a good girl," David admonishes, his frustration evident. "She works hard in school, hardly ever complains, and always does what's right."

David's confidence in me makes me smile.

"No, she can't go," his wife huffs. "I can't explain why, but she just can't go."

"Marina—" David begins, but immediately is interrupted.

"NO! NO! NO!" Mom shouts as she storms back into the house, leaving David on the front porch by himself. Feeling sorry for his father, Ando goes out to be with him.

"You can play with my hacky-sack," I hear him say as he tries to be comforting. "It used to belong to Andrew, but he gave it to me."

"Thanks, son," David replies, and I hear the smile in his voice. "I really needed this."

♪♪♪

Pleasantly surprised, I complete my homework in record time, eager to return to my grandfather's journal. The story is fascinating; however, I cannot quite figure out if both of my grandparents were crazy or not. The idea that my grandmother dictated this preposterous story to my grandfather, who then transcribed her memories into this journal, not only terrifies me, but captivates me. All this talk of Sirens just confuses me further.

Frantically, I search for the box which is hidden underneath my bed.

The clock reads 8:11 p.m. as I begin to read:

One day, while we enjoyed the serenity of Anthemoessa, the goddess Demeter appeared to my sisters and I, her daughter Persephone, close by.

"To what do we owe this visit, great and wise Demeter?" My younger sister, Leukosia, always the articulate one, speaks first, her long flowing blonde hair stroked by the wind's invisible fingers.

Demeter smiles in her customary gentle fashion.

"Sisters of the Sea," she often referred to us, "I require a great favor."

"Anything," we all answer simultaneously, as we often do.

This time, my elder sister Ligeia steps forward, bowing low.

"Ask anything of us, our lady." Ligeia, the boldest and loveliest of us, her emotions known to be as fiery as her crimson locks, exclaims, "We serve you without question!"

Leukosia and I chime in unison, "We serve you without question."

"Then watch over my most prized possession." Demeter gently maneuvers Persephone closer to us. The young goddess grins and we know we will give our lives for her.

For decades, just as promised, my sisters and I watched over Persephone like she was our own offspring. We taught her the songs of the birds and the adventurous nature of the ocean. Persephone loved to explore our island, gathering wild flowers and playing with the many animals she would encounter on her walks. The young goddess would *always return before dark, always carrying new items she'd found on her trek.*

"Lena!" my brother bangs on the door, disturbing my reading.

"What is it?" I snap, wanting to return to the story my grandfather has so masterfully laid out.

"I need help," he states, his voice muffled behind the wooden barrier.

"What kind of help?" I huff, shaking my head.

"Alfredo wanted me to throw him up in the air and he accidentally got stuck in the fan," he confesses meekly.

Rolling my eyes at him, I tuck the journal under a pillow and leave to assist my brother and his teddy bear.

"I'm on my way," I reply, opening the door to see Ando smiling appreciatively. "Let's go save Alfredo."

Approximately five minutes later, I return. Eagerly, I fetch the journal from its hiding space and begin reading:

One day, darkness came and Persephone had not returned. Ligeia and I began searching every inch of

Anthemoessa, hoping she had just lost track of time, as young-ones often do, while Leukosia swam around the island in case Persephone had gone to the limestone masses to practice her songs, but she was nowhere to be seen. After hours of searching even the darkest crevices of the island, we summoned the goddess Demeter to explain our predicament.

"Oh, noble Demeter," we three say in unison. "The innocent maiden has been lost."

We bow low almost to the point of our faces touching the dark, fertile soil.

Demeter's expression suddenly turns from calm and peaceful to misshapen and distraught. High above, the clouds begin to compress into a huge, gray form, ominous and deadly. Anthemoessa begins to shake so violently the needles on the millennia-old Cypress trees begin to fall. Even the hundreds of multi-colored birds abandon their lofty resting places, fleeing their precarious perches.

"You were to look after Persephone!" Demeter yells. "Instead, you have lost her!"

Tears roll down her face in waves, cold and salty. As they began to soak into the earth, the ground starts to harden and turn icy. Before our eyes, the thick carpet of grass covering the entire island begins to whither and turn from bright emerald to dusty brown. An unsympathetic, savage wind sweeps over the land, destroying every lavender blossom, lemon tree, wild oregano plant, honeybee, and butterfly in its path. In seconds, our once flowery home is turned into a barren wasteland of ice and snow.

Leukosia, the Precocious, dares to step forward, face stained with tears of her own.

"Dearest Demeter, goddess of the grain, let us continue the search for the maiden," she begs in a sad, soulful tone.

Finally finding my voice, I step forward and humbly kneel at Demeter's sandaled feet.

"Gentle Demeter, Goddess of Fertility; give us the tools to find your child. Let us search every valley and mountain peak of Gaia for young Persephone."

Red-headed Ligeia bows next; face almost as red as her hair.

"We will find her, no matter where she may be. And we will punish anyone who has harmed her," she adds angrily, nostrils flaring with each difficult breath.

To our relief, Demeter's tears lessen as she ponders our heartfelt words. The goddess closes her red-rimmed eyes, contemplating her next move. My sisters and I hold our breath, wondering what awful punishment will befall us, but the patient goddess restrains her rage.

"Because I know your hearts are true to me and to Persephone, I will grant your wish." Demeter's features soften as she turns to the heavens, arm outstretched, and announces, "To you sisters three...I give to thee...wings of a bird...to give you flight."

Quite unexpectedly, I feel something wriggling beneath my skin, like a worm breaking free of the earth; a wave of terror crashes over me. My sisters are both screeching in agony as Demeter watches calmly. Before long, two large, eagle-like wings appear on each of us. Outstretched, they are twice the length of our arm span. To my delight, the tips of my wings are painted in shimmering aquamarine. Ligeia's wings are streaked with a bold red that resembles a ferocious sunrise after a violent storm. As imagined, Leukosia's feathers are highlighted in varying shades of golden hues, just like those adorning her fair locks. Curiously, we willed them to move...which to our amusement they did, beating and flapping on command.

Filled with excitement, I will myself to rise and I did, several feet into the air in fact. Soon all three of us were soaring through the heavens, trying out our new appendages. Inspired by the song birds for eons, we had learned how to sing like them, but now, graced with the power to fly, we embraced that feeling of freedom we had never experienced before. Finally, we were complete.

As gracefully as possible, we landed back on solid ground, ecstatic about our ability to soar. Impossible to stop them, tears begin to well up, blurring my perfect vision and causing my aquamarine irises to sparkle like meticulously polished jewels. I'd never been so sad and so joyful at the same time. With a steady voice, the goddess spoke softly, her tone ridden with anguish.

"This gift will help you with your search for Persephone. I hope your journey is successful."

In a cloud of smoke, she disappeared, leaving us surrounded by snow and destruction and a new determination to find our beloved Persephone...

Tired from the day's events, compounded by the sad tale, I slowly close the journal. The scent of worn leather still lingers on my hands. As if under its well-woven spell, I trace its decorative sigma with a lone finger. This cannot be possible, any of this, and although my mind tells me otherwise, my heart and soul reaffirm that nothing is impossible.

CHAPTER EIGHT

I t is a few minutes before midnight, and I cannot sleep. Dreams of goddesses and sea nymphs plague my thoughts. Missing the voices, I leave the window open again, but no songs visit me. For the second night in a row, Mom and David are in their room quarreling. I can hear them from downstairs. Mom has never been this upset with David until tonight. In fact, I cannot remember them ever disagreeing. Do not get me wrong, they have little tiffs here and there, but never ones that last this long.

As expected, the front door opens, and I hear someone pacing across the weather-worn wooden planks of the porch. I look out just in time to see David sitting on the grass a few feet away from the entrance to the descending rocky staircase. Soon after, another set of footsteps warns of Mom's approach. As I watch from the open window, she glances up and spots me.

Panicked, I race back to bed, quickly sliding under the covers. I even add snoring to complete my performance.

A few minutes later, she opens the door just enough to make sure I am in bed, then softly shuts it again. With abated breath, I wait a couple minutes as Mom checks on Ando, then goes back down to the first floor to her own room. The pipes begin to shake as her shower is turned on.

Unable to quiet my mind, I lay on the soft mattress, allowing the night's events to sink in. Mom is behaving so strangely, but I guess I have been acting similarly. I do not want to eat; the smell of cooked food makes me sick. I am always tired and men in general aggravate me beyond words. Even thinking about males, including my favorite television star, makes me angry.

Am I coming down with the flu? I self-diagnose, getting more concerned with my failing health.

As I close my eyes, a gust of salty wind slithers in through the open bedroom window, causing the sheer white drapes to dance. Like before, it beckons me, filling me with an unnatural need for independence…freedom from the constraints of this room…this life.

"Come to us, Selena," it whispers. *"We need you. You need us. Don't be afraid. It is your destiny. It is inevitable."*

"No," I murmur, covering my head with one of my pillows. "Leave me alone."

"The sea needs you and you need the sea. Come to us and you will be complete. Come to us…"

Determined to find the source of the voice, and also to check on David, I make my way back to the window, but he is no longer there. In the distance, the surf sounds loud and violent. Quickly, my vision adjusts to the outstretching darkness and focuses on David briskly walking in the direction of the carved stairs.

Then, a sudden dark thought strikes me.

"Dad, please stop!" I shriek, not caring if they ground me. As fast as possible, not even stopping to grab my shoes, I run downstairs, across the noisy living room floor, and out the front door. I am running so fast that I trip over my own feet and fall at least twice before reaching the edge of the cliff where the steps are located. "Daddy! Come back!"

Afraid of tripping again, I walk as carefully as possible down the steps holding on to the protruding uneven cliff surface.

Overhead, clouds gather in front of the moon, blocking the only light. It is almost impossible to see now.

"David!" I roar, hoping he will hear me call him by his first name and turn around to scold me.

Gingerly, my foot finds the stony surface below. Trying to locate David, I squint, but he is nowhere around. Desperation fills me as I dash to the water's edge and peer down into its shadowy, churning surface. Without warning, he surfaces, gasping and fighting against the current.

"Hold on, Dad!" I shout, looking around for something to use as a life preserver. Once more, his form disappears beneath another wave. Something down deep in my soul kicks in as I dive headfirst where David last appeared. The coldness of the water shocks me a little, but determined to save him; I hold my breath as I will myself to plunge downward, even more terrified at my situation.

Why didn't I take those swimming lessons at the Y when I had the chance?

Eyes burning from the salt, I look around underwater, surprised that I can actually see. A few feet above me, swirls of bubbles dance among the current, creating a star-like pattern.

Focus Selena, focus!

It is then that I see my stepfather floating down to the sandy bottom. I kick as hard as I can against the rocks, and to my astonishment, I descend rapidly, fast and powerful; my arms pumping like pistons in an engine.

Moving with purpose, I reach his figure swiftly, but he has already stopped struggling. Panic-stricken, I grab him around the chest and head toward the surface when a flood of terror engulfs me as something grabs my leg. With a swift kick, I try to break free, fueled by the need to get him up to the surface. I keep kicking my leg as hard as I can. Whatever it is, will not release me. In fact, the grip tightens.

Dear God! Please don't let it be a shark!

In a last attempt to reach the surface, I secure David in one hand and reach down with my free one, and there, around my ankle, cold, icy fingers are wrapped. Attempting to engulf me, a red seaweed-like mass begins to float around me, blocking my way. Petrified, I open my mouth to scream, forgetting I am underwater and salty liquid rushes in and I swallow in a panic.

This is how it ends for me; I think. *Another drowning victim!*

Thankfully, I am still holding David. With all of my remaining strength, I push him upward with the hope that he will at least float up to the surface. Then, as rage replaces horror, I grab the pale fingers and pry them open. With a mind of their own, the red spirals retract as a face appears below. It is a woman with long curly red hair and hypnotic aquamarine eyes. She looks at me curiously and slowly releases her grip. Wanting to get back to shore…no, needing to get to the shore, I swim to David's body and grab him under the armpits.

Somehow, I manage to pull him out of the water and onto the rocks safely. Frantically, I put my ear to his chest. There is no heartbeat. My stomach lurches as I feel for a pulse, but find nothing. Remembering my CPR training from summer camp, I tilt his head back, squeeze his nose, and breathe into his mouth. Next, I find his sternum and begin rhythmically pumping.

One…two…three…four…five. Breathe, dammit! I do this process just like the camp counselors taught me when I was younger.

"Please, God, don't let him die," I pray. "David, you better start breathing on your own!" I begin to whimper, but the sound gets caught in my throat. "Breathe…breathe…please breathe!"

Relief fills me as David starts to cough uncontrollably, seawater spurting from his mouth. Overwhelmed with joy, I hug him, releasing every distress-filled tear I have. Loud sobs keep coming, bursting with the agony at the thought of losing him. From nowhere, Mom flies down the steps, followed closely by Ando. Upon seeing us, her expression changes from anger to alarm to sheer horror as David lies on the wave-smoothened rocks gasping for air.

"David! Selena! Oh, my goodness!" Mom hugs us both tightly. "When I couldn't find the two of you in the house, I never imagined you'd be down here...David..."

She kisses his damp face.

Ando hugs me, then Dad, and then Mom. He is not crying, but I can see the sadness in his eyes...those mesmerizing aquamarine eyes; just like the eyes of the woman in the sea...just like mine.

Without a word, our mother helps David back up the steps to the safety of the house and settles him on one of the dining chairs. Luckily, his breathing is back to normal for the most part. Exhausted by the night's events, Ando sits on the chair beside him, yawning as he colors a get-well card. Instead of his usual talkative self, he stays uncharacteristically quiet. When he finishes, he takes it with him to the living room. A few minutes of complete silence passes before the rest of us realize my little brother has fallen asleep on the sofa, his picture on the coffee table, teddy bear propped under his head like a furry brown pillow.

"What were you doing down there?" Mom interrogates as she pours David a hot cup of coffee. He takes a long sip as steam rises off of the dark liquid in a serpentine motion, while color begins to return to his cheeks.

"It was the strangest thing," David begins; his thoughts are far away, reliving the event. "I was sitting on the porch thinking about our argument and enjoying the scent of the ocean when this song starts to play. It was so soft and alluring, like it was serenading me."

Mom turns a sickly green hue.

"This song called to you?" she counters.

"Yes," he answers with a dismissive smile.

"And you went to find it?" I ask, feeling nauseous again, but this time not from hunger.

"Yes," he speaks, but the word fades into the air. "I can't explain. The voice wanted me to come to it. It kept singing to me like a sweet, angelic child. At first, I tried to ignore it, but somehow it took hold of me."

Carefully, David fills his mouth with coffee.

"Do you remember the words?" Mom and I question in harmony.

Dad stares at us, then suddenly narrows his eyes.

"I'll never forget it," he promises, and there is a short pause as he closes his eyes and begins humming a peculiar song. Then he sings, *"Don't be afraid…come with me… into the sea… in the ocean waves we'll play."*

With this confession, my saliva goes down the wrong pipe and I choke as my body convulses from the sudden assault on my lungs. Still carrying that same sullen expression, Mom helps her husband to the bedroom and returns to find me still sitting at the dining table. I watch as she lowers herself on the chair beside me. Unwilling to meet my gaze, she pours herself a cup and swirls the warm beverage. I can tell that she wants to pace, but she wills herself to stay in her seat. Her eyes glisten from the florescent light above.

Just like my stepfather, she begins humming the same little tune, seemingly unaware of what she is doing. Compelled to join in, I hum along with her in the same way; our voices intertwine until they are one: sad, yet strong. Over on the couch, Ando stirs. We realize what we are doing, but something urges us on. Ando moves again, this time changing his position as Mom and I continue; trapped in this musical loop. Suddenly, Ando sits up, rubs the sleep out of his eyes, then comes to us; his teddy bear was still clutched in his arms.

"Why are you two making so much noise?" he pouts with a perturbed sigh.

I gaze at his tired expression and ask, "Did it call to you?"

"No," he grumbles. "I've been trying to sleep and you keep making noise."

Then, quite annoyed, my brother turns and stomps upstairs to his room. David, on the other hand, walks out of the bedroom in a weird trance. Zombie-like, he walks towards us and stops when he reaches our human barrier, then lethargically, he turns on his heels and walks to the front door. Mom and I immediately release hands and stop humming. Dad looks around, unsure of where he is or how he got there.

"Honey, are you alright?" Mom stands as if to go to him, and then stops.

"I don't know," he responds. "I was getting ready to take a shower, heard that beautiful song again, then the next thing I know, I'm out here."

He shakes his head.

"Weird," he grumbles, then turns around.

Seemingly lost, he goes back to the room, mumbling under his breath in Spanish about losing his mind. David must be really upset because he usually only speaks in Spanish when he is really angry or excited.

"What's going on?" I demand, not caring about my tone of voice.

"What do you mean?" my mother feigns innocence unconvincingly.

"Your weird disappearing act…the strange voices coming from the sea…the voices that don't seem to worry you…"

"Selena—"

"*What?*" I snap without thinking. "You need to tell me! Whatever you are trying to hide from me…just tell me, please!"

"You won't believe me…" she blurts. "…you're not going to believe me."

I watch wordlessly as my mother goes around the entire house, making certain that all of the doors and windows are securely locked.

"W-we don't have to w-worry about Ando being lured," she stammers to herself, completely forgetting that I am only a few feet away. "He's immune to the call, b-but David is another story."

Unsure of what to do, I venture to the second floor to check on Ando, who snuggles beneath a *Spiderman* comforter. A black tuft of hair sticking out is the only evidence that he is there. That makes me smile.

Returning to the bottom floor, I decide to peek in on David. Even he has managed to fall asleep. As I stand watching, a soft groan escapes his lips as he tries to get comfortable. I am certain it is because his chest is sore from CPR. In my opinion, a few bruised ribs are better than the alternative.

"How did you know that something was wrong with David?" Mom unexpectedly appears behind me, making me jump.

"I've been leaving my windows open at night," defiantly I inform. "I heard you two arguing. When you checked on me earlier, I was pretending to be asleep. After you left to take a shower, I looked out of the window and saw Dad heading toward the stairs. Something just didn't feel right, so I followed him."

"Thank goodness you did because he almost..." the usually well-composed woman chokes back a sniffle. Taking my hand, she leads me to my room, sits down on the disheveled bed and begins to sob.

"Mom," I say shyly. "When I was under the water… something scary happened."

Quickly, she wipes her face with the back of a trembling hand and tries to regain her composure.

"What happened?" she sniffs.

"Well, my first thought was that he got too close to the edge, slipped, and bumped his head on the rocks." I pause.

"Continue," Mom pleads.

"So I jumped in after him," I continue. "I was down there…looking for him…I was in the water for a while…"

"Keep going," she encourages, coming to a standing position.

"Then I saw him… down at the bottom… so I swam down to get him, but…"

"But what?" She watches my animated facial expressions and accelerating breathing as she takes a step in my direction.

"When I was swimming, I felt powerful," I admit. "I felt like I was… like I was at home."

"What happened next?" She takes another step towards me.

Trying not to leave anything out, I recall the exact details.

"I got a hold of David and was trying to swim to the surface, which was amazing in itself since I can't swim." I know I am being long-winded, but I do not care. "I was almost to the surface when something grabbed my ankle. I thought it was a shark for sure, but when I touched it...it was fingers; long pale fingers."

"Go on," she urges with wild eyes.

"It was a woman, I think, holding me," I relay. "She had unnaturally long, red hair and bright aquamarine eyes... just like ours."

The room goes deadly silent. Mom's face is ashen, and I can almost hear my own heartbeat. I already know who it is; she does too.

"It was Ligeia, the eldest of *The Three,*" I whisper before she does. "I think she recognized me."

"Why do you say that?" she asks, voice filled with unease.

"She looked at me, smiled, and then released me," I sigh. "I don't know if that's a good thing or a bad thing."

For a long time, my mother says nothing, then quickly closes my bedroom windows and locks them.

"She did recognize you, because you are the spitting image of me and Yaya Parthenope."

I stare at her trying to understand the implications of her statement.

"Parthenope, you mean the dark-haired sea nymph in Grandpa Theo's book? She was my grandmother?" I laugh uncontrollably. "That's a good one, Mom."

On a mission, she takes the journal from the nightstand and quickly scans the pages. Without a word, she hands it to me.

On the last page is a sketch of a beautiful woman standing on the bow of an ancient Greek sailing vessel. Jet black curls frame either side of her face; her aquamarine eyes partially hidden by unusually long ebony lashes. The woman has high cheekbones like a model and a flawless olive complexion that glows even in the dark. Everything about her is graceful and poised.

"This is you when you were younger." I gently touch the yellowing pages. "You are so beautiful. Was this in Greece?"

Mom smiles, but shakes her head.

"That is not me," she reveals, shocking me.

Not thoroughly understanding, I inspect the sketch again.

"It has to be you because I have never posed for this." I frown.

She giggles.

"That is Yaya Parthenope... my mother, your grandmother, several hundred years ago."

CHAPTER NINE

Dad speeds to St. Peter and Paul's like a racecar driver trying to win the *Daytona 500*. In the back seat, Ando and I are buckled in holding on for dear life. We left home late because David had a flat tire.

"Dad, stop driving like a maniac!" I squeal, my right hand gripping the overhead bar.

"You're gonna crash the car!" Ando chimes in.

"We won't enjoy the swim meet if we're dead!" I bark, gripping the handle tighter and closing my eyes. "I'm not trying to be mean or anything, but it's true."

"Sorry," the usually composed marine scientist slows down as we pull up to the thick iron gates of the school.

"How do I look?" I ask for the umpteenth time, fidgeting with my top.

"Lena, we already told you that you look fine," Ando rolls his eyes.

"Fine as in fine, or fine as in *Fine*?" I ask for clarification unsuccessfully.

Finally, David looks at me, irises gleaming with mischief.

"What's the difference?"

"Fine, is just okay. *Fine* is like hot!" I explain, but David is still confused. I think of another example he can relate to.

I got one!

"Fine is Martha Stewart," I expound. "*Fine,* is Salma Hayek."

"Oh! *Ella esta muy caliente!*" The man finally gets it, chuckling. "Without a doubt, you are the Salma Hayek one."

From my peripheral vision, I spot Jenny and Nicole waiting for us at the entrance. It is so weird seeing them in regular clothes. Quickly, I kiss Dad on the cheek, hop out of the car, and wait for Ando to join me. Why he is moving so slowly? I have no idea.

Before we get too far from the vehicle, my stepdad rolls down the window.

"What time does the movie finish?" He questions for the tenth time.

"It ends a few minutes after ten," I remind for the tenth time.

"Mom and I will meet you in front of the Cineplex at a quarter past ten," he glares, overly concerned.

"Okay...stop it," I roll my eyes.

"Hey!" David calls out.

"Yes?" I reply anxiously.

"If Andrew tries to kiss you, give him a right hook just like I taught you!" He jabs the air to illustrate, and I roll my eyes again.

"Please stop worrying about Andrew trying to kiss me," I reassure the overly protective man, but secretly I hope he does make a move. "I'm sure that's not going to happen."

"Do you have your cell phone?" he interrogates.

"Yes," I huff and stomp my left foot to emphasize my aggravation. "I have my cell phone with me, so everything is copasetic."

"Copasetic?" Dad repeats with a loud belly laugh.

I stick my tongue out at him playfully, causing him to guffaw.

"Stop being such a dad!" I shout after him as he slowly drives away.

Nicole finally spots us and waves.

"Lena, they're here!" Ando shouts, seeing them too.

Ignoring my request to stay beside me, my brother takes it upon himself to run ahead to meet them. Eagerly, Jenny picks him up and spins him around. When she finally puts him back down, he is too dizzy to stand. His adorable, boyish giggle fills the air.

"Hey maggot!" Jenny teases while he catches his breath.

"Hi amoeba!" Ando teases back, still looking wobbly.

Nicole hugs him and he giggles again. I think he has a crush on her, but he tries to hide it. He is such a guy!

"Oooh! You look like something out of a fashion magazine," Jenny jokes, bumping me with her hip.

"Thank you, thank you!" I bat my eyes flirtatiously, then curtsy. "Both of you look gorgeous, too."

"Your outfit is beautiful." Nicole touches the silver beading around the neckline of my halter top. "How long did it take to put this ensemble together?"

"This old thing? I just threw this together," I fib, giving her a wink.

Little does she know; it took me over an hour to pick out this outfit. In all honesty, I changed at least five times. I even went through my mother's closet. At the very last minute, I decided to wear my dark blue jeans, white halter top, and a cute pair of sandals. I even used Mom's hot iron to straighten my hair; surprisingly, it looks very cute.

"What about me?" Nicole interjects. "How do I look?"

She spins around to show off her new tan cargo shorts and navy scoop-neck t-shirt. Usually, she wears her hair up in a bun, but today she is sporting a sleek down-do. Jenny also looks attractive in her blue plaid Bermuda's and white tank top; her hair, which is usually worn straight and pulled back into a high ponytail, in now loose and sporting perfect spiral curls.

"No guy could resist us." I lower my voice and strike a sexy pose like I've seen on TV. They strike similar poses and we all burst out laughing. Just then, Amy walks by with her father, Stuart Jacobs, who is Dad's boss at Ocean World. They stop to greet us and Mr. Jacobs takes my hand, giving me a big smile.

"Hello, Selena!" Mr. Jacobs states enthusiastically. "It's nice to see you again,"

"Thank you, Sir, it's good to see you too," I lie, not wanting to be offensive. "Hi, Amy."

Amy smirks, then turns to her father.

"I'm going to find some seats," she croons to her dad, then slowly saunters in the direction of the bleachers.

"You have to excuse my daughter," Mr. Jacobs tries to justify his daughter's rude behavior. "Amy's shy around new people. Give her some time, she'll come around. She really is a good girl."

"I'm sure she is." I smile, but it does not reach my eyes.

Tension bounces between us as we stand uneasily, wishing the other person would end the conversation.

"I hope you all enjoy the meet," he concludes, then quickly skulks away, just like a little rat.

"Amy's father seems okay," Nicole tries to paint him in a more positive light when she sees the revulsion darken my features.

"He's a lot nicer than she is, that's for sure," Jenny agrees, glancing over her shoulder at the tawdry blonde and her rodent of a father.

"I don't know yet," I say uneasily. "There is something about him that doesn't sit well with me. The way he bullied my father the other day at Ocean World…it just wasn't cool."

"C'mon, let's go look at some hot swimmers," Jenny moves her eyebrows up and down in a funny sort of way.

♪♪♪

Immediately, Ando runs ahead of us to find some seats. To my delight, Andrew and Mike have already saved us four seats in the front row of the bleachers. Amy and her father are sitting all the way in the top row. I wave to her, but she just gives me a dirty look.

"What did I do to Amy to make her hate me so much?" I ask out loud.

Both Nicole and Jenny turn in Amy's direction and wave to her, too. She pretends not to see them. Like children, they giggle and turn forward, facing the pool again.

"Isn't it obvious?" Jenny chuckles.

"Isn't *what* obvious?" I sulk.

"Amy has had a crush on Andrew since the third grade," Nicole explains. "And he's never given her a second look—"

"But that changed about two months ago when they ended up on the school dance committee together. Coincidence, I think not. Everyone knows Amy joined the committee to be near Andrew," Jenny interrupts.

"For as long as I can remember, Amy's been mean to me and Jenny," Nicole jumps in again. "Then all of a sudden, she starts acting really sweet to us and showing up to all of the swim team hang-outs. Andrew likes going to the skate park...next thing you know, Amy's suddenly interested in skateboarding."

"I guess she thought she was wearing him down or something, so she asked him to the dance—" Jenny blurts as she turns her cell phone to vibrate.

"What dance?" I interject.

"The Homecoming Dance in November," Jenny nudges Nicole, who is searching the pool for Mike.

"Oh, but then this new girl shows up one day, and she's beautiful, funny, smart, and has the voice of an angel." Nicole stretches her neck to get a better view as she resumes her search for Mike.

"Andrew begins hanging out with this new girl and Amy, being the skank that she is, decides that this girl needs to stay away from her property," Jenny takes over once more.

Both girls snap their fingers at exactly the same time, startling me.

At their informative narrative, my brow furrows as I mull over everything that has been laid at my feet. Andrew, Amy, me: everything!

I think I feel a headache coming on.

"But Andrew hasn't asked me to the dance," I respond awkwardly.

"Not yet," Jenny sings like she is the lead soprano of an opera.

"Okay, I understand that Amy likes Andrew, and she is upset because he doesn't want her, but that isn't my fault," I state under my breath.

"It doesn't matter," Nicole blurts as she spots Mike doing a warm-up lap on the far side of the pool and waves.

"Why doesn't that matter?" I make a face like I have just sucked on a slice of lemon.

"You are getting in the way of her plans," Nicole grins.

Jenny, who was chatting with Ando, becomes animated.

"Yeah, girl, Amy is used to getting everything she wants and right now, she wants Andrew," Jenny pinches Nicole's arm, causing her to flinch.

I sigh.

"If she wants him so badly, then she can have him."

"But Andrew wants you," they both announce together.

Their ability to know what each other is thinking is truly amazing. I would not mind having that ability. Then I would never have to be alone.

"So, what should I do?" I fret, hoping for some good advice.

Before I can stop her, Jenny pinches my arm and points to someone in the pool waving at us. It is Andrew; with his goggles on it is really difficult to recognize him. We wave back, including Ando, who stands up so Andrew can see him.

"Good luck!" my brother bellows as he jumps up and down like a fighting kangaroo.

Suddenly, Nicole turns to me, her expression no-nonsense.

"Do you like him or not?" Nicole probes seriously.

"Yes," I blush. "I like him a lot."

"Good to know!" Nicole smiles omnisciently.

"Then forget about Awful Amy and give Andrew a chance," Jenny adds and successfully closes the topic.

♪♪♪

Andrew and the rest of the St. Peter and Paul's swim team won fourteen out of fifteen races. We are almost hoarse from cheering so loud. Everyone, especially me, is elated to be hanging out together.

After the meet, we end up at MT's Pizza Parlor. The restaurant is crowded, and all of the tables are filled. Mike and Andrew bring everyone pizzas and drinks while a dark-skinned gentleman in the kitchen assembles more pies. Near the soda dispenser, an attractive chestnut-haired woman fills red plastic tumblers with ice and beverages.

"Why are Mike and Andrew serving us?" I ask, wondering if this is a self-service restaurant.

Nicole finishes chewing before she answers.

"Mike's parents own this restaurant."

"He works here after school and Andrew works part-time on the weekends," Jenny adds.

"The Taylor's treat the swim team to free pizza after every meet. They are the nicest people...down to earth, you know?" Nicole chimes in again.

"That's so sweet," I smile, loving the kind gesture.

Shortly after, Andrew comes over to the table wearing a pair of beige Dockers and a black button-down polo; his eyes are extra green this evening. His hair is still damp from earlier and he smells like a combination of Y cologne and chlorine, but for some reason the combination smells nice on him.

"How are you doing?" Andrew beams, resting a stack of paper napkins in the middle of the table. "I should have warned you about how crazy it was going to be, but I didn't want you to cancel."

"I'm having fun," I divulge, wiping my hands on a napkin.

"What about you, Andover?" Andrew teases. "How are you doing with all of these girls?"

Ando makes a face.

"They keep talking about how cute you are," my little brother rats us out without a second thought.

I choke and almost spit out my soda as the girls quickly change the topic. Andrew blushes as he turns and heads back towards the busy kitchen, but Jenny stops him before he can escape.

"What time does the movie start?" Jenny questions, her face red as well.

Andrew checks the clock.

"It starts in a little over an hour," he tells. "Mike's mom is going to drop us off."

Mike comes over next.

"How's the pizza?" he questions, already knowing the answer.

"Really good!" Jenny praises, licking her lips; making everyone except Mike blush.

The tolerant teen ignores her, all of his attention fixated on Nicole.

"What about you, Nicole?" his hazel eyes lighting up. "Is your food okay?"

"It's the best pizza I've ever eaten," Nicole practically moans from the incredible taste.

Jenny just looks at them and shakes her head.

"Nicole," she taps her on the shoulder. "Doesn't Mike look handsome?"

Nicole gives her a stern look.

"Yes, he does, Jenny."

"Is that a new shirt?" Jenny continues, and Mike nods. "Doesn't the green in his shirt bring out the flecks in his eyes?"

Beads of perspiration suddenly appear on Nicole's upper lip. Mike looks like he is sweating, too. Jenny, on the other hand, is cooler than a cucumber. I am just glad she is not harassing me.

"And Mike…" Jenny continues. "Don't you think Nicole looks amazing?"

"She always looks like an angel," Mike stares at Nicole, eyes dancing playfully, which makes us all smile.

"Hey, you two slackers!" Mr. Taylor yells from the kitchen. "Get back to work! You can flirt with pretty girls later. We've got hungry people to feed."

Before we can request more food, Mike's mother brings us another pepperoni and mushroom pizza.

"Selena, this is my mom," Mike introduces, smiling proudly, revealing his dimples.

"How do you like Isla Flora, Selena?" Mrs. Taylor asks as she wipes her hands on her apron, hazel eyes twinkling.

"I wasn't sure I'd like it here, but it seems to be growing on me," I reply, glancing in Andrew's direction.

"I'm glad." Mrs. Taylor places the tray on the table. I realize then that Mike has her eyes and her smile. Then she announces in Italian: *"Finisci di mangiare!"*

"It means eat up!" Mike translates.

Sweetly, Mrs. Taylor kisses him on the cheek.

"My dear," Mrs. Taylor addresses Nicole. "My son told me that he asked you out, but you turned him down. You know that you're destined to be my daughter-in-law. What's the problem?"

Mrs. Taylor winks at her playfully and now it was Nicole's turn to change color.

"Umm...well...umm..." she glares at Jenny, cheeks glowing.

Seeing this, Mike scoots his parent away.

"Thanks a lot, Ma," he grumbles. "I think I hear Dad calling you."

Trying to ignore the awkwardness of the moment, Nicole grabs another slice and takes an enormous bite. Ando, who thinks stuffing your mouth should be an Olympic event, looks at her and snickers. Andrew, who is now blushing for his best friend, leads Mike away from the table to the kitchen. Mike's milk chocolate complexion makes it difficult to tell when he is embarrassed, but we can see it in his expression.

"C'mon, Casanova," Andrew states in a fatherly tone. "Get back to work."

At a loss for words, Nicole is still taking large bites of her food. Her best friend stares at her, then, without provocation, punches her on the arm.

"Why didn't you tell me Mike asked you out?" Jenny huffs.

Nicole finishes swallowing the large mouthful before responding.

"I didn't want you to be mad at me," the shy young lady confesses. "I know you like him, too."

"I don't like him," Jenny responds emphatically before rolling her eyes.

"But you're always teasing him and making kissing faces at him and tickling him." Nicole tries to wash down a chunk of pizza with her drink.

"I do that because it makes him uncomfortable," Jenny laughs. "He's the shyest boy I know, and I think it's funny that he gets all flustered when I do those things."

"So…you don't like him?" Nicole confirms.

"No, you moron, I don't like him like that," Jenny reconfirms. "So go out with him already."

"I don't think that's a good idea," Nicole's voice lowers.

"Why not?" I jump into the banter. "He's a great guy."

"Suppose we start dating, end up breaking up, and then we end up hating each other and six years of friendship goes down the toilet?" the teen rambles.

Then she pauses to gather her thoughts.

"If that happens, we'll be forced to divide up our friends," she continues. "Andrew would hang out with him and you and Jenny would support me. I'd rather have him as a friend than nothing," Nicole informs gloomily.

I look at Andrew and think the same thing.

Jenny punches her again.

"You've thought about this way too much."

As we continue our conversation, the bell on the front door jingles, making us all turn to see who it is. My heart sinks as my rival for Andrew's affections, along with two other female students, enter the restaurant. Jenny, staying true to her character, starts gagging loudly as they pass our table.

Nicole just looks Amy up and down.

"She wasn't wearing that outfit at the meet," Nicole whispers.

Ignoring our disgusted stares, Amy struts across the restaurant, blonde hair teased like a lioness's mane, wearing a much too tight black tube top, black leather mini-skirt, and tall, black hooker boots. Let us just say that the outfit does not sit well with the patrons in the restaurant; however, most of the guys are drooling all over their slices of pizza. Richard—the boy who made those inappropriate comments on my first day of school—

starts whistling. Amy winks playfully at him, but makes a beeline to Andrew, who is wiping down the counters.

"Three slices of cheese pizza, please," Amy places her order with Andrew, who is looking very uncomfortable. She pays with a fifty and says: "Keep the change."

More uncomfortable than before, I turn away.

♪♪♪

For the rest of the evening, Amy relentlessly flirts with Andrew. The other girls in her entourage are busy making their way from table to table like a couple of bothersome gnats. I feel the need to throw up.

In mid-sentence, Amy suddenly looks at her watch.

"We have to go," she whines. "My dad is picking us up in a few minutes."

To my delight, Andrew seems relieved.

"Have a good night," he replies coolly, but is not fast enough to avoid her reach.

More than annoyed, my eyes automatically narrow when she touches his arm.

"I heard you were going to see a movie tonight," Amy begins.

"Yes," he answers politely, but glances over at me.

"Which one are you going to see?" she pries, still running her neon painted fingernails over his bare arm.

Andrew gulps.

"We're going to check out the re-release of Star Wars at the MCA," he replies, moving his arm away.

Obviously clueless, Amy leans over the red Formica counter and kisses him on the cheek; uncaring that her boobs are practically falling out of her top.

"Maybe I'll see you there," she coos, then snaps her fingers and her friends come running. Without a glance back, all three strut out of the restaurant, butts swinging like pendulums on a grandfather clock.

♪♪♪

About an hour later, Mrs. Taylor drops us off in front of the theater a few minutes before the movie starts.

"Mike, I'll pick you and Andrew up right here after the show," she reminds with a bright smile. "Have a good time, everyone."

She waves goodbye and drives off, leaving us standing around unsure of what to say next.

Andrew speaks first.

"Selena, I swear I didn't know Amy was going to be at the pizza parlor."

"It's okay," I believe him. Trying to hide my jealousy, I look up at the bright neon Cineplex sign on the front of the building. "Andrew, what movie theater did you tell Amy we were going to again?"

"I told her we were going to the new MCA theater across the street from the college," he blushes, and we all start laughing. "You know, the one on the other side of town?"

We buy our tickets at the Cineplex box office. Actually, Andrew buys tickets for me and Ando. I try talking him into letting me purchase Ando's, but he refuses.

"I invited Ando, so it's my treat," Andrew grins, handing my brother his ticket.

Like a true gentleman, Mike tries buying Nicole's ticket, but she runs in front of him and buys her own. Jenny just shakes her head again. We wait for the sassy redhead and then go inside the popcorn-scented lobby. The place is practically empty for a Saturday night. I guess everyone wants to check out the other theater.

Andrew buys popcorn and sodas for himself, Ando, and me. Jenny and Nicole combine their money and buy a box of *Goobers* and two bottled waters. Mike gets two hot dogs, loaded nachos, a candy bar, and an extra-large lemonade.

"I can't believe you're still hungry," Nicole comments about the quantity of food he has.

"I'm starving." The teen takes a bite of one of the hot dogs.

"But didn't I see you eat an entire large pizza earlier?" Nicole questions with a wry smile and a tilt of her head.

"I'm a growing boy," he admonishes indignantly.

"Mike, your mom and dad are so sweet," I inform with a flashy grin. "I didn't know you're bi-racial."

His expression hardens as he looks at me

"So what?" Mike snips. "Do you have something against mixed-race people? Tiger Woods is mixed you know? So are Mariah Carey and Dwayne *'The Rock'* Johnson.

"Plus, a whole bunch of people that I can't remember right now," he educates defensively.

Jenny glares at him and shakes her head.

"Mike's a little sensitive when it comes to that subject," she chimes in. "When we were in elementary school, some stupid kid teased him about it."

I'm horrified!

"I didn't mean to offend you," I apologize sincerely. "I don't know what I am. I may have some Greek in me, but I'm not really sure. It doesn't matter. At least that's what my mom tells me."

"No worries, girl," his demeanor softens, and he gives me a wink, letting me know that he has accepted my apology. "So, you're not sure what your background is?"

"No, I never knew my real dad," I mumble. "David is my stepfather, but I love him like he's my real one."

"Oh, now I'm the one who's sorry for going all crazy on you," Mike apologizes as well. "It's just difficult for me to understand why some people have such a problem with people of different races loving each other."

"Love is love," Andrew adds. "It doesn't matter what color you are."

Mike gives him a high-five and then continues:

"It's awesome having more than one heritage," he laughs. "Mom's side is Sicilian, so when my uncles and aunts get together, there's a ton of food."

He spaces out, licking his lips.

"There's all types of pasta, antipasto, tons of seafood, and incredible Sicilian desserts."

Andrew nods in agreement.

"Also, when we get together with Dad's family, his Southern heritage comes through," Mike reminisces. "They make the best smothered pork chops I've ever tasted and when both sides combine, especially on holidays, the food blows my mind."

Lost in the memory, his eyes close as he thinks about all of that food. Andrew punches him in the arm and Mike returns to us.

"It's the best of both worlds," he finishes with a cheesy grin.

"It does sound amazing," I agree, loving his description.

"I never got to know my parents," Jenny notifies sadly.

"Why?" I ask.

Nicole answers for her.

"Jenny's parents died in a car accident when she was a baby."

"I live with my grandparents," Jenny adds.

"I'm so sorry," I gasp, giving her a quick hug.

Andrew, feeling left-out, joins the conversation. "My parents are divorced."

"Now you guys are starting to depress me." Mike rubs his temples. "How did this conversation get so dark?"

Our entire group becomes quiet.

"I'm multi-racial," Nicole tries to lighten the mood. "My father is Chinese and my mother is Black and East-Indian."

"No wonder you have those amazing almond-shaped eyes," I compliment with a wide grin as Nicole flutters her long eyelashes at us.

"Yeah, and that's why she's so short," Mike teases while patting the top of her head.

"I'm not that short!" Nicole sneers indignantly, hands on her hips.

"You're like a midget," Mike pokes.

Her eyes are fixed on him with a death-stare.

"I'm five-two!" she growls.

"You are a pixie," he chuckles heartily, throwing his head back. "I can pick you up and carry you around in my pocket."

"Just try it, you Jolly Green Giant!" she counters.

Mike tries to actually pick her up, but she slips under his long arms and evades his attempts.

Jenny and Andrew look left out as they glance around the room, shuffling their feet.

"I'm Irish and Cherokee," Jenny perks up.

"That's a good mixture, Sweetie," Mike puts his arm around her shoulder.

We all look at Andrew.

"Well…my father is English and my mom's background is Scottish. So I guess that makes me—"

"Just a fly white boy!" Mike interrupts and then they high five again, making everyone laugh.

"Are you guys ready to go see this movie, or what?" I ask, enjoying the company. "The females of this very diverse group would like to sit down and enjoy the show."

"Come on, Vanilla Ice," Mike grabs Andrew and puts him in a headlock.

"Let's go," Ando agrees, taking Nicole's hand and pulling her to the theater.

"Ando, are you going to sit next to me?" Mike begs.

"*Orrr,* why don't you sit next to me?" Nicole suggests, encouraging with a sweet smile.

"Okay!" Ando agrees happily, continuing to hold her hand until we find our seats.

Jenny turns to Mike.

"How does it feel losing her to a kindergartener?" she jabs.

The incredibly jolly high schooler ignores her and sits on the other side of Nicole. Andrew and I sit down near Jenny. Without hesitation, he brushes popcorn off of my seat. The trailers start just as we all settle down. As the previews start, I glance around and notice that there is only one other couple in the theater. Fifteen minutes later, the movie starts. Out of the corner of my eye, I see Andrew searching for my hand, but it is dark, so he accidentally grabs my thigh.

"Sorry," he apologizes emphatically.

"No problem," I whisper back. At last, he takes my hand in his and we sit contentedly for the rest of the show.

♪♪♪

Mike's mom, Nicole's parents, Jenny's grandparents, and our mom and dad are waiting for us when the movie releases. My heart sinks. Truthfully, I was hoping to talk with Andrew about the movie. Not wanting to be teased by his folks, Mike gives Nicole, Jenny, and me tight hugs then picks up Ando and spins him around. Andrew, however, stands nervously playing with the sleeves of his swim team jacket.

"I had a great time," I state, looking at my feet.

"Me, too," Andrew does the same.

"Guess I'll see you at school on Monday?" I mumble shyly.

"Definitely," he kicks at a pebble, avoiding eye contact.

Amused at the situation, Jenny and Nicole are giggling a few feet away.

"Kiss her already!" Jenny suddenly shouts, causing Nicole to step on her foot to shut her up.

"Bye, Selena," Andrew kisses my cheek, gives Ando a high-five, sticks his tongue out at the girls, and climbs into the backseat of Mrs. Taylor's SUV. Right away, he rolls down the window and sticks his head out as they pull away.

"I forgot to tell you that you look really nice tonight!" he shouts, facing glowing as he waves goodbye.

CHAPTER TEN

All the way home, Ando cannot stop talking about the swim meet, eating pizza at Mike's pizza parlor and all of the fun we had at the movies. He keeps telling our parents when he grows up he is going to join the swim team and work at MJ's Pizza Parlor, just like Andrew and Mike.

"I had a great time!" he keeps repeating.

I had a great time, too. Even I forgot about nightmares and strange voices calling to me at night. Being a teenager is complicated enough without thinking that I have inherited some sort of mental illness or something much worse. In fact, the best part of the evening was just hanging out with the gang, being silly, and eating pizza. The entire day was normal, uneventful, and completely wonderful.

When we are inside, David takes Ando upstairs to get ready for bed leaving Mom and me downstairs alone. I wait in the kitchen until they disappear before going out to talk with her. I find her sitting outside on the porch enjoying the coolness of the evening; her black hair blowing like a billowy sail across her face.

"So, you haven't told me about the date," Mom playfully teases me.

"It was a lot of fun," I blush.

"Did you get to know Andrew a little better?" She probes energetically.

"Yes, I did," I grin. "He's a great guy."

"I'm happy that you've made friends," she smiles, tucking her hair behind her ears.

"I need to ask you a question." I sit down next to her on the front porch.

"Go ahead," she encourages, gently brushing my locks from my eyes.

"How can we be…what you say we are?" I ask, still not believing.

Mom seems puzzled, and a bit confused concerning what exactly to say.

"We are the descendants of the Sirens," she states with confidence.

"Do you actually believe that?" I query. "Or could our family truly suffer from mental illness?"

"You know, that's crossed my mind quite a few times," she jokes with a genuine smile, then sobers. "But there is no debating what we are."

"But Mom…there's no such thing as Sirens," I answer firmly. "The ancient Greeks made them up to explain things they didn't understand. That's all."

Mom plays devil's advocate: "There are so many things in this world that can't be explained, Selena. Some things you just have to accept. This part of us, you'll just have to accept on faith."

"Suppose I can't, Mom?" I admonish. "Everything that happens in nature can be explained."

Mom sighs as she searches for the right words.

"So how would you explain the voice that calls for you at night and the lady that you saw in the sea when you rescued your father?"

"I was probably hallucinating," I mock myself. "After all, I was holding my breath for quite a long time; my oxygen was low, which made me think I saw a woman. It was probably seaweed."

That explanation sounds reasonable to me.

"What about the way you charmed the male students in your Chorus class with your singing?" she exhales loudly.

"Well, maybe I'm just a natural singer," I shrug.

"And how do you explain what happened with David?" she adds with amusement.

"David's been under a lot of stress lately: new job, new home, more responsibilities at work," I explain. "All of these things could have contributed to him sleepwalking. There have been many clinical studies about the link between stress and sleepwalking."

She pauses, gathering her thoughts.

"So how do you explain having the same nightmare every night?"

I contemplate that question for a few seconds before answering.

"The nightmares began when we moved into this house," I remind. "I'm sure that they are occurring because I'm not used to sleeping in a strange place."

Mom makes a low whistle.

"Wow!" she exclaims. "You are one smart kid! Those are all great explanations, but I have one more question."

Bracing for her next move, I fold my arms across my chest.

"What is the question?" I chirp.

"How could David have heard the song that called him to the ocean? The same song you have been hearing?"

I stop, suddenly realizing Mom's implication.

"Wait...how do you know about the voices and the song?" I probe.

"I know about them because I hear them too," she dryly confesses.

Her words make me shiver.

"Stop! It's not true! It's just crazy stories that Yaya told you when you were young."

"Do you remember when we were humming the other night and Dad came out of the room all hypnotized?" Mom probes, her voice unfaltering. "How do you explain that?"

"I didn't tell you that night, when David almost drowned. It took me over ten minutes to find both of you. How long were you in the water?"

"I don't remember." I blink, unsure. "It seemed like forever."

"And what about my incident with the reef sharks?" Mom nervously smooths the wrinkles on her nightgown with her hands. "I knew exactly what to do to get them away from your father and that child. I told them to clear a path for me and they did. Remember the angel fish at the observatory? I was talking to it."

Mom starts making that same weird clicking sound with her tongue.

"Please stop!" I plead, anger beginning to take over. "Stop it! It's not true!"

"You can try to explain all of those incidents, but that doesn't change who we really are...*what* we really are." Before I can object, Mom takes my hand. "Come with me."

Silently, we walk hand in hand to the side of the house, down the staircase, to the rocky shoreline. Tonight, the moon is only at quarter fullness; there's not a cloud in the sky. Carefully, Mom sits near the edge.

"Sit next to me," she instructs, offering her hand to me.

Obediently, I put my hand in hers. The ocean is calmer tonight, which makes me feel better about being so close to the edge. After I settle beside her, she smooths my hair and kisses my forehead.

"Whatever happens, I need you to stay calm, okay?"

I nod.

Then she closes her eyes and takes a few deep, cleansing breaths as she clasps her hands together. I watch, mesmerized by her serenity, her beauty, her strength. Then her lips part and a soft, mournful tune begins to form. Before long, her body starts to rhythmically sway: back and forth…back and forth. The song has no words, only sounds, but the sounds have more emotion than I have ever heard.

Unable to focus on anything else, I sit enthralled by her perfect pitch and unnatural range as she sings; alto, bass, and soprano all at the same time. Tears begin to roll down her cheeks, landing on her thin cotton nightgown. It is then I realize that I am crying too. Every emotion inside of me erupts as I listen to her song, like lava bursting forth from a slumbering volcano.

As she continues, the wind begins to blow harder, so hard in fact, that I almost toppled into the water. Terrified, I grab a hold of my mom, who is still in a deep trance. I feel the spray against my face and wish she would stop whatever she is doing. It is then I see bubbles begin to appear in the water nearby. Frantically, I shake my mother, trying to make her stop, but it is too late.

As the bubbling subsides, two heads pop out of the churning sea. Unable to do anything else, I hold my breath as the women look at me and then at Mom. One has long blonde hair, with lips pink like coral, and the other's red hair reminds me of the horizon at sunrise, crimson with streaks of gold. Both have the same piercing aquamarine eyes as my brother, mother, and me. Saying nothing, they simply bob silently in the surf.

Suddenly, my mother opens her eyes and smiles, and then reaches a hand towards them. The blonde beams happily, swims toward her and they touch hands, palm to palm. She looks at me and makes the same clicking noise to my mother, who grins and clicks back.

"Reach out, palm facing her," Mom instructs.

Nervously, I present my palm.

"It's okay," she reassures. "She won't hurt you."

I do as she requests, even though my entire body is shivering and my palms are now dripping with sweat. The woman's hands are smooth like polished shell. She clicks at me, but I do not understand.

"This is my daughter, Selena," Mom answers, and the woman laughs and clicks some more. "Yes, she looks just like me."

Mom turns back to me.

"Selena, this is your grandaunt, Leukosia."

"The precocious one," I add, and Leukosia nods graciously. I quickly turn to my mother, who looks relieved that our meeting is going smoothly. "Does she understand what I am saying?"

"Of course, I do," Leukosia answers, her voice delicately sweet, yet has a strange, amplified resonance to it; angelically lyrical like what I imagine the most heavenly instruments to sound like.

"Selena, named after the Moon goddess," she purrs, her gaze lingering on my face. "How appropriate. You were born during a full moon, after all."

Oddly, her voice seeps into my head and makes me dizzy. Leukosia notices my condition and stops speaking. My mother clicks to the other woman, who continues to examine the scene. Nervously, I hold my hand out to her, palm open, her hypnotic eyes fixed on me. I blink and she is beside me, hand touching mine.

"I am Ligeia," she says with that same hollow lilt, but her voice is a bit lower than her sister's.

"We've met before, remember?" I acknowledge her coldly. "You know, the other night when you tried to kill me and my father?"

She nods dismissively and takes her hand away.

"You speak your mind…another quality you have inherited from Parthenope," Ligeia informs proudly.

With my thoughts racing, I turn to Mom.

"The other night when I followed you here, what were you doing?"

"I went for a swim," she admits bashfully.

"Did you swim with them?"

"Yes," she answers. "I couldn't fight it anymore; the need to be close to them…I didn't want to fight it."

"Is that why you've been disappearing all of the time?" I feel suddenly upset with her. "You've been sneaking off to be with…*Them?*"

"Yes," Mom replies meekly, refusing to lock gazes.

Thankfully, Leukosia breaks the uncomfortable repartee.

"Marina used to love swimming with us before… " she pauses, then changes her comment. "Do you remember when we followed Cristoforo's ships all of those years ago? What arrogance he had, thinking he was the first to discover this place!

"We have swum these waters for over a millennium; humans have only charted these waters for a millisecond of that time. What gives them the right to go around claiming pieces of the world like everything belongs to them?" she scoffs. "They are so self-centered!"

"Who is Cristoforo?" I ask, intrigued by the change in conversation.

"Cristoforo Colombo," Ligeia repeats, then clicks at Mom, who translates.

"They are talking about Christopher Columbus," Mom informs in a rush of words. "When I was around your age, we found three ships near modern day Cuba. They thought they were near India, but they had miscalculated."

I stare at her in disbelief as my head begins to swim.

"Mom, you knew Christopher Columbus?" I gasp.

"Yes, we all did," Leukosia emphasizes. "In fact, you did spend a lot of time speaking with him. Did you not, Marina?"

My mother nods.

"He got shipwrecked on Jamaica because of me...I didn't mean to do it," she sulks. "It was late one night, and I went out for a swim. The night was so calm and peaceful that it inspired me to sing, so I stopped in a shallow cove and began my song. Cristoforo and his men heard me and ran aground."

"It took decades for you to get over that mishap," Ligeia laughs.

"I couldn't stand the guilt," my mother blushes. "I spent many evenings conversing with Cristo, talking about his family and the terrible consequences his discovery had on the indigenous people."

"Marina felt so guilty in fact, that she promised to name her first son, Fernando… after Cristo's own little boy," Leukosia finishes the account.

"Would you like to go for a swim with us?" Ligeia offers at last, grinning mischievously.

"No thank you," I answer firmly. "After what you tried to do to David and me the last time—"

"It was an accident," Ligeia sounds offended. "I was calling for Marina and David heard my song. When I grabbed you, I thought I was grabbing your mother. You are the spitting image of her, if you had not noticed."

Confused even more now, I dare ask the scowling woman, "Why did David say the song called to him?"

Before my eyes, Ligeia's features darken.

"The song is *not* specific to each individual. Human males hear what they need to hear. Each person hears their own message even though our song is the same," she explains. "On that night, David was upset. He needed comforting and our song called to that need within him."

"So, you didn't mean to drown him?" I ask, full of relief.

"No, we did not," Leukosia shakes her golden locks as she quickly turns to Mom. "I did not realize your *Human* is so susceptible to the call."

Ligeia studies Mom, eyes fixed.

"You need to take care of that before he gets hurt," the Siren insists.

"What does she mean, Mom?" I ask. "What exactly should you *'take care of'*?"

"Humans can become immune to a Siren's song if they are exposed to it a little at a time for a long period of time," my mother explains.

"Then why don't you do it?" I blurt, not understanding why she would not want to keep him safe.

Ligeia looks disapprovingly at her.

"Because that would mean Marina would have to tell him what she is and that might not bode well."

Mom sits silently.

"Selena, are you ready to come with us?" Leukosia inquires, eager to get me into the sea. "You will be perfectly safe. I promise."

I make the mistake of glancing in Ligeia's direction, and am taken aback by the wicked grin she is wearing.

"Perfectly safe," the red-head smiles, but it does not reach her eyes.

"I can't swim," I advise, humiliated to admit this to mythological sea creatures.

"When you were trying to save the Human…I mean David…did you notice how long you were under the water?" Ligeia asks.

"It was only a few minutes," I answer, unsure of the exact time.

"You were under for more than ten," Ligeia smiles.

"That's impossible!" I dispute her words with a scoff.

"You are one of us, dear child, whether or not you choose to believe," Ligeia chastises, then dives back under the waves.

Leukosia turns to my mom, her expression saddened.

"She must learn about who she is. Then she can make her own choice." She touches palms with Mom again. "Just like your mother did, just like you did."

"It's too soon," Mom shakes her head angrily, hands balling into clenched fists.

"You cannot fight it anymore," Leukosia continues. "She will be with us...one way or another. It is inevitable."

CHAPTER ELEVEN

"What did she mean by that? I would have to make my own choice...my own choice about what?"

"I'm tired, Selena," Mom walks quickly back to the house. "We'll talk about it another time."

"I need to talk about it now!" I demand forcefully.

"Selena..." Mom continues ahead, determine to end the conversation.

"You can't just introduce me to my long-lost aunts, who, by the way, are epic beings of death, and expect me to just wait for answers. I want answers right now, tonight, this minute—"

"Selena Thermopolis, I said not now!" Mom shouts and a thick blanket of storm clouds begins to roll in from the sea. Glancing toward the heavens, I realize that the moon is hidden again. My mother's features are stern and I realize the depth of her anger. "I said we will discuss this at another time."

Slowly, her expression calms, causing the sky to become clear again.

"Okay," I reply meekly.

"Goodnight."

"Goodnight, Mom."

"Selena," she adds sternly. "I don't want you going back down there without me. Do I make myself clear?"

"Crystal," I confirm.

♩♩♩

Sunday morning breakfast is quieter than usual. Mom woke early and made a huge meal of pancakes, eggs, sausage, bacon, and orange juice. The mouthwatering aroma wafts upstairs, waking Ando and me. David was the last one out of bed and he still looks a bit tired. Ando also looks worn out, but for another reason.

"I heard you and Mom singing last night," my inquisitive sibling murmurs as we make our way downstairs together. "You were so loud."

"Did you feel the need to come to us?" I probe.

"No, I felt the need to go to sleep and couldn't because of all of the noise."

"I'll try not to disturb you anymore," I reply, baffled by his harsh tone.

With this promise declared, I then stick my tongue out at him, making him burst into wild laughter.

"Good morning, baby," Mom leans over and tries to kiss him on the forehead as we enter the kitchen, but he moves his head away.

"Morning," he replies grumpily, which is totally out of character for him.

"Did you sleep well last night?" Mom asks, surprised at his foul mood.

"No, I didn't," Ando states rudely.

I study him, trying to figure out what is wrong.

"Why are you being so mean?" I interject, feeling very protective of our mother.

"Leave me alone, Lena!"

"Stop being such a little jerk and I will!"

"Everything is always about you!" he barks. "It's not right that Mommy trusts you more than she trusts me. I hate you!"

"Fernando David Theodore Marquez!" It is never good when Mom or Dad calls you by your full name. "That's quite enough! Apologize to your sister and to me, or go back upstairs until you are willing to be more agreeable!"

To both of our surprise, Ando gets up from the table, pushes his chair in, and stomps up to his room without another word. David comes out of the bedroom just in time to see his five-year-old stomping up the stairs, mumbling all the way.

"What's wrong with Ando?" he frowns, giving Mom a quick kiss.

"Just woke up on the wrong side of the bed, I suppose," she shrugs.

"Breakfast smells delicious," David comments as he inhales deeply. "Is it a special occasion or something?"

"Why do you say that?" Mom asks, suddenly sounding guilty.

"It's just that we haven't had a big breakfast since we moved into this house," he interjects as he joins me at the table as Mom reddens.

"I guess it's starting to feel more like home now. Everything is unpacked, most of the repairs are finished, and things are settling down." Mom happily sighs. "I have my husband, kids, and a new career…what more do I need?"

She kisses Dad longer and more passionately than she has in a long time. Wanting the mushiness to cease, I clear my throat.

"Should I leave the room?" I josh, right before Mom throws a dishtowel at my head while David blushes.

"Do you want me to go and get Ando?" I query, wanting to give them some privacy.

"Please," Mom responds, still smiling, as she wraps her arms more securely around my stepfather's waist.

It is nice seeing them so happy. The last few months in Columbus were tense between Mom and David, to say the least. Money was tight and trying to sell the house was not easy. We had it on the market for over four months before we had a nibble. Now, with Mom trying to keep her family secret, the tension is back again. At least we will have some normalcy this morning.

♪♪♪

Ando is in his room hiding in his make-shift tent he constructed using Mom's new sheets. I hear his old battery-operated radio playing in the background and the crunching of goldfish-shaped crackers—his favorite snack—coming from behind the cloth covering.

"Hey, little brother," I announce as I slowly enter the tent. "Mom and Dad are waiting for us to eat. She cooked your favorite foods for breakfast."

"I'm mad at you!" he growls, taking me aback.

"Why are you mad at me?"

"I saw you and Mom talking with those ladies' last night."

My heart begins to race.

"What ladies?" I feign innocence.

Angrily, he glares at me, unsure of why I am being secretive.

"Lena, the ladies in the sea," he pouts. "One had blonde hair, and the other had red, and they were really pretty, remember?"

"Yes," I admit with a lump in my throat. "Mom and I were talking to two ladies' last night, but we thought you were asleep."

"I was trying to sleep," he sighs. "But Mom was singing so loud that I got out of bed to see what was going on. When I couldn't find either of you in the house, I went down the stairs to the shore."

My eyes automatically widen.

"Mom forbade you to go down there!" I gasp. "It's dangerous."

"You go down there!" he scolds. "Who are they?"

Unexpectedly, my temples are beginning to throb from lack of sleep and all of this arguing. In the end, we both sit in silence, debating who should speak next. Ando is looking at me, waiting for a response. Not wanting to say too much, I close my eyes trying to find the right words, but there does not seem to be any that fit the subject of being related to fish people.

"I think you should ask Mom," I insist instead. Clearly annoyed with me, he releases a small sigh and turns the volume up on the radio.

"Tell Mommy and Daddy that I'm not hungry." Ando pulls out a *Spiderman* comic book from under his sleeping bag and begins to read.

♪♪♪

Downstairs, Mom and David have already started eating without me. The food smells so good that my stomach begins to growl. They both look at me as I rejoin them without my brother. Famished, I help myself to a little bit of everything on the table.

"He still doesn't want to come down for breakfast," I inform, chewing on the end of a tasty sausage link. "Mom, you need to talk to him."

"About what?" she manages with a full mouth.

"Oh, about our two new friends we recently started hanging out with," I reply, getting a pat of butter for my stack of pancakes. Without being asked, David passes me the maple syrup.

"He saw?" Mom's mouth opens in disbelief.

"Yup," I confirm, taking a bite of the soft golden discs drowning in sweet liquid.

My stepdad is looking curiously at us, but he continues to eat his breakfast. His eyes, however, look first at Mom, then at me, like he is watching an invisible tennis match going on between us.

"He says he saw us talking with them recently," I continue after swallowing.

Mom leaves the table without another word and goes up to Ando's bedroom. David watches silently at the show playing out. Finally, he chuckles softly to himself.

"Why are you laughing?" I smirk.

"It's just funny that you and your mom are trying to be so covert, like spies or something. I think it's hysterical."

Finding it funny too, I stick my tongue out at him and he mimics me playfully. We both laugh, and I could not imagine our lives without him; I just could not. Whatever Mom has to do to keep him safe, she had better do it and do it fast.

♪♪♪

To my surprise, Ando stayed in his room for the entire day, playing in his tent and munching on snacks he had hidden in his room in case of emergencies. I had never seen my brother so angry before; it is so unlike him.

After dinner, Mom and Dad take a walk while I remain at home to watch over Ando and also to read more of Grandpa Theo's journal. Never in a million years would I have imagined that Sirens were not just stories in books, but were actually real and very much of an influence on the mortal world.

Quickly, I find the entry I had left off at:

In the months that followed, Leukosia, Ligeia, and I searched every snow-capped mountain top, every ice-covered valley, and every barren field on

237

every continent, but to our dismay there was not a trace of the lovely Persephone.

Our bodies grew weak from the lack of food, water, and sleep. Most importantly, our souls yearned for the serenity of Anthemoessa, covered with its purple, lavender and rolling hillsides. I think most of all; we missed our precious songbirds; their cheerful tunes filling the air. My soul felt heavy without them, but no matter how tired or homesick we became, our priority was to find Demeter's beloved child.

Days began to drift into the next until six months had seen the Earth under its icy prison. Relentlessly, we sang her favorite songs, hoping that Persephone would hear our familiar melodies and reveal her hiding place. One day as we searched, our songs echoing against the snow-covered mountains, the goddess Demeter appeared.

"Dear sisters of the sea, you no longer need to search for Persephone."

"But why?" I asked, confused by the request.

"Hades stole Persephone from the island. He wanted her for his queen, but she was so sad in the underworld without the trees, without the ocean, without the birds and their heavenly songs, and without the three of you... her companions... her friends."

Leukosia began to weep, tears of salt and relief. Ligeia cursed Hades, the god of the Underworld, for his boldness and swore vengeance upon him, but I stood quietly. My head filled with curiosity.

"Demeter, ruler of the harvest. What has become of Persephone?" I ask, bowing.

"My daughter will be allowed to visit the Earth for half of the year, then she must return to Hades for the rest."

As Demeter spoke, I could see the snow beginning to melt giving way to the sleeping dirt below. The clouds began to part allowing Apollo to pull his chariot across the sky melting the frost. Blades of grass pushed their way out of the ground while inch worms began to till the soil. Before long, the Earth awoke and stretched her graceful arms, ready to don her Spring cloak.

Then Demeter smiled for the first time since Persephone had disappeared.

"I give thanks to you, my sisters. Persephone also sends her gratitude. It was your songs that Hades heard that helped to soften his heart, for he knew how much she was missed and loved."

Ligeia kissed her hand.

"We are forever your servants, dear Demeter."

"And the wings, dear goddess," Leukosia spoke. "What is to become of our wings?"

Demeter smiled.

"They are yours to enjoy," she answered, then vanished before our eyes.

We were ecstatic as we flew back to Anthemoessa. It took us two days to reach home, but the joy we felt when we returned was so intense that the only way to express it was through song. We sang so loudly and so beautifully that every bird on the island flew out to meet us, singing just as loudly. Our lives would return to normal, learning new songs and enjoying our island paradise. Of this, I was certain.

♪♪♪

I am not sure what time I fell asleep, but the sound of singing wakes me; my alarm clock shows a few minutes before midnight. Outside is bright as the Moon smiles lovingly upon the Earth. The entire sea is shimmering like someone scattered loose diamonds over its writhing surface. Bursting with anticipation, I grab my robe and sneak out, excited to see the Sirens again.

I stop briefly, realizing Ando's door is open. I poke my head in, expecting to see him sleeping peacefully, but his bed is empty. Worry batters my soul as I run down to the shoreline in a frenzy, praying that he is safe. In front of me, moonlight illuminates the entire sky almost to the point of it being daytime.

Cheerful laughter is coming from near the edge of the rocky coast. Spurred by concern, I race toward the sound. Breathlessly, I search the water. To my relief, floating happily in the surf is Ando assisted by Ligeia and Leukosia.

"Hi, Lena!" he greets, still in the same carefree position.

"Ando, I thought you were…you can't keep coming down here like this!" I chastise sternly, feeling my pulse return to normal, but he tunes me out. "Mom would punish you if she knew you were down here!"

"We would never do anything to harm him," Leukosia swears in her most soothing tone.

"Fernando Marquez!" I insist, using my most parental voice. "Get out of the water right now before we both get into trouble!"

"Come in with us," Leukosia urges, ignoring my comment.

"Let us show you the world that you come from," Ligeia encourages.

"It will be fine," Leukosia promises. "Come into the sea."

Hesitantly, I lower myself over the edge and into the water; it is as cold as winter's first frost. Ligeia offers me her hand, and I accept. This makes her smile; I did not think smiling was possible for her.

"Stay close," Ligeia instructs, and I nod my understanding.

Beside me, Leukosia takes Ando firmly by the hand as we dive under the waves.

♪♪♪

Below, another world exists. I watch in awe as silvery moonbeams pierce the watery surface, illuminating the alien world, stretching as far as the eye can see. All around, groups of neon painted coral donning various shades of orange, copper, emerald, and aquamarine glow like an underwater black light has been switched on. Farther away, long tentacles of seaweed sway to the movement of unseen currents running their course.

My heart feels like it will burst from the joy I feel. I hold my breath, trying to enjoy the moment, when out of nowhere, a feeling of panic comes over me. Distracting me, Ligeia makes that strange clicking sound with her tongue, then points to something in the water. The object is moving quickly in our direction; it looks like a torpedo that has been jettisoned from an old-World War II submarine. In its wake, the sea parts on command. A few seconds later, it is close enough to recognize. I smile, realizing it is a dolphin, smooth and sleek. A second dolphin appears and then a third; soon an entire pod surrounds us.

Ando wants to swim to them, but Leukosia holds him at bay. Disappointment fills his eyes. Ligeia clicks again and the smallest dolphin in the pod swims up to Ando and allows him to touch his flipper. Another pod member cautiously approaches me. Rather bravely, I touch its beak, gently exploring its smooth exterior; there is a small scar near its right eye. I am guessing it was made by a boat propeller. The idea makes me furious.

Without warning, Ligeia lets go of my hand. Unsuccessfully, I kick my feet, trying not to sink to the sandy bottom, but the current is strong, and it pulls me toward open water.

Damn it! Why did I let them talk me into this?

Surrounding me, long red seaweed-like locks sway weightlessly in the water, catching my attention. Still flailing my

244

limbs, I look up to see Ligeia motioning to me. Her demeanor is calm as she keeps opening and closing her mouth, releasing bubbles into the surrounding water. Not comprehending her instructions, my lungs are starting to feel like they will explode. Then that foreboding tingle in my legs begins once more. The pain is so severe that my vision becomes blurry as dizziness engulfs me. Before I know what is happening, everything begins to fade.

Similarly, to falling asleep, my eyes close and comforting darkness embraces me. Shortly after, I feel a muffled thud as my body bumps against something hard. Then I feel the sensation subside. Fearing that I will see the pearly gates, I open my eyes and realize I am sitting on the shell-covered sea bottom; my lungs taking in oxygen from the surrounding water. An itchy sensation calls my attention to my feet, and that is when I notice it.

To my amazement, there is a thin membrane of skin stretching across each small gap between my toes, similar to a duck's webbed feet. Bending down, I touch the newly grown skin; it tickles. Fascinated, I check my hands and the same webbing is in between my fingers. Somehow, this makes me smile as I swim back up to my aunts and Ando.

The pod of dolphins has left already, probably frightened away by the spectacle I caused. Leukosia clicks at me, but I still cannot fathom what she is trying to say. Finally, my body reaches the surface, and for some reason, I cannot breathe regular air; my gills are on fire!

With lightning speed, Leukosia and Ando rush to my side. With a concerned expression, the gentle blonde touches my chest with one hand and pumps several times, which somehow activates my lungs and I begin to breathe normally once again. Ando seems to be experiencing some difficulty breathing too, but Leukosia touches his chest in that same manner and he too returns to normal.

"What's happening to us?" my brain revs, trying to grasp what is going on.

"It will take a few more times before you can smoothly transition," Ligeia states shortly.

"Transition? What is that?" I beg.

"To transition is to automatically go between using your lungs and your gills," Leukosia patiently explains.

"Our…gills," I repeat in disbelief.

"Yes, now that you have been exposed to us, you have experienced your first transition," Leukosia clarifies calmly. "It is when your body realizes that your gills are there for a reason, and because of your natural survival instincts, they activate."

"So… you're telling me that I've always had gills, but just never needed them before now?"

"That is correct," she nods. "You had to experience nearly drowning in order to shock your body into using them."

"Why couldn't I breathe when I came up to the surface?" I probe, doubtingly.

"Because you are not used to traveling between worlds yet, so it takes a bit longer for your lungs to acclimate," Leukosia continues.

"After a while, they will transition without hesitation." Ligeia smiles more now, and I realize that she is not as scary as I first believed.

"How did you get them to transition by touching us?" I inquire, feeling more at ease.

"It is one of our gifts," Leukosia grins.

"Okay…but what about that awful sensation that happens when my legs get wet?"

"That is also a part of the transition," both clarify at once. "The webbing between your toes and fingers will help you swim faster. They are like fins on a fish, and with them you will be able to out-swim anything in the water. In time, you will grow used to the sensation."

Filled with questions, my mind surges until I believe it will explode.

"And how do I get rid of them when I get out of the water?"

"For now, you will have to dry them off completely, but as you gain experience, you will be able to access them at will," Leukosia smiles with great pride.

"I want to go again!" Ando squeals; completely delighted by the adventure.

"That is enough for now," Ligeia says in that no-nonsense way of hers. "You will have more opportunities."

"It is time to go back," Leukosia adds sadly. "Before your parents miss you."

Ando gives her a hug before swimming back to the shoreline.

"I'm curious," I say out loud. "How is it possible that we are so different?"

Leukosia shakes her head.

"You still do not believe, young one."

"You two are descendants of ancient sea nymphs, whether or not you choose to accept it," Ligeia boasts with an off-handed wave of her hand.

"You both have the blood of the Sirens coursing through your veins," Leukosia states proudly. "Our blood… your mother's blood… are the blood of the Sirens. Ando is only part Siren, so his abilities may be limited, but he is still one of us."

"And me? I'm half Siren too," I acknowledge with a hint of disdain.

Leukosia and Ligeia look at each other and start that infernal clicking.

Leukosia looks at me with surprise.

"It is time that you discuss this subject with Marina."

Back to his regular adorable self, Ando helps pull me out of the water. I kneel, hand outstretched, palm open, like Mom taught me. They smile, happy at my gesture. Rather unexpectedly, Ligeia touches my palm with hers; her once cold aquamarine eyes were now warm with emotion.

"You cannot fight us, Selena; it is futile for you to try. We are a part of you just as you are a part of us, one part of a whole, one part of *The Three*. Like Parthenope and Marina, you belong to the sea no matter how much you wish you did not."

She moves her hand, and I feel cold once again.

"Sooner or later, you will join us," they announce in unison. "Once again, it is inevitable."

Leukosia touches my hand. Then they slip gracefully beneath the waves.

CHAPTER TWELVE

Today was almost a perfect day, *almost*.

Our mom dropped us off at school with time to spare, and I was able to hang out with the gang before the first bell rang. Next, I got a perfect score on my science quiz and earned a free homework pass from one of the nuns for picking up trash that some nimrod threw on the floor in front of the main office. Then my arch nemesis, Amy, tripped over her own feet as she entered the room, causing everyone to chuckle. As a bonus, she also received after-school detention from Miss Khan because she would not stop talking with her friends instead of paying attention to the lesson that was being given.

I have never seen our teacher lose her temper until today. Not only did she raise her voice (which she rarely does), but she actually removed her glasses, pinched the bridge of her slender nose, and mumbled something that sounded similar to a prayer in another language. It was then that the entire class closed their yappers and shrunk into their seats. After Miss Khan berated the rude teen, she returned to her normal, laid-back self like a switch had been thrown. Right now, I wait on pins and needles for her to explain why she wanted me to stay after class to 'talk'.

I happen to glance down at my hands and they are trembling.

"Selena, thank you for staying to see me on such short notice," Miss Khan apologizes unnecessarily. "I know you have to go to P.E., so I will be brief."

"Am I in trouble?" I probe, feeling a pit growing in my stomach.

Miss Khan laughs.

"Good gracious, no," she removes some sheet music from her briefcase and hands it to me. "The title of the piece is called *Ali d'angelo,* or Angel Wings."

Quickly, I glance over the words.

"It is written in Italian," I say, quickly scanning the page.

"Yes, opera originated in Italy," she grins.

"I can't speak Italian," I remind with a chuckle.

"You don't need to," she honors me with a bright, toothy smile. "I have a copy of the song on CD performed by Giada Pomodoro; a famous Italian opera singer."

Overflowing with anxiety, I shuffle my feet as I think about what my mother will say.

"All you need to do is memorize the words and voilà," Miss Khan explains with a flourish of her slender, tanned hands.

"I don't know," I mumble, thinking about the ramifications it may cause.

"Selena, you are my best singer, and I truly want you to be the featured soloist for the concert." She pauses. "Are you interested?"

"If I say no, will I fail the class?"

"Of course not," she reassures. "I just think this would be a great opportunity for you, possibly even lead to a college scholarship in the future."

"I don't think it is a good idea," I reply, nervous of the effects my singing has on the male population. After all, having guys throwing themselves at your feet sounds good in theory, but in reality, it can be quite bothersome. "Maybe one of the other girls in class, like Amy, could do it. She would jump at the chance to have a solo. Ask her."

"Selena, you have a strong, multi-ranged voice that would be perfect for this song," she compliments.

"I need some time to think it over," I add, glancing at the exit.

"Why don't you take the CD home with you and listen to the piece, then give me your answer tomorrow?"

Miss Khan's sweet disposition makes it difficult to say no.

"I'll listen to it, but I'm not promising anything," I tell with a frown.

"Don't you think you should share your gift with the world?" Miss Khan asks as I was almost out the door.

My frown deepens.

"I don't think it's wise," I utter, right before my hands begin to sweat.

♪♪♪

True to their word, Nicole and Jenny are waiting outside the classroom. Jenny is snacking on an apple. Nicole is biting her nails nervously.

"Are you in trouble?" Nicole wonders, naturally assuming the worse.

"No," I say firmly. "Miss Khan wants me to do a solo for the winter concert."

"That's great!" She hugs me prematurely.

Jenny notices my worried expression

"Why aren't you jumping for joy?" she questions. "Any singer worth her salt would be doing cartwheels right now."

"I get stage fright," I lie.

"Don't worry your pretty little head. We will help you to get over it." The two sing in harmony. Jenny's soprano range and Nicole's alto range actually sounds really good together.

"How long have you been practicing that little musical tidbit?" I smile.

"We came up with it while we were waiting for you," Jenny replies before taking another bite of the red-skinned fruit.

"It was impressive, wasn't it?" Nicole jokes.

"Oh, extremely impressive." I make a face like I have just eaten a sour pickle.

Playfully, Nicole hooks our arms together like we're a couple walking down the aisle, while Jenny pretends to be the flower girl and begins throwing invisible flower petals at our feet. Sister Amelia, nun and vice-principal of the school, suddenly rounds the corner.

"Good afternoon, Sister," Nicole and I politely greet her. She smiles and nods.

"You look very nun-like today, Sister," Jenny jests in her playful way.

"Jennifer," Sister Amelia tries not to smile, instead she only looks at all three of us, shakes her head, and continues her penguin-like stroll down the hallway.

♪♪♪

All three of us have physical education after lunch. Even with our horsing around, we reach the P.E. field only a couple of minutes late. Thank goodness, Miss Khan gave us a pass so we would not be counted as tardy. Immediately, I hand Coach Johnson the late excuse from Chorus.

She reads it rapidly then informs, "Okay, girls, please join the class in the auditorium."

"No fieldwork today, Coach?" Nicole queries, grinning from ear to ear.

"No, today both classes are watching a video about physical development and so on." Coach Johnson seems nervous about the whole topic. "Girls, go on in and find a seat."

Not wanting to get on Coach Johnson's bad side, Jenny grabs our hands and makes a beeline towards the gym. Inside, the air-conditioned gymnasium rows of boys and girls are sitting watching an obviously boring and embarrassing health video. Most of the guys are watching intently. The girls, on the other hand, are chatting among themselves and making faces.

We scan the space, trying to find Andrew and Mike. Finally, I spot them sitting at the very top, both doing homework from other classes and taking in the scene happening on the bleachers below. As if he senses me, Andrew looks up and waves us over. Before we can reach to their location, Amy takes a seat between them.

"Oh, my gracious… that little bit—," Jenny begins. I place my hand over her mouth before she can finish her expletive.

"It's okay," Nicole whispers. "We'll find somewhere else to sit. Don't make a scene."

Nicole looks directly at Jenny, whose face is turning the same color as her hair.

"Come on, you little firecracker," I say coolly. "We'll talk to them later."

We soon find a seat on the bottom row of the bleachers and begin watching the remainder of the film. Unable to control ourselves, we laugh at the silly cartoon characters and the corny lines. Out of the corner of my eye, I see Andrew looking over at me. He smiles and makes a funny face. Mike sees us too and waves. Amy, on the other hand, continues to chat with Andrew while finding any excuse to touch him. It is all I can do not to walk over to her and punch her straight in the mouth.

Grr!

Unexpectedly, another thought occurs to me, and I scan the area, making sure no teachers are around. Closing my eyes, I begin to hum… nothing of importance… nothing with words, just a soft tune.

Nicole, Jenny, and the other girls are totally unaware, but to my surprise, every male, including their coach, is transfixed on me. Quietly, they stand and head in our direction, and before I know what is happening, every male within ear-shot is sitting around the three of us smiling, talking and flirting. Jenny is in heaven while Nicole is nervously observing the unusual display.

"Why aren't you all watching the show?" Coach Johnson yells, disturbing my tune.

As soon as I stop, the boys come out of their hypnotic daze. Scratching their heads in confusion over their behavior, they return to their seats, all except Andrew and Mike, who have relocated from their previous positions. Guiltily, I look back at Amy, who is livid and making the most horrible face. Unable to help myself, I smile, then turn back around to watch the video.

♪♪♪

A few hours later, the bell rings announcing the end of the school day. Happily, I say goodbye to Nicole and Jenny and head downstairs to meet my brother outside of his classroom. On padded feet, Amy appears next to me as I walk through the crowded hallway. She is so close that I feel her boney elbow nudge me in my ribcage and see the fillings in her teeth.

"Listen, you little mongrel," she outwardly insults. "Don't think I'm just going to sit back and let you take over my life!"

"What are you talking about?" I blather, not knowing what else to say.

"Don't play dumb with me, Serena."

"My name is Selena," I boldly correct through gritted teeth.

"Whatever," she sneers, offhandedly waving me off like a fly. "I always perform the winter solo, always! I have the best voice in class."

"Well, I guess Miss Khan doesn't agree with that statement," I reply coldly.

"Don't make me angry," the blonde threatens. "I can make your life a living hell. Do you understand me?"

"Maybe it's time to give someone else a shot?" I shrug as Amy continues walking beside me. Enraged, she clears her throat, then turns to face me.

"I hear Dr. Marquez loves working at Ocean World," she begins. "I had the opportunity to speak with him over the weekend."

"Is that right?" I ask, trying to maneuver through the procession of students.

"We had a nice long chat about you," she coos. "He is a very nice man. Smart too. Oh, and he is incredibly handsome."

"What's your point?" I hiss loudly; my tone causes her to pause before continuing.

"He was telling me how much he loves his job...*really* loves his job. Yup! We were talking...in his office...just the two of us."

I don't like where this is going.

"Get to the point, Amy."

"Well…we talked for over an hour, and then afterward I gave him a hug and a kiss on the cheek," she sneers.

"Sooo?" I snarl, beginning to lose patience.

"How would it look to the everyday sap if a handsome, educated family man was accused of doing something naughty with a sixteen-year-old high school girl?" Amy confidently bemuses like a cat toying with a helpless mouse. "And not just any sixteen-year-old, oh no! The boss' daughter, of all people."

I stop suddenly, causing a backup of students.

"Are you threatening my father?" I hiss, stunned at her boldness. My cheeks begin to heat up. "You wouldn't dare—!"

"I could, and if you don't back off, I will." Amy walks away, then stops before reaching the stairs. "And another thing: Andrew belongs to me."

"According to Andrew, he's not dating you!" My voice escapes, becoming unnaturally high pitched.

Once more, she smiles, eyes twinkling. Out of the blue, Amy makes a dejected face and suddenly tears begin to roll down her cheeks.

"'Daddy! I don't know what happened! One minute, Dr. Marquez and I were talking and the next…h-he was kissing me…and touching me! I was so scared!'"

Then, just as quickly as they appeared, her tears stop. Making her point, Amy wipes away the rivulets of warm liquid, picks up her books, and walks away whistling happily as she goes.

"Hey!" I yell, running after her and grabbing her arm with all of my might without caring who else sees. Not knowing my newfound strength, she screams in pain. The sound echoes through the now practically empty hallway, but I do not care. "You mess with my family and I'll—"

"You'll what?" she growls. "I'm just giving you the facts. One word to my father and Dr. Marquez is history, and in this economy, who knows how long it will take him to find another job?

"Your family will have to move again. It's such a shame," she purrs, then yanks her arm away.

On the verge of violence, my face heats and sweat beads appear on my upper lip.

"Don't you *ever* threaten my family!"

Outside, dark rain clouds are rolling in toward the school. Crashes of thunder and flashes of lightning can be heard in the distance. Ignoring me, Amy opens her backpack to look for her umbrella. I am finding it hard to breathe; everything around me seems to be spinning.

Then Amy turns her back to me.

"It's not a threat, it's a promise," she starts to leave, but pauses long enough to add. "One more thing, heifer: I always get what I want. Andrew is mine."

"He's not your property, Amy, regardless of what you might think!"

"I wouldn't bet on that," she jabs me once again, then turns on her heels and leaves.

♪♪♪

Ando is playing with the hacky sack while we wait for a lull in the weather. Still agitated by the confrontation with Amy, I stand watching the storm. Nasty clouds still loom aggressively overhead, pelting the school with quarter-sized raindrops. What a day to have to walk to Mom's new office to catch a ride home, especially with Amy's words still rattling around in my head. Then, to my delight, I spot Andrew coming towards us with his backpack carelessly thrown over one muscular shoulder; eyes glimmering with mirth, full lips turned up in an enthralling smile, absolute perfection.

"Hey! Slow down!" Andrew quickens his pace, trying to catch up to us as we speed walk up the main street of the island. "I heard you got the winter solo," — he pants breathlessly— "Congratulations!"

"I'm not going to accept the solo," I announce bluntly.

"Wait, what? Why not?" his eyebrows scrunch up. "You're the best singer in the whole school."

"I don't want to put in all of the extra practice time," I distort the truth. "I have to keep up my GPA if I want to get into Harvard."

"I understand," Andrew sighs, exasperated. "But colleges also want students who are active in clubs and organizations, community service, music, the arts...*singing*." –he nudges me with his elbow— "It'll look great on your transcripts: '*Winter Soloist*'."

Feeling the surge of anger beginning to grow, I snap: "I said I don't think I'm going to do it!"

"Okay, no problem!" Andrew looks at me with bewilderment, hands raised in a defensive pose. "Anyway, if you haven't heard already, the homecoming dance is coming up in a couple of months and I was wondering if you'd like to be my date?"

Instantly, my heart sinks.

"I'm sorry," I hear Amy's threats echo in my mind. "But I can't go with you."

"Has someone else asked you?" Andrew looks disappointed.

"No, no one asked except you," I reply, continuing my journey to Mom's office, my brother in tow.

"It's alright if you can't dance, we can just sit and talk."

"I can dance," I sigh, getting frustrated.

"Then why won't you go to the dance with me?"

"I said, I can't go with you!" I snap sharply, taking both Ando and Andrew aback.

"Sorry," he pauses sheepishly before he asks the next question. "What about just going with me to Mike's party? His family is getting together for his parents' anniversary and they gave him permission to invite a few friends. Their get-togethers are amazing; food, music, probably a live band."

"I can't."

"Nicole and Jenny are going to be there," he comes at me with a new hook.

"I already made plans," I respond indifferently.

Andrew seems disappointed.

"Think about it?" he urges.

If I don't break things off now, I never will.

"Listen, Andrew, I don't want to go out with you," I say as sternly as I possibly can. "I don't want to hang-out or talk to you outside of school. I have to concentrate on my studies. You're a distraction that I can't afford right now."

"A distraction?" he repeats. "When did I become a distraction? I thought you liked me."

"That is really arrogant of you!" I chastise with narrowed eyes. "Who do you think you are…God's gift to woman-kind?"

"No…well…maybe," he smiles, trying to lighten the mood.

"Well, you're not, so just go back to your groupie!" I growl. "I hope you two will be very happy together."

On the verge of crying, I grab Ando's hand and begin walking faster up the street, leaving Andrew standing alone, staring at me in disbelief.

CHAPTER THIRTEEN

S everal weeks have gone by with no real problems. My brother is his usual adorable self, except for the fact that he has introduced the aunts to junk food. They seem to truly enjoy spicy chips and anything containing chocolate. I made the mistake of finishing the last bag of *Doritos* and was given the silent treatment for over a week.

Sirens can really hold a grudge!

Mom and David have become sneakier when and how they argue. They have resorted to glaring stares and rolling of eyes instead of their normal verbal tirades. I do not know if they are better or worse. I try not to contemplate on it too much.

On the other hand, things have been relatively quiet at school since my volatile confrontation with 'Awful Amy.' Determined to keep my word, I have practically ignored Andrew except for when we were paired up in math class to play *'Calculus*

Jeopardy' and even then, I only spoke when absolutely necessary. It was agonizing to be so near to him, yet so far away.

Just as I expected, Amy wastes no time chasing Andrew. No sooner had we stopped seeing each other than she was there to pick up the pieces, regardless of Andrew's protests.

"I wish I could just walk up to her and smack the ugly off of her!" Jenny makes a fist and punches Nicole on the arm for emphasis.

"What was that for?" Nicole punches her back.

Helplessly, I watch as Amy sits next to Andrew at the lunch table in front of us, batting her heavily applied mascara-laden eyelashes and smacking her gum. Andrew looks uncomfortable, like a bait fish being lowered into a tank of bass. He waves at me, but I look away.

I feel a tap on the shoulder and turn to see Mike. Without being asked, he sits down beside me; his tray was only half full. Nicole stops eating her tuna fish sandwich, waiting for Jenny to stop making kissing sounds.

"Stop that!" Nicole shoots her an angry glance.

"Why aren't you sitting over there?" Jenny interrogates, taking a bite of her ham and cheese hoagie.

"I don't like the company," Mike grimaces.

"So why is Andrew over there without you?" Jenny questions again.

"I think he's trying to make Selena jealous." Mike looks directly at me. "Is it working?"

Like a ninja, I peek at Andrew and Amy and lose my appetite.

"I'm not hungry," I declare, excusing myself from the table. "I'm going to go to the courtyard to do some studying."

"Do you want us to come with you?" Jenny asks as she stuffs the last bite of a Twinkie into her mouth.

"No, it's alright," I watch as Amy begins giving Andrew a neck massage. "I'll talk to you two later. See you later, Mike."

♪♪♪

Unable to purge that upsetting event from my mind, I race downstairs. Thankfully, the courtyard is empty except for a couple of teens kissing on one of the benches. I recognize the girl from my Calculus class; the boy I haven't seen before. Their kisses are so passionate. I immediately vision Amy and Andrew lip-locked together up in the cafeteria.

"Give you any ideas?" I glance up to see Andrew standing over me, smiling.

"I thought Amy was massaging the tension out of your *neck*," I retort sarcastically.

Quite amused, he laughs.

"You're jealous," Andrew teases.

Immediately, my eyebrows hitch and my eyes widen.

"*Jealous*? Of you and Amy?" I huff indignantly. "Ha! Don't flatter yourself."

"We haven't talked in nearly a month," he mentions.

I frown.

"I've been busy," I act extremely blasé.

"You've also been avoiding me," he adds with a wry smile.

"I haven't been avoiding you," I feel my dander rising. "It's just your paranoia working overtime."

Andrew's smile disappears as he queries.

"Then why haven't you returned any of my phone calls?"

"Oh...did you call?" I ask coyly, with extra contemptuousness thrown in. "Did you get permission from Amy?"

He laughs mockingly, making me want to give him a right hook to the chin.

"You wanted to concentrate on schoolwork, remember?"

270

"I remember." I begin reading my library book.

"Yup, you are definitely jealous," he continues.

"I'm not the jealous type." I look him directly in the eyes…those hypnotic emerald-green eyes and those perfectly shaped lips.

Focus, Selena, focus!

"Jealous, jealous, jealous," he mocks.

Unwilling to be assaulted by his verbal punches, I gather my belongings and begin walking to the stairs. Andrew walks beside me being annoyingly bubbly. The scent of his cologne intoxicates me, and I wish I could grab him and kiss the arrogance right out of him.

"Selena," he steps in front of me, blocking the entrance to the stairwell. "Whatever I did to make you so angry, I apologize."

A perturbed sigh escapes me.

"You didn't do anything," I blurt, sadness engulfing my entire body.

"Then why don't you want to keep seeing each other?" he questions in a sweet, boyish manner.

"Amy told me that she would get my stepfather fired if I kept dating you," I finally admit.

"Wow! She pulled that card?" He genuinely seems shocked that she would go to such extremes. "Don't worry, I'll talk to her."

"And say what, exactly?" I ask with raised eyebrows. "Listen, my family doesn't need any more problems than it already has. If she wants you so badly, she can have you, and she can have the Winter Solo as well."

"What am I, a piece of meat?" Andrew glares. "Am I supposed to just sit around while you and she decide who I'm going to be with? This is ridiculous!"

He moves from the stairs; body language is tense and clearly agitated.

"When you figure out what's important to let me know," he snarls.

"Andrew, my stepfather worked hard for this position and I won't put it in jeopardy," I justify my position. "I'll see you around."

Out of time, I push him out of the way and head to my next class.

♪♪♪

The ride home with David and Ando is quiet. We spend most of the time in silence. Unfortunately, Dad seems unnerved.

"Did Mom tell you two if she had a meeting or something scheduled for today?" he finally asks; running his left hand through his hair like he often does when frustrated.

"No, sir," I answer truthfully.

"Ando, did Mom say anything to you?"

"No, Daddy," Ando looks at me curiously.

"I haven't heard from her the entire day," David grips the steering wheel tighter. "She called in sick to work. She's not answering her cell phone. I'm getting really worried."

♪♪♪

We pull up to the front of the house in record time. David drove like a racecar driver, swerving around cars and racing around sharp mountain roads. Honestly, I wanted to bend down and kiss the ground when we made it home safely.

"Selena, call your mother on the house phone," my stepfather commands. "I'm going to call the police."

Frantically, we all run inside the house. Immediately, I go to the phone, but before I can begin punching the numbers, Mom walks nonchalantly into the living room from the kitchen and plops down on the sofa.

"What's the matter with you all?" she asks from the living room couch, unaware of our panic-driven state.

Stupefied, my stepfather stares at her in amazement. In a petrified state, he stands in the doorway looking as though he has just seen a ghost; clearly off-kilter at the sight of his carefree spouse.

"What are you doing home?" he interrogates gruffly. "I've been trying to get a hold of you all day. Your secretary said you called in sick, but you never called to let me know."

"What the hell is going on, Marina?"

"I'm sorry I didn't call to let you know I wasn't at work," she pacifies. "But I didn't think it was a big deal."

"Of course it's a big deal!" he barks. "I'm your husband and I need to know if you're staying home! Not as a control thing, but because I love you and want to make sure you're safe, that's all!"

"Fine, next time, I'll let you know what's going on," Mom replies caustically, very much out of character.

At first, we all stood around staring at her; our mouths gaping as we wonder why she was acting so strangely. Ando, I think, looks more frazzled than the rest of us. Without a word, he goes upstairs to his room and closes the door. David storms off next as he takes refuge in his office, slamming the door behind him. The impact makes the first-floor windows shake. Me, I am left staring at the woman who, up until a few months ago, was the glue that held our family together, but is now the one who is pulling it apart.

CHAPTER FOURTEEN

Things have been getting very tense between David and Mom. They have been arguing more and more with every passing day. My mother has not been able to concentrate and is always disappearing. The only place that Ando and I feel at peace anymore is on the front porch where we like to play jacks.

David is constantly asking: *'Where were you, Marina?'* while my mom is always answering with: *'I've been working, David.'* It is like a dance between two cobras, and Ando and I are caught in the crossfire.

Tonight, my brother and I sit on the porch waiting for the latest argument to finish. Ando rests his head on my shoulder as I gently run my fingers through his wavy, dark hair. Mom and David are in the living room, unaware of their eavesdropping offspring.

"I was working. I've told you again and again...why don't you believe me?" Mom grabs a couch cushion and angrily fluffs the material.

"Why are you acting so distant, Marina? So secretive," he frowns. "I went to your office to surprise you with dinner, since you've been working so hard lately, and your secretary said that you had left over two hours ago."

"I had to pick up a few art supplies for a project that I'm working on," Mom tries to pacify.

"It was after eight!" David counters. "The only art supply store on the island closes at six!"

"I'm sorry!" she yells at the top of her lungs, causing the window to vibrate. "I didn't know that I was married to a detective. What am I, some kind of prisoner or something? Do I have to check in with you every single second of every single day?"

"Stop overreacting!" David yells back. "That's all you do lately... yell and overreact! Oh, and don't forget, sneak around."

Mom throws the cushion back onto the couch.

"What are you implying?" her arms fold defiantly across her chest.

"Are you having an affair?" he whispers, almost choking on the words.

"Now you think I'm having an affair?" Mom's voice lowers.

David stands perfectly still, his eyes glistening, but no tears appear.

"I don't know what to think," he callously admits. "You disappear for hours at a time and when you do show up...your hair is wet and your clothes smell like day old fish."

"I would never—" Mom begins, but is suddenly interrupted.

"Marina, tell me what is going on?" his voice softens. "Ever since we moved to this place, you've been different."

Without warning, Mom rushes out of the house onto the front porch. The spot has become their favorite place to argue; something about the salty air and the smell of the sea, perhaps. David rubs his temples in a vain attempt to clear his head as his wife begins her usual pacing. Both are oblivious to my brother and me already occupying the porch.

"I don't know what you're talking about, David!" Mom yells. "I'm the same person you married! I haven't changed!"

Ando and I look at each other, knowing her words are untrue. She has changed. Her demeanor is more caustic...more impatient...and extremely cold.

"Where have you been going so late at night?" he asks, not really expecting an answer.

"I told you, I go for walks," Mom lies.

David shakes his head in disbelief.

"You go for walks at midnight?" he shakes his head again. "Do you honestly expect me to believe that?"

"Yes," she responds with a loud exhale.

Pushed to his limit, he covers his face with his hands, trying desperately to calm his growing temper.

"I don't believe you, Marina."

"Fine, don't believe me," Mom sighs. "I'm just your wife."

"Yes, you are my wife and we've been married for eleven years...*eleven* years, Marina." David begins to pace. "I thought I knew everything about you, but obviously I don't."

Sadness shadows his appearance as he stares at her.

"What could be so terrible that you can't tell me?" he huffs his agitation.

Mom suddenly stops dead in her tracks. Her reaction makes us both jump. David cannot take his eyes off of her; neither can I.

"I'm a Siren," she reveals without any hesitation. "You know—a sea nymph?"

Slowly, David sits silently contemplating her answer, then bursts into uncontrollable laughter.

"Like a mermaid?" he retorts.

My mother instantly frowns.

"First of all," she huffs. "*We* do not have tails or bad attitudes."

"Be serious," my stepfather sneers.

"I first saw you off the coast of Anchorage," Mom continues, ignoring his strange expression. "You were documenting the migratory patterns of Orcas. If memory serves, you were wearing a red and black plaid long-sleeve flannel shirt, a brown leather aviator jacket and a pair of blue jeans."

She laughs as the memories come rushing back.

"Oh, and you were also wearing a pair of silver-framed glasses. I didn't think that someone could look nerdy and sexy at the same time, but somehow you managed to."

David's mouth drops open.

280

"How do you—"

"I didn't realize you were there at first; I was too engulfed in watching a family of Orcas playing. They looked so happy that I burst into song. A few minutes passed when I heard a loud splash nearby; being nosy, as you well know I am, I swam in the direction of the commotion and found you lying face down in the icy ocean."

David opens his mouth to say something, but Mom raises her hand and he stops.

"I pulled you back into the boat and checked for a pulse, but there was none. I touched your chest, and you began breathing again. Before you opened your eyes, I dove under the boat to hide. I watched as you took the boat back to the harbor and waited until the ambulance came to take you to the hospital."

David is completely dumbstruck.

"How could you possibly know all of that?"

"I told you...I was there," Mom states steadily. "That's how I know."

He shakes his head again.

"That's impossible. I must have told you—"

"I swam to that harbor every day for a month to see you," she informs with a grin. "Every day you'd bring a thermos of hot chocolate and roast beef sandwiches with mustard. You'd always manage to get mustard on your shirt."

Mom laughs jovially.

"Sometimes you would bring that old battery-run, radio slash cassette player that Ando has now, and sing along to the oldies. The Temptations were your favorite group. You'd listen to 'I heard It Through the Grapevine' every single day."

"Marina—"

"I never knew that humans could be so gentle, so kind, and I fell in love with you," she genuinely praises. "I fell in love with you, David, and I knew I had to be with you somehow."

Mom's eyes glaze over as she relives the memory of falling in love with him.

"So, I went to my aunts and told them that I had fallen in love with a mortal just like my mother had," she gushes. "But they forbade me to see you."

David watches her, his face void of emotion.

"They said that no good could come of it," she rambles, voice filled with raw sentiment. "If I gave up the sea I would eventually die, they reminded me, but I didn't care. I wanted to be with you even if it meant my death."

"What do you mean...*your death*?" David inquires with confusion. "What are you talking about, Marina?"

"I am the daughter of a Siren, an immortal being. I could have lived forever, but instead I chose a mortal life. I chose to live as a human being and to experience all that that entails... pain, hurt...death."

David's expression changes to terror.

"Okay, stop! This sounds too crazy," he snaps, his cheeks flushed. "What you're saying isn't possible."

Stiffly, he gets up to go back inside the house; the floorboards creak under his weight, but Mom halts his exit.

"I guess I have always been fascinated with humans: their customs, traditions, and their families," she reminisces. "After all, a thousand years is a long time not to experience love, and I wanted so much to be in love."

"Marina, you were already an up-and-coming model when we met, and you had already had Selena." David's words can't be disputed.

"After Hera took away the Sirens wings and cursed them into the sea, Parthenope felt the loss hardest of all. She stopped singing to Zeus, which sorrowed him deeply."

"Zeus," he pauses, scratching his head in confusion. "The god from Mt. Olympus?"

"Yes, the very same deity you learn about in school," Mom replies. "Parthenope's depression weakened all of the sisters; their angelic songs ceased and they no longer graced the world with their music."

"Wait," he retorts, rubbing the back of his neck. "Don't you mean Poseidon? Isn't he the ruler of all the *'fish-folk'*?"

Mom's body stiffens and her lips roll into a jeer.

"Pfff!" she scoffs indignantly. "Poseidon started all of this, that son of a Kraken!"

David looks troubled.

"Marina, stop! Please stop this nonsense."

Attempting to hold it together, my mom takes a deep breath.

"Parthenope was his favorite, and it hurt his heart to see her in pain, so the ruler of the gods blessed Parthenope with the ability to create life. In fact, she was the only one of *The Three* that could reproduce.

"A year later, she met a Roman sea captain named Marcus Antonius during one of his trading voyages. Marcus' ship, The

Song of the Sea, was lured to its demise when it sailed too close to Anthemoessa."

"What is Anthemoessa?" David asks, his voice sounding shaky.

"Anthemoessa is a flower-filled island off the coast of Italy," Mom informs and then realizes that David still does not believe her. "Today, the island is called Capri."

"Capri...we honeymooned in Capri," David remembers.

"Should I continue?" Mom pauses.

"Why not?" David states sarcastically.

Mom takes a deep breath, her right foot tapping a staccato with hands clasped together.

"Unfortunately, Marcus was the only survivor, but he was badly injured. Parthenope nursed him back to health. He was stranded on Anthemoessa for almost a year; however, during that year the two fell deeply in love. Shortly after, Parthenope gave birth to a daughter."

His wife pauses, clears her throat like she often does when she is nervous, and then continues her tale.

"Marcus named their daughter Marina, which is Latin for 'From the Sea.' The little girl was me, half-human... half Siren, a gift from mighty Zeus."

"You expect me to believe this?" David speaks calmly. "That you are the daughter given to the mythological Siren by Zeus himself, fathered by a Roman mariner."

"Yes, because it's the truth." Mom reaches out to touch his hand, but he pulls away.

"When we met, you were a model," he states flatly.

"I followed you to Ohio, found a modeling job in Columbus, and met you at the fundraising dinner the marine biology department threw at the University of Ohio a month later," she rambles without taking a breath.

"And what about Selena?" David motions in my direction, causing Mom to focus on me; her cheeks redden with embarrassment. My curiosity peaks as well. "Was she another blessing from Zeus?"

Mom sits down on the porch steps and I move closer to her trembling form.

"As Parthenope's offspring, I inherited the same blessing to bear children."

"So...who's Selena's father?" David asks snidely. "Davy Jones?"

Mom says nothing, which causes David's temper to rise. The strain between them is growing, and I cannot do anything to squelch it. Through all of this, my mother seems unusually calm.

"Selena has no father," Mom whispers.

"You're lying!" David yells.

My mother's mouth drops open like she has just been slapped, and immediately her eyes well with tears as she stands staring at her husband in disbelief. She blinks several times before taking another much-needed breath.

"There has always been *The Three*," she says flatly. "Since the creation of Mother Gaia, there has always been *The Three*. They are the embodiment of nature, passion and apathy... vengeance and forgiveness... hope and despair. Their bond as sisters hold them together.

"Those are *The Three*...Parthenope the Compassionate, Ligeia the Passionate, and Leukosia the Mediator. One cannot survive without the other two. In order for me to live as a human, I had to give them a third. I had to give them back balance or they would have died. So, I willed myself to have Selena."

"What does that mean?" David demands in barely a whisper.

"Regardless of Parthenope meeting Marcus, she could have created life from her own essence by splitting her cells into a smaller entity; essentially creating a miniature version of herself without any male assistance."

David's eyebrows hitch as his face turns ghostly pale. I can imagine the conflicting thoughts battering his scientifically rational brain. After all, the man has a PhD in Marine Biology and Chemistry. He has been a scholar trained by the best of his field. The man is a master of hypothesizing and test studies, and all of this sounds like hocus pocus and fairytales. Basically, what my mother is selling, he surely is not buying. In fact, knowing David, he probably thinks she is just losing her mind.

"You willed yourself to give birth to Selena?" He chuckles like a lunatic. "She just appeared?"

"No," Mom shakes her head. "Because I am half-human, Selena developed and grew in me just like a regular baby, only much faster."

Unable to hold my tongue any longer, I bolt to a standing position.

"But I wasn't a regular baby," I whisper, almost in tears. "I'm...I'm a freak."

"No," Mom soothes. "Even when you were still inside me, I felt your strength...your power. I knew you would be much greater than I."

"I'm a freak?!" I repeat as tears now roll down my cheeks.

David looks at me with despair. He looks as if someone stabbed him in the heart.

"Marina, stop this insanity!" he begs. "Look what you are doing to our child!"

Mom takes David's hand and begins walking toward the side of the house. As they disappear from view down the rocky staircase, I hug Ando, who sits quietly next to me on the porch stairs.

♪♪♪

What seems like an eternity passes before they return. David appears first; his eyes are dark, and his facial features are pale. Mom rushes past Ando, and me, runs upstairs and returns moments later with Grandpa Theo's journal.

"Here, read this!" she orders. "It will answer most of your questions about who I am!"

David stares at her dumbfounded, unsure of what to say or do. He leaves us standing on the porch, but we quickly follow.

Silently, he goes into the bedroom and takes an empty suitcase from the closet. As we watch in horror, he throws most of his clothes into it. With a tear-streaked face, Mom stands in the doorway, speechless.

A few minutes later, David steps back into the living room with a sickly sallow expression.

"Ando, Selena, go and pack some clothes," he growls.

"Daddy, why do we need to pack?" Ando pleads. "Where are we going?"

"We will discuss it later," David replies without emotion. "Just go pack."

Obviously shocked, Ando looks at him and then at Mom, terrified at what is happening. Our mother tries to smile, but tears are running down her face. She wipes them with the edge of her t-shirt.

"Ando," Mom speaks softly. "Do as your father says."

My brother stands for a moment wondering what to do, then runs upstairs to get his stuff, but Mom and I stand our ground.

"Selena!" David's anger is growing. "What did I say?!"

"Daddy, please don't leave!" I beg, sounding childish. "Can you please calm down?"

At my request, he takes a deep soothing breath and tries to rein in his temper. With trembling fingers, he presses his throbbing temples and glances between Mom and I. I cannot believe this is really happening.

I hate being a Siren!

"I need some time, Selena," David glances at Mom. "Please, get your things and let's go."

"I can't leave her," I answer protectively.

Understanding my dilemma, David hugs me tightly.

"No matter what happens, you will always be my daughter... always," he reminds.

Mom is crying even harder now.

"David, please stay," she touches his arm, but he pulls away. "We can work it out."

"Ando, let's go, hurry!" David calls, trying to get around her body without hitting her with the suitcase; his hands still clutch the journal.

An eternity passes before Ando comes downstairs carrying his bag and teddy bear.

"Daddy, I don't want to leave Lena and Mommy!" he pouts angrily.

Ignoring his plea, David takes him firmly by the hand.

"The sisters are really nice," Ando adds. "They let me play with dolphins!"

David looks at me, then at Mom.

"You and Ando went down there, to swim, with those... creatures?" he reprimands. "Do you know how dangerous that was?"

I feel the tears begin.

"I'll never go to see them again," I promise. "And I'll make sure that Ando doesn't either. I won't sing ever again! We can be a normal family. Just please don't leave!"

Without another word, David takes Ando to the car, loads up the vehicle, and pulls out of the driveway, leaving us in the dark.

The wind is beginning to strengthen; rain-laden storm clouds are coming in from the east. Fat cold raindrops land on the ground all around me, then begin to darken my blue V-neck. The clouds seem to be expressing everything that I cannot... that *she* cannot. Mom's heart is breaking. Even without our mental connection, I can feel it, and apparently, Mother Nature feels it too.

CHAPTER FIFTEEN

The house is quiet without David and Ando, much too quiet.

For the past week, I have slept with Mom in her bed to keep her company. She cries practically every night, then falls asleep for a few minutes, only to wake to begin another round. Mom has been doing that a lot since they left. She and I worry because he has not called yet, and I do not have the heart to tell her that I do not think he is going to.

Sadly, I know how she feels; Andrew and I have not spoken in over two weeks. What makes it worse is that I have to see him every day in school, in every period except for P.E. Both Nicole and Jenny think I am crazy for being so stubborn.

"Don't let Amy intimidate you," Jenny said yesterday at lunch.

"Yeah, Selena," Nicole agreed. "If you want to be with Andrew, then fight for him."

Even non-violent, shy, Mike encouraged me to stand my ground.

"Walk up to her and slap her right on her smug face," he growled, nostrils flaring.

We all laughed that those words actually came out of his mouth. I think he impressed Nicole with his newfound aggression. After that, she kept glancing in his direction with a goofy grin on her face.

"Mr. Taylor," Jenny punched him on the arm. "I didn't know you had it in you."

"It's the Italian in me," Mike smiled as he did his best *Robert Dinero* impersonation. "*'You wanna a piece of me?'*"

Needless to say, we laughed until Jenny fell off of the bench and had to go to the nurse's office. Thank goodness she did not get hurt; however, she did turn red when everyone in the cafeteria turned to see what all of the commotion was. Even with all of that, none of my friends understood that Amy would do anything to get her talons into Andrew, even lie and get David fired, or worse, arrested. I am certain that Mr. Jacobs would do it just to keep his little girl happy.

The little rodent!

This morning, as I fantasize about various ways of defeating my blonde rival, the toast pops up and out of the toaster, breaking my train of thought. Temporarily forgetting my current fictitious revenge scenarios, I decide to scramble some eggs for us, but Mom refuses them at first. After several minutes of nagging, I finally convince her to eat before going for a swim with the aunts, but instead of going down to the sea, she waits for me on the porch.

"Is breakfast almost ready?" Mom hollers from outside.

"Almost!" I reply, feeling rushed.

Quickly, I turn my attention to the task of smothering the pieces of bread with butter and jelly, piling the scrambled eggs on top of the sweet condiments, and then make my way to the front porch. The scent of the food makes my stomach grumble. For some inexplicable reason, I am extra hungry lately. Mom thinks it is because I am having a growth spurt, but I play it off. I am not stupid enough to tell her I have been sneaking off for midnight swims with Ligeia and Leukosia every night for the last two weeks.

"Mom?" I swallow my first bite of breakfast as we sit on the steps.

"What is it?" she asks; bracing herself for the unknown, mouth full of the delicious scramble.

"If you created me to complete the Sirens…" I state, needing to know the answer no matter how difficult.

My mother's body visually tenses as she huffs.

"Just say it, Selena."

"Why didn't you leave me with them?" I ask, the question burning on my tongue.

Slowly, she releases a held breath and a faint smile appears on her perfectly shaped lips.

"I had every intention of leaving you," she acknowledges. "But once I held you in my arms, I couldn't."

"Oh!" I smile. "How did the sisters take the news?"

"Let's just say that a tsunami almost destroyed Sri Lanka that year," she replies, shaking her dark locks. Shocked by this newfound revelation, my jaw drops and hangs there for a few seconds.

"They caused that catastrophe?" I gasp, shocked at the news.

Mom nods, her expression humorous.

"The first year we were away from the sisters was an unusually active storm season," she admits guiltily.

Feeling the need to change the subject, I query: "I know how Yaya met Grandfather Marcus, but how did she meet Grandpa Theo?"

My mom thinks for a long moment before answering.

"Well…my mother sent me with my father when he was rescued from Anthemoessa, knowing that she could not abandon her sisters. Father was heartbroken, and so was she. She was allowed to visit us twice a year; once during the winter season then again in the summer. Father stayed true to her for his entire life. He passed away from pneumonia when I was sixteen human years old, and I went back to the sea after he died. There was nothing that really tied me to the humans except for him.

"Centuries passed, until one summer while Parthenope and I were swimming off the coast of Isla Flora, we heard singing. It was a deep voice with a familiar Greek accent, singing folk songs reminiscing of days of old when Zeus' lightning bolts made the world quake."

"It was Grandpa Theo who was singing," I say, not surprised, remembering when he was alive and all the lullabies, he sang for me and Ando. He had a superb singing voice. Now, knowing that he was able to tame a Siren, I feel even closer to him.

"Yes, it was, and right then and there is when she revealed her true form to him and he accepted her without doubt," Mom reminisces as she becomes misty-eyed.

"Too bad David didn't do the same," my voice quivers and I am unable to stop it. "I mean, accept you for *You*."

"Yes," her tears resume. "That would have been wonderful."

♪♪♪

After breakfast, the aunts take us for a short swim to a nearby islet located in the deep harbor of Isla Flora, approximately a quarter of a mile offshore. The excursion, so far, has been lighthearted and frivolous as Leukosia takes the time to give brief descriptions of the surrounding underwater topography and marine life native to the waters surrounding our lush tropical area. Ligeia, on the other hand, swims beside my mother, catching up on everything that has happened since they were last together. It is wonderful to see Mom so casually laid-back and at ease.

"Kick off harder, Selena!" both aunts instruct in Siren at once, their eyes sparkling even on the dusky ocean bottom.

"I did!" I snap, feeling like the odd Siren out.

Aunt Ligeia rolls her expressive eyes and barks several quick clicks, followed by one whistle and an elongated clack.

Not understanding, I perch my hands on my hips.

"Could you please repeat your last comment?" I request as calmly as possible in Siren. Mom insists that I must practice the complicated language even though it does not come naturally to me yet.

Again, she makes the same noises, but this time much faster, and then has the nerve to 'harrumph' me.

My mouth drops with shock.

"That's uncalled for!" I chastise; my annoyance at its peak.

Aunt Leukosia snickers a few feet away while she heals the dorsal fin of a young nurse shark that was recently attacked by a much larger shark of another species. According to the nurse shark, it was an Oceanic White-tip with a chip on its shoulder the size of a whale shark.

"Aunt Leukosia? What did Aunt Ligeia just say to me?" I interrogate the much nicer sister.

"She said that you have as much grace as a lame hermit crab who snacked on a piece of decomposed human trash," the blonde snickers.

"Huh?" I sound with confusion. "What in the world does that mean?"

Behind me, I hear my mother giggle and I turn in her direction.

Gracefully and with absolutely no effort at all, Mom hovers a few feet above the soft, sandy ocean floor, watching my first 'lesson' on being a proficient Siren. So far, I have been practicing how to call my gills and webbing, speaking and translating Siren, as well as sharpening my telepathic skills. You would think that it would be easier after all of these months, but according to Ligeia, I am *not* a quick study. Leukosia, on the other hand, is a tad bit more supportive. She claims that it will all fall into place, eventually. I certainly hope so.

"Ignore your aunt," Mom comments flatly. "She's in a bad mood."

I snicker.

"When is she not in a bad mood?" I tease, feeling vindicated when the red-haired Siren's mouth gapes just as mine did.

Ligeia throws another jibe at me.

"Are you a Siren or a moray eel?" Ligeia blusters with a touch of hostility.

Again, I glare at her, not understanding.

"What?"

"Moray eels are notoriously sensitive," Mom shrugs with a chuckle. "And they always tend to overreact."

Unable to hold it in, I laugh out loud.

"I see!"

♪♪♪

Tired of being confined to training in the small alcove below our house, the aunts have brought us to one of their favorite spots. The island is roughly a half of a mile in length and the same in diameter, which, according to the aunts, is where they 'live' when in this part of the world. It is a pretty place full of birds, lizards, and insects (lots and lots of insects), and there is a bubbling stream that flows out of the ground that provides fresh water. Everywhere the eye can see are edible flowers along with a small grove of coconut palms. Not surprisingly, the entire island is surrounded by the most amazing sea creatures that I have ever seen.

"Where do you sleep?" I question, surveying the surrounding sea.

"Over there." Ligeia points to a crack in the rocky base of the land formation.

"Where?"

"There is an underwater opening that leads to a roomy cavern beneath," she informs dismissively.

"Can I see it?" I ask hopefully.

"That depends on how well you perform with your lessons today," Aunt Ligeia smirks.

Movement in my peripheral vision gets my attention and I turn toward it. Filled with excitement, I point to a strange animal swimming nearby that sort of resembles a chunky dolphin, but unlike a dolphin it is armed with a protruding tusk jutting out of its head. Right now, he is currently making small talk with my mother.

"What kind of animal is that?" I clickity-clack with excitement.

Mom pauses from her lively conversation.

"This is Aalik," she introduces with a wide grin. "He is a narwhal."

The creature nods proudly.

"Aalik, this is my daughter Selena."

"Nice to meet you, Aalik," I reply, giving a nod of acknowledgement to the medium-sized, toothed whale with the large protruding canine tooth.

"Come here," Mom requests, motioning with her hands. "He is harmless."

Not believing that anything with such an intimidating tusk could possibly be 'harmless', I hesitate.

Mom smiles, the only true smile that she has made since David and Ando left home.

"Don't be afraid," she coddles with several drawn-out clicks and whistles. "He's very sweet."

Taking a deep breath, I slowly swim toward the unique looking marine mammal, getting his back rubbed by my mother.

"What should I do?" I clack and then click.

"Touch him." Mom smiles and takes my trembling hand, placing it on his tusk.

I follow her instructions, not making any sudden motions and being careful not to get in front of him for fear of being skewered.

"He has a tusk like a spear," I giggle as I run my hand along his weaponry.

Mom shakes her head.

"This is actually an enlarged spiraled tooth that has sensory capability and up to ten million nerve endings inside," she continues, obviously enjoying our lesson. "It can grow as long as ten feet."

"Wow!" I interject enthusiastically.

My interest is definitely at attention.

"Do all narwhals have these?" I question, recognizing why David is so fascinated by marine biology. A pang of sadness hits me, but not wanting to ruin this experience, I push it to the back of my mind.

"Usually, it is found on males," she educates like a knowledgeable scientist. "But some narwhals can have up to two tusks, while others may have none."

"He reminds me of a unicorn," I whisper, not wanting to offend him.

Mom snickers as she puts her finger to her lips, silently to warn that he might overhear.

"Is he native to these waters?" I ask, turning to the aunts.

"No," Leukosia answers sympathetically. "Poor dear has a terrible sense of direction."

"Apparently, he wanted to explore and wandered too far away from home," Ligeia adds.

Temporarily unable to remember my basic Siren language, I turn to Mom.

"How do I ask: where does he come from?"

She grins, then leans in close to my ear and whispers.

With newfound confidence, I utter a series of clacks and chirpy sounds. I think Aalik actually…smiles back?

Mom is trying to control a belly shaking laugh and Ligeia and Leukosia are blushing and chuckling too.

"What's wrong?" I ask, my face red and hot.

"Basically, you asked him if he wanted you as a mate," Ligeia snorts underwater, causing a stream of bubbles to escape her perfectly shaped nose.

"Did I?" I blush, holding back a snort of my own.

They all nod, including Aalik.

"Try again," Leukosia encourages with a playful wink. "However, this time, only clack twice and shorten your chirps."

Grateful for the advice, I give her a thumbs-up and try once more. This time I get it right. Proudly, I give myself a mental pat on the back.

Aalik puffs up his chest before answering my question.

"I...year-round live...in waters Arctic waters around Greenland," he states with a thick accent. "Me sorry...me not speak Siren too good."

I give him a gentle rub over his smooth skin.

"That's alright," I grin. "Neither do I."

CHAPTER SIXTEEN

L ately, the only thing that keeps my mind off of David, Ando, and Andrew is being in the sea. Underneath the waves, my thoughts are still…my heart is at peace…my purpose is clear and, in those moments, all that matters is the freedom it offers.

Today is my first day away from the protection of the shoreline. The Sirens have found a more secluded area in a nearby mangrove on the southeast part of the island. Here I feel safe, like I am in my own baby-Siren nursery, which is very similar to a shark nursery in that I am allowed to explore without fear of predators making a meal of me and that I can freely practice my abilities. Actually, we share this mangrove with baby lemon sharks and hawksbill sea turtles. In this area, Leukosia, Ligeia, and Mom teach me everything they know about my new watery playground.

I am a quick study, even if I do say so myself. I have almost mastered their strange click-clack language now; I can even call the nearest dolphin pod to me. One time, I clacked when I should have clicked and accidentally called an extremely cranky bull shark. Fortunately, Ligeia is even crankier and was able to convince him that it was in his best interest to find another meal. It is comforting to know that not even a seven foot, three-hundred-pound male bull shark wants to get on Ligeia's bad side.

Actually, Ligeia's attitude has softened quite a bit in the last month. She smiles more; sometimes she even laughs. Last week, she allowed me to accompany her on a late-night excursion to the other side of the island to check on a visiting flotilla of loggerhead turtles.

Leukosia, on the other hand, has always been friendly, but lately she has been overly emotional, to the point of bursting into tears at the slightest thing. If I did not know better, I would think that she was premenstrual.

Determined to be a better Siren, I have been diligently practicing, in my opinion, the most challenging skill of calling the webbing between my fingers and toes at will. It is incredibly difficult, but I have been able to do it twice now. It is easier to control the webbing when I am dry, when they get wet. Those darned things take forever to disappear. Last week, I was washing dishes and water splashed on my feet; it took almost ten minutes of towel drying to make them go away.

Transitioning between my lungs and gills is the most painful part of my aquatic experience. Sometimes the pain is so extreme that I lose consciousness before either one will kick-in. Several times, I have woken up on the sandy sea bottom to three sets of aquamarine eyes glaring at me; it is extremely uncomfortable, not to mention embarrassing.

"Will this ever get any easier?" I puff, trying to transition my breathing on command.

"It will in time," Ligeia answers, her melodic voice tickles my ears.

Mom suddenly surfaces, holding an aluminum soda can and a plastic grocery bag.

"I wish people would be more careful with their trash," she states casually.

"Humans don't care about the negative impact they have on the earth," I answer rather coldly. "They will not stop until the world is a lifeless ball of nothing."

"Selena, that is a terrible thing to say," Mom defends.

"You know that I'm right," I continue.

"Believe me, Selena; mankind has come a long way this past century," she conveys. "Advancements in medicine, agriculture, technology; they have a lot to be proud of."

"Could you be any sappier?" I smirk with an indignant air that catches me off guard.

Ligeia comes to my mother's aid.

"It is true," the blonde concedes. "Not all men are destructive or unkind."

"Are you kidding me?" I blab, overwhelmed by her words of praise toward mankind in general, men in particular. "All men are destructive."

"Selena!" Mom gasps. "You don't really mean that!"

"Yes, I do."

"Do you think Ando is like that?" Mom questions, giving me a surprised expression.

"Of course not!" I snip. "Ando is part Siren. He doesn't fall into the same category."

"Your father is a wonderful man too," she reminds.

"He is not wonderful!" I raise my voice, which surprises her and the aunts. "David destroyed our family when he walked out on us! I hate him!"

Mom slaps me across the face without warning; if it was any harder, it might have knocked me out.

"Don't you ever say that again! Do you understand me, Selena?"

I stare at her defiantly, refusing to blink, unable to stop my eyes from welling with unshed tears.

"What is the matter with you?" Mom stares at me disapprovingly.

"You are both feeling the effects of the sea," Leukosia interrupts, teary-eyed. "The longer you are in the water...the longer you are near us, the colder your hearts will become."

"Your dislike of humans will also grow as well as the need for solitude," both aunts say simultaneously. "I believe you have been having these kinds of emotions as well. Is that true, Marina?"

My mother nods.

"What about you, Selena?" Their eyes lock onto me.

I do not answer.

"As Sirens, our hearts must be cold. Immortality makes it so," Leukosia adds. "We are of this world, yet apart from it.

"Marina, since you are half-human, the effect will take longer to influence your emotions, but Selena...Selena is only a quarter human; she will lose her humanity faster."

A tear rolls down Leukosia's cheek, surprising Mom and me.

"We, on the other hand, become more susceptible to human emotions the longer we are with you and other humans." Leukosia's eyes glisten. "Your humanity warms our hearts."

"That is why Parthenope and my mother fell in love," I mumble. "Because they were infected by mortals."

"I do not think 'infected' is the correct word," Leukosia evasively corrects.

Both sisters add: "Parthenope was always fascinated with humans; even before she met Marcus, she would follow passing ships, listening to conversations between crew members."

Ligeia flicks water into the air with her webbed feet, while Leukosia gazes aimlessly into the night sky.

"She wanted so much to be human...to love and to be loved," they conclude.

Memories of Andrew come to mind, his gentle eyes, his warm smile, his firm, tight, umm, muscles. Even the way his dimples appear when he laughs, or the way he rambles when he is nervous…are all adorable. Like a lightbulb being flicked on, I feel like my normal self once again.

"I don't want to be cold-hearted," I admit, allowing myself to discard the hateful ideas.

"It is our nature, young one," Leukosia regains her composure.

"What about dying?" I wonder out loud. "If you are immortal, how can you die?"

The sisters look at each other and click-clack their answer. Mom translates.

"We can choose to leave the sea…live like humans, but with this choice we also become susceptible to disease, hunger and pain. We begin to age and eventually, well, we die."

"But if we stay in the sea, we remain immortal," they both respond.

"Is that what you chose to do?" I ask Mom. "To live on land, like a human, giving up all that you are?"

"Yes, to be with David, I would do just about anything," she stares longingly at her wedding ring.

The sisters' glance at each other and then at my mother, their expressions grave until finally asking:

"So, you would truly give up immortality in order to live a short, painful life that will only end with old age and death?"

"In a heartbeat," she smiles wistfully.

"So, if I wanted to live forever, I would have to return to the sea?" I interrogate the aunts.

"Yes," they nod. "You would have to leave everyone and everything you have ever loved and live with us."

"What happens when it is just the two of you?"

"Eventually, our powers will weaken," Ligeia emphasizes offhandedly. "We will lose the ability to communicate with sea life and our moods are more likely to cause terrible storms, things such as those. Then we will die...probably turning into sea foam or some other such useless nonsense."

"It is a slow and agonizing death too tragic to speak of," Leukosia stifles back a sob.

"Worst of all, we will lose the ability to sing," the Sirens advise together.

"What's so bad about that?" I sneer; my humanity begins to lapse again.

My aunts begin clicking and clacking and clacking and clicking until Mom speaks out.

"We are the embodiment of music, the Song of the Sea. Melpomene the Muse created the Sirens by giving birth to us in the sea...singing as we came forth into the world. At that moment, *The Three* sang and created the Song of Gaia; the Song of the Earth.

"We are the voice of the Earth in physical form," they speak as one. "Without song, we have nothing; without us, the Earth will wither and die."

"But you won't die if it's just the two of you?" I verify, hoping to get the answers that I need.

Leukosia frowns.

"We begin to age, of course much slower than that of humans, but without *The Third* we will age a year for every decade of Man, so yes, eventually we will die. However, if we are reunited with *The Third* before death, we will return to our naturally youthful state."

"The gist of it is: if you don't have a third Siren, you will die," I summarize sadly. "And once dead, you can't come back?"

Both sisters nod in acknowledgement.

"Come on," the brash crimson-haired sea nymph changes the subject. "There is something we would like to show you."

Without hesitation, I hold tight to Leukosia's hand, suddenly afraid of being alone.

♪♪♪

The water is warmer than it has been; it feels like I am swimming in a bathtub rather than the sea. Timidly, I open my mouth and allow a flood of the bitter, salty substance to enter. I gulp, panic-stricken as it slithers past the tongue, down the esophagus, and finally into my lungs. Terrified, I begin to flail at the thought of my gills, not remembering to do their job. This time, Leukosia does nothing except wait.

My vision is becoming blurry again, but instead of passing out, I begin concentrating on activating my gills. Suddenly, like a switch being thrown into the ON position, oxygen begins filtering through my body. Looking down at my hands and feet, I see that ugly honey-colored webbing emerges from beneath my skin and I smile.

Finally, I've embraced my inner fish!

We swim for at least a half an hour toward the open ocean. Nothing can be seen of the shoreline or of the mangrove cove anymore; all that remains is darkness and the soft song of a calm sea. Above us, delicate strands of moonlight reflect off of the water, creating a hypnotic light show, while more determined beams pierce through the liquid barrier to illuminate the darkness below. Even the small Xeno crab clinging to a clump of tangerine-hued whip coral seems to be enjoying the magical light show.

Nothing could be more perfect.

Up ahead, I notice a dark gray shape in the distance, and as we swim closer, I realize it is a wrecked oil tanker. The outer hull is covered with barnacles, starfish, and other mollusks; the eerie silence surrounding the wreck fills me with an unexpected uneasiness. Sensing my reservations, Leukosia tightens her grip on me and my apprehension disappears.

The gorgeous blonde nymph points in the direction of a hole in the hull large enough for us to fit through. She enters first, looks around, then motions for me to follow. All of the hairs on the back of my neck stand on end without warning. I have seen scenes like this in scary movies whereas soon as the diver enters the shipwreck, a giant man-eating monster bites their head off. Blocking the image, I inhale, allowing a large amount of oxygen to filter through my gills and cautiously begin to explore; staying within sight of my aunt.

Inside, it is pitch black, but my eyes swiftly adjust as though I am wearing special underwater goggles. A strange smell creeps into my nostrils, and I realize it is the scent of decay. It permeates every nook-and-cranny of this submerged tomb. The odor is repulsive, and it takes a few seconds for my siren-senses to decipher the decay as marine in nature, not human. A feeling of relief fills me, and I grin, delighted by my newly found abilities.

Aunt Leukosia lets me wander through the rusty hallways looking into each room of the once active vessel. Beneath us, schools of multi-colored fish meander in and out of the wreckage, their bodies gleaming under glimmers of moonlight penetrating through small holes in the metal from the surface. On the ceiling, there are dented areas where the tanker must have first impacted the ocean floor before coming to its final resting place, and within these areas, patches of rust had formed, creating intricate lace-like patterns. In awe, I run my hands along the rusty metal walls enjoying the many variations of smooth to rough to jagged; much like a blind person would read Braille, trying to imagine the events that led up to this tragedy.

Further into the tanker, in the captain's quarters, I come across pictures of the men who served onboard. They wore tan uniforms and funny looking hats. All of them are smiling, and I wonder how soon after this picture was taken that the tanker sank. Something deep inside of me hopes they had all gotten off of the ship unharmed.

Several clacks followed by one click come from my aunt's direction. Overwhelmed by our new environment, I try desperately to translate the ancient Siren language. I come to the conclusion that she is either saying: 'I want a tuna fish sandwich' or possibly 'It's time to leave.' I choose the second translation and head back toward the entrance, out the hole and up to the surface.

The wind has gotten stronger since we began our adventure. Instinctively, I close my eyes, concentrating on activating my lungs, which normally would take a minute or two to complete this task, now almost immediately, they begin to take in the cool mid-October air.

Leukosia smiles, her eyes filled with pride.

"The Moon Goddess has given us a beautiful night for exploring," Leukosia's words sound like the beginning of a song.

"Have you ever loved a person?" I dare ask.

"No," she retorts. "Never."

"Why are there always three Sirens?" Curiosity fuels my words.

"*We* were created as *The Three*…three sisters…*We* are three parts of a whole. Zeus made us to watch over the watery depths, to take care of the animals of the deep, and for millennium we have."

"How do you feel now, Tia Leukosia?" I probe. "Are you happy?"

Tia, I have learned, is the Greek word for 'Aunt', and almost glowing, she explains on a breathy note:

"Now…We are whole."

CHAPTER SEVENTEEN

Miss Khan corners me before I can escape the classroom.

"I need an answer, Selena," she inquires again after class.

"An answer about what?" I pretend not to remember about the solo.

"You know what," Miss Khan frowns at me, not falling for my phantom amnesia. "Will you be performing the solo for the Winter Concert?"

"I'm still not sure, Miss Khan," I pout, not wanting her to know about my problems with Amy. "I want to, believe me. Nothing would make me happier than to sing, but I'm in an impossible situation. If I accept the solo, I risk my father losing his job at Ocean World."

"Ah, yes, Dr. Marquez is my mother's friend. She speaks very highly of him and that is quite rare." Her eyes suddenly narrow. "Why would your father lose his job over a school concert?"

"Amy threatened to get him fired," I answer, feeling the need to unburden myself. "She said that she would lie to her father and say David made advances toward her."

Miss Khan's eyes seem to glow red for an instant, or it might have been the fluorescents. Whatever it was, causes her demeanor to change from mild and meek, to aggressive and stern. The sudden change causes the hairs on my arm to stand up, which is never a good sign.

"I'll take care of Miss Jacobs," Miss Khan smiles aloofly.

"How—?"

"Don't worry about it," she adds sweetly. "I've dealt with my share of monsters."

Something tells me to trust her, so I do.

"Okay, I'll perform the solo!" I accept with enthusiasm.

"And what about the aria?" The teacher grins with anticipation.

"Of course," I coo as my excitement grows by leaps and bounds. "I would be honored."

"Good!" Miss Khan claps and then returns to her normal self.

"Thanks again, Miss Khan."

"Selena," she calls, stopping me in mid-stride.

"Yes, ma'am?"

"The next time you run into a problem like this, or any other problem that you can't handle, just let me know, okay?"

"I will," I say joyfully, but at the same time there is a growing apprehension in the pit of my already nervous stomach. In my haste to exit the room, I almost knock over a trash can on my way out the door. I cannot explain it, but something about Miss Khan today frightens me.

♪♪♪

Nicole and Jenny are waiting for me right outside the Chorus room door. During the brief trek to the cafeteria, I excitedly tell the girls about what happened, but they blow it off with a wave of their hands.

"She's probably just going to give her detention or something like that," Jenny says.

"It would be hilarious to see 'Princess Amy' scrubbing toilets," Nicole makes a cleaning action as we sit at an empty table.

"I don't know," I add. "She had this strange look in her eyes, a wildness. I can't describe it, but whatever it is, I'm glad I'm not Amy."

"Try not to think about it anymore," Nicole states as she examines her lunch, leftover kung-pao chicken, and fried rice.

Mike walks over, smiling nervously.

"Nicole, may I speak with you for a moment?"

"Sure," Nicole seems just as nervous.

"In private, please?" He offers her his hand, and she takes it.

Jenny and I watch as they walk over to a secluded part of the lunchroom.

Moments later, Nicole returns with a huge grin on her face.

"Well?" Jenny and I ask at once.

"Well, what?" Nicole repeats coyly.

"Did he ask you to homecoming?" I cannot control my excitement.

"Maybe…"

"Spill it Wong," Jenny demands.

"Yes, he did!" she squeals with delight. "We're going to the dance…*together!*"

"It's about time!" Jenny slaps the table.

"Now you're the only one who needs a date," Nicole informs.

"What do you mean: *only one*?" I turn to the blushing teen. "Jenny, do you have a date already?"

"Yes, umm, sort of," Jenny turns a darker shade of pink.

Getting annoyed, I place my hands on my hips and start to tap my right foot, just like Mom does.

"What does *umm sort of* mean?" I prod. "Do you have a date or not?"

"I do," Jenny stares into her cheese and broccoli soup.

"That's wonderful!" I beam. "Why didn't you tell me?"

"I don't think you are going to approve of my date," she refuses to make eye contact.

"Why? Is it Andrew?" I gulp, not really wanting to know the answer. "It's alright if it is... I mean, I don't care who he goes with, just as long as it's not Amy."

"No, I wouldn't do that to you," Jenny reassures.

"Well, if it isn't Andrew, then who is your mystery date?"

Several long, pregnant seconds pass as she shifts uncomfortably in her seat.

"It's Richard, okay!" she finally reveals, embarrassed. "I'm going to homecoming with Richard!"

"Richard?" a giggle escapes my lips. "The jerk from Calculus?"

I begin laughing uncontrollably, causing everyone in the cafeteria to turn in our direction. Jenny's face turns bright red, immediately making me feel guilty.

"I'm sorry, Jenny," I giggle again, trying to stifle all-out laughter. "If Richard is who you want to go with, then I promise to be nice to him during the dance. I'll even talk to him if you want me to."

"That would be fantastic!" Jenny hugs me tightly around my neck. "He's really sweet once you get to know him."

"I'll take your word for it." I squeeze her back.

"Selena, what about you?" Nicole's attention is now on me.

"I don't really want to go to the dance," I fib passively; not wanting them to make a big deal about it. "I just agreed to it because you two wanted to go. I'll stay home with my mom."

"No, homecoming is amazing!" Nicole claims sternly, but with much excited enthusiasm. "The school holds it at this incredible hotel that overlooks Frenchman's Reef, so it will be gorgeous! There will be a live band and a DJ, great food, and of course there will be the King and Queen Ceremony. You can't miss it!"

"What am I supposed to do while you and Jenny are dancing with your guys?"

"Let's be clear: Richard is only my date for the evening," Jenny emphasizes firmly. "He's *not* my boyfriend."

"Regardless of title, you will still be a couple for the evening," I remind. "I'll be the fifth wheel."

"You can share Mike with me," Nicole offers sweetly. "He's not my boyfriend either."

"That's a good idea; share Mike with Nicole. I'm sure he won't mind," Jenny glances over at Mike, who is staring at Nicole.

"Thanks, but no thanks," I reply, a little grossed out. "It seems too weird. I'll go, but I'll go stag…by myself."

"Are you sure, sweetie?" Nicole seems concerned.

"I'm positive," I state confidently. "That way I can dance with all of the dateless guys at the dance."

"There is a reason they are dateless, Selena." Jenny points to a table of rather plain looking guys playing chess instead of eating.

We laugh.

♪♪♪

I pick up Ando from his class at the end of the day, but instead of waiting for Mom, we are waiting for David, who insisted on taking me for the weekend.

"How is the new apartment?" I grill Ando.

"It's nice," he answers in a hushed tone. "It has a swimming pool and tennis courts."

"How's Dad liking it?"

"I don't think he likes it very much because he's always saying that it doesn't feel like home," he explains.

Sadly, I kiss Ando on the forehead.

"We miss you guys, too."

"Hey, Andover!"

I glance up to see Andrew running toward us and try not to smile as he approaches.

"I got you this," he hands my brother another blue and yellow hacky-sack. "I heard you lost the other one."

My brother took the hacky-sack on a swim with the aunts and ended up giving it to a dolphin.

"This is mine, to keep?" Ando beams and high-fives Andrew, who refuses to look at me. "Thanks!"

"Hi, Andrew," I try to get his attention.

"Hi," he replies, without looking in my direction.

I try again.

"No swim practice today?"

"Nope," he replies in a flippant tone.

"The weather is getting cooler," I babble uncomfortably.

"Yeah," Andrew still has not looked at me.

For several seconds, we stand awkwardly, both looking at our respective shoes.

"I have to go, Mom's waiting for me," he turns to leave.

"Andrew, wait! Don't go yet!" I bellow, not caring who hears. "I'm so sorry that I let Amy get in the middle of us and I'm sorry for treating you so meanly the last time we spoke. I've got so much family drama going on, you couldn't possibly imagine."

"Like what?" He waits for an answer, but none comes. Annoyed, he rolls his eyes and begins to walk away again.

"Are you going to the dance?" I blurt, hoping he will wait.

"I haven't decided yet," he shrugs, then quickly turns and begins walking toward his mom's office.

"See you later, Ando!" he shouts over his shoulder.

Ando looks at Andrew and then at me, his expression worried.

"Call for him, Lena," my brother orders.

"What?"

"Call for him; make him like you again."

"No, you don't trick people into caring for you." I continue watching Andrew's form getting smaller in the distance; an overwhelming feeling of grief comes over me, causing my heart to ache. "That's just wrong."

At that moment, I notice Amy coming toward us; her face is placid and cheerful, which is very unlike her. Nervously, I scan around, trying to decide whether to run or wait and take whatever horrible thing she has to say to me. Taking a deep, calming breath, I steady myself for her wrath.

"I know you," Amy says politely. "It's Selena, right?"

"Selena...right." I stand perfectly still, so as not to provoke her.

"I just wanted to apologize for the way I've been treating you," she declares sincerely, catching me off guard. "I remember what it's like to be the new kid in school. It's not fun."

I blink several times before swallowing the lump in my throat.

"No, it's not," I manage to speak.

"Well…" she looks around in sort of a daze; her pupils resemble dark, round orbs, like they have been dilated. They are as big as saucers. "I only wanted to apologize again for being such a douche to you."

Then she blinks like a robot

"Have a good weekend," she gleams and just as abruptly as her entrance, she walks up the street, still looking like a lost puppy or a child who has lost its parent. I want to run to her and ask if she is alright, but the strange apology still lingers in the air, heavy and unsettling. I do not know what to make of it. Thankfully, David arrives soon after, a welcomed sight as far as I am concerned; my link to the mortal world…my anchor.

"Hey, there!" he beckons from the truck. "Come on, let's go!"

Respectfully, we climb into the truck. The smell of salt water and fish welcomes me back. It is the most comforting smell in the world.

"Hi, Dad," I give him a squeeze. His hair smells of the sea.

"I've missed you so much," he says, giving me an almost stifling bear hug.

"That happens when you don't see someone for almost a month," I jibe as I fasten my seatbelt.

"Let's not fight," he requests, glancing over his shoulder at Ando, who is still playing with the hacky sack.

"Sorry," I whisper. "It's been one of those days."

Up ahead, Andrew walks slowly up the street, never looking back.

"Should we give Andrew a ride?" David notices him as well.

"No, I don't think he wants to be anywhere near me right now."

"Why?" he questions. "Did you to have a fight?"

"Dad," I sigh loudly. "I don't want to discuss it right now."

"I know, it's not cool to talk about boys with your dad," David says slyly. "But I used to be a teenager, so I could probably give you some great advice about them."

"Okay," I smile at his comment. "Amy Jacobs, you know...your boss' daughter?"

"Yes, I remember her," he replies, pulling away from the curb. "We spoke for a few minutes a couple of months ago. We were talking about you, as a matter of fact. She seems very nice."

"Believe me, she's not," I reprimand. "Well, Miss Khan offered me several solos in the Winter Concert after she heard me sing."

"Selena, you sang..." David is mortified. "...in front of *everybody?*"

"I didn't know what I was capable of back then," I try to look at him, but cannot. "I didn't know that I was a Siren, for crying out loud."

Needing to unburden my guilt, I tell David all about the aria and the way it affected the guys who heard me sing. Most of all, I explain that if I had known then what I know now, I would have never, ever sung it in the first place."

Dad reaches over and touches my hand, trying to comfort me.

"Singing is a part of you, I understand that," he informs, looking at my brother. "Ando has explained about the aunts and the call of the sea, but most importantly he's explained why Mom couldn't come to me about all of this."

Confounded, I turn around in my seat to look at Ando, who stops playing momentarily, his aquamarine eyes shining under the curtain of onyx lashes.

"I've been singing for Daddy," he states, looking directly into my eyes rather unapologetically.

"*Ando!*" I snap. "Why would you do that? It's dangerous for mortal men to hear our call."

Ando shakes his head defiantly.

"No," he explains. "Tia Leukosia and Tia Ligeia told us that men who are exposed to the call, a little at a time, over a long period will become used to it."

David nods in agreement.

"I asked Ando to sing to me a little each day."

"How long has this been going on?" I probe, still stunned.

"About a month now," David admits with a broad smile.

"How do you feel when Ando sings?"

"I feel lightheaded, like I'm floating on a cloud, but not like I felt that night."

"You mean, on the night you almost drowned?" I wipe away the tears streaming down my cheeks.

"That's why I want to try an experiment with the two of you this weekend," he continues, eyes glued ahead.

Skeptically, I frown.

"What type of experiment?"

"I want you to sing for me," he requests with a thin smile.

"No, Dad, definitely not!" I rebuke, willing the tears to stop. "I have no control over my powers. I'm older and stronger than Ando, and when I'm upset…" I pause, gauging his reaction, "…my mood messes with the weather and not in a good way."

Exasperated, I release an extremely long exhale.

"I don't even know how to control it," I sniffle. "I'm afraid that I might kill you."

Quickly, he pulls the Jeep to the side of the road and turns to face me.

"I can't do this without your help, Selena." David takes hold of my hand. "I can't come back home until I can build up some resistance to *The Call*. I need your help."

Every instinct I have tells me not to do this, but knowing it is the only way David can return home, I guess it is something we will have to try.

CHAPTER EIGHTEEN

After a very uncomfortable dinner, David, Ando, and I make our way from the apartment overlooking Buccaneer Bay to a secluded beach fifteen minutes away from his apartment complex. It is a few minutes past seven, and the white sand beach is deserted except for a flock of seagulls diving several yards offshore.

"I want you to know that I'm doing this under protest," I remind uneasily, remembering the night when I fished David out of the sea unconscious and near death.

"We have to try, Lena," Ando looks at me sternly.

"I know we do," convincing myself to continue.

Hesitantly, I begin to walk closer to the shoreline when my stepfather halts me. His expression is uneasy as he clears his throat and runs a nervous hand through his thick hair. Deep inside, I hope he is going to tell me to forget about this dangerous task we are about to begin.

"What's the matter?" I question. "Have you changed your mind?"

Unwavering, he shakes his head.

"Actually, I wanted to ask your opinion about something extremely important," his mood becomes more serious.

I swallow hard, wondering what is wrong now. Ando, seeing my concerned facial expression, stops kicking sand and waits for our father's response. All three of us seem to be holding our breaths.

"What's your question?" I mumble, biting my lower lip nervously.

"I know we've discussed the subject of adoption a few times in the past," he begins expeditiously. "And I know we had to postpone it due to the move— "

"Yes!" I interrupt before he can complete his thought.

David smiles, his eyes glistening.

"Good!" he beams. "Because your mother and I have already filed the paperwork with the courts."

My brows arch.

"Even though you are separated?" I frown.

"One has nothing to do with the other," he informs confidently. "You were, are, and always will be my daughter."

Elated, I hug him so tightly that he cries out in chuckling spasms of discomfort. I guess I did not realize how much I wanted to be his legal daughter, for me to be a real part of the family. Mom, David and Ando are all blood related. I am the only one who does not share that blood-connection…that fleshly bond that only blood relatives share. Way down in my soul, I must have truly wanted this, needed this.

"Ouch!" he loudly complains, bringing me back to the present. "I'm human! Don't use your Sireny-strength on me!"

I snicker at his request.

"I'll remember to treat you with kid-gloves," I jibe, my heart soaring, knowing that he still loves me just as much even though I am technically a conundrum of all things normal.

As we giggle and joke around, the wind picks up speed. The trees wiggle to and fro as their branches are assaulted by the strengthening gusts. Finding the weather odd, I glance up at the sky just in time to see thick clouds passing by. A storm is approaching and not one accidentally created by my emotions.

"We need to get started with this experiment before the weather worsens," he grimaces, removing his glasses and handing it to Ando.

"I'm ready," I inform, wiping my sweaty palms on my shorts. "I think."

My brother tucks David's glasses in his front shirt pocket, careful not to damage it.

"What should I do first?" David asks, his voice filled with anxiety. "Should I sit down? Should I go into the water? What's the procedure?"

"You're asking the wrong person." I rub my temples, feeling a massive migraine developing. "Okay, you sit down and Ando will sing for you. That way, I can see how his call affects you."

"That's a good idea," David praises, sitting cross-legged while he waits anxiously for Ando to begin.

Slowly, my brother sits beside him, closes his eyes and begins a low, sad tune. His boyish voice rises and falls like the waves themselves. The song rings with sorrow, and I begin to realize what Mom and Dad's separation is doing to him. Sometimes it is easy for me to forget that he is only five; a mature five-year-old, but a five-year-old nonetheless.

Through all of this crazy tumultuous family drama, he has been a trooper. He is supportive of both our parents and, most of all, to me. He is my best friend, regardless of his age.

Tonight, the moon is high in the sky, but is covered with a spooky blue haze resembling fog. Wanting to ward off bad luck, I mutter a short prayer all the while grasping my black pearl pendant in my left palm. The clouds keep covering the moon and it is difficult to see David's face in this dim light.

"How are you doing, Dad?" I call out, my voice echoing against the swaying palm fronds.

"I'm fine, not a single urge to go into the sea," he declares happily.

"Great, but we still don't know if Ando's call has any serious sway on men, after all, he is the first male Siren," I remind them both. "He's only a quarter Siren. Maybe his call is not very strong."

"My call is strong!" Ando pouts as he throws a shell at me, but I dodge it.

"Don't get mad at me," I chuckle. "I'm just trying to figure this out."

"Okay, Selena. It is your turn," David urges. "Sing for me."

"I still don't think—"

"Don't worry," he reassures. "I'll take full responsibility for whatever happens."

"How can you take responsibility if you're dead?" I sarcastically mumble under my breath.

"I heard that," David surprises me. "C'mon, let's get this over with."

Wary of this plan, I sit down near the water's edge, enjoying the cool liquid; remembering family picnics on the beach and Sunday mornings in the park. Closing my eyes, the sensation of my voice rising up into the heavens fills me with joy and everything that makes me happy begins to take form in this one song. From far away, I hear a small voice calling to me. I can barely understand it, but something tells me to open my eyes.

Slowly, I open them and it takes a couple seconds for them to focus, but it is enough time for me to witness David striding out into the surf; completely oblivious to what is happening.

"No!" I scream as loud as I can. *"David! Stop! Stop!"*

Unexpectedly, I feel all of the blood in my head rushing down to my stomach as it begins to churn. David stops in mid-stride, waist high in the surf.

"What the hell?" His voice is filled with anger and disappointment in himself.

"That's it! No more experimentation!" I squeal, not caring if I am carrying on like a child throwing a tantrum. "This is not your lab or some sort of game we're playing! When I *sing*, men can die! That's the drill: *'To follow a Siren is to follow death!'*"

Furiously, I begin pacing and flailing my arms above my head as the sand gives way below my feet and I barely notice. My entire family has lost their minds. Mom— unwilling to deal with the fact that our lives are going to hell in a handbasket—has chosen to immerse herself in all things Siren, including eating raw seafood straight out of the sea and swimming with the aunts nude. My brother has appointed himself the role of mediator, which has taken a toll on his normally sweet disposition. During this visit alone, he has snapped at me at least a dozen times, and has even kicked me in the shin when I accidentally bumped into him while at the grocery store and apparently, my stepfather has now developed a superhero complex and believes he can accomplish something no man has ever done before: *fight against the call of a Siren!*

Pfft!

Worst of all, I am so desperate to fix my dysfunctional family that I am willing to put David's life in jeopardy.

"What?" David grabs me by the shoulders. "Who told you that?"

My eyes widen and my cheeks flush.

"Every book! Every article! Everything I've read has told me that Sirens are *death!*"

David sighs loudly; the sound is painful to hear. It is the sound of heartbreak. I should know, it is a friend of mine.

"I don't care," he says calmly. "I love you, and your mother and Ando, and I will do anything…absolutely *anything* to be with the three of you. I wouldn't want to be alive if I couldn't be with you all. So, let's try it a few more times, but this time I want you to only sing in short bursts. Got it?"

Resolute not to cry, I sniffle back the tears.

"I got it," I whimper, suddenly understanding the weight of his words.

I guess that is what love does to you; it makes you do crazy things.

♪♪♪

After an hour or so, we walk back to the apartment; all of us are still shaken up over the night's events. To my surprise, David only tried to kill himself six more times. The last few times he was able to *'will'* himself to stay on the sand, even though it took every ounce of his mental prowess to accomplish this task. Regardless, I was proud to be his daughter.

"Goodnight, Daddy," Ando gives David a hug and kiss, then turns to me. "See you in the morning, Lena."

He sounds like himself again...adorable.

"Sweet dreams, baby brother." I squeeze him tightly, enjoying his shampoo-scented locks.

David and I wait until he is out of earshot before beginning our conversation.

"Are you thirsty?" he queries, heading to the cramped, yet neatly kept, galley-style kitchen with contemporary white appliances and cabinetry. There are no windows on that side, just some potted herbs to decorate the counter.

"Some water please," I answer, taking a moment to truly examine his new apartment.

Although it is a two-bedroom, two-bathroom corner unit, it does not have a lot of space. From the outside, you get the impression that it is much larger than it is.

The living room has two rectangular windows and a glass door that leads to the balcony that has a partial ocean view. Attached is a cramped alcove that contains a built-in eating unit with storage in the bench seating. The main area is sparsely furnished with a second-hand sofa and loveseat combo, an old college trunk that he is using as a coffee table which is anchored by a plain, grayish-blue area rug worth twenty dollars, if that much.

The only other niceties are the bunk beds in the second bedroom where my brother and I stay when visiting.

Throughout the entire space, the walls are lightly dusted with stucco and painted in neutral beige, while the floors are carpeted in a darker hue of the same color. There are no adornments anywhere, not even David's framed collegiate distinctions. The only decoration is a framed picture of Mom, Dad, Ando, and me when we went on vacation to The Grand Canyon.

"Why haven't you decorated?" I question nosily.

He grins like a goofball.

"I don't plan on being here for very long,"

Instantly, I feel better.

"That's a terrible photo of me," I scold, in shock.

David laughs as he brings us two glasses of water and a paper plate with a few double chocolate chip cookies, my favorites. Actually, anything containing chocolate is fine with me.

"How long do you think it will take before you are totally cured?" I ask.

"I'm not sure," David responds a little too quickly. "Not too long, I hope."

"Does Mom know we're doing this?"

"No," he smirks.

"Afraid to tell her?" I tease.

He smiles.

"Wouldn't you be?" he responds nervously.

"You should tell her," I gently urge. "It will give her some hope. Right now, she has nothing."

"She has you, and she still gets to see Ando."

"It's not the same," I educate with a frown.

"I want to surprise her."

"Right now, all she has are the aunts and the sea. I can see it in her eyes. I can hear it in her voice," I state firmly. "The call of the sea will consume her. I know it will."

David sulks.

"What about you?"

"Sometimes, I wish I could lose myself in it," I answer honestly. "When I'm in the sea, it's like I've found the missing part of me. I'm a complete being. On land, I feel like a fish out of water, no pun intended."

I laugh, causing David to laugh too.

"That's how I felt when I met you and Marina," he grins. "You made me complete."

CHAPTER NINETEEN

The following day, David and Ando drop me off at the mall around noon to go shopping for homecoming dresses with Nicole and Jenny. He and Ando decided to go see a movie as their own guy outing; free of the weary glances of a girl. Honestly, I do not mind.

After visiting three department stores, we decide to take a break at the food court. Jenny is content eating a hot fudge sundae smothered with extra whipped cream and nuts. Nicole is eating a non-fat frozen strawberry yogurt with soy nuts, mumbling that at least she will be able to fit into her dress. I, on the other hand, have a craving for sushi and ravenously devour eight Hamachi Nigiri in less than three minutes, along with an order of dragon rolls.

"Slow down, Selena," Jenny begs. "You're going to choke on that Yellowtail, and I don't know the Heimlich maneuver."

"Sorry," I apologize, slowing down a bit. "I'm starving."

Nicole stares at me strangely.

"What's the matter?" I ask; mouth full of spicy fish and wasabi.

Nicole makes a confused expression.

"I thought you hated raw fish," she announces with an upturned lip, reminding me of Elvis Presley, the bygone singer.

"Yeah," Jenny agrees, stopping momentarily from her dessert.

Mindlessly, I shrug, continuing to chew my snack.

"Weird," Nicole mumbles, then takes a dainty bite of her frozen treat.

Needing to change the subject, I swallow what is left in my mouth in order to talk without fear of bombarding my friends with chum. Knowing them, Jenny would probably laugh while Nicole might roll her eyes at me. I never imagined that I would make such good friends so soon. The thought makes me smile.

"Which dresses have we decided on?" I question as Nicole takes another bite of her frozen yogurt.

"Nothing that I've tried on speaks to me," Jenny confesses, wiping a gooey glob of fudge sauce from her chin with her napkin. "All I know is that I want a black dress."

"Why black?" I ask, wiping the extra wasabi from my lips, wondering why it does not hurt.

"Black doesn't clash with my red hair. I think I'm going to get the black cocktail length dress at Latham's."

Latham's Department Store had an amazing selection of homecoming dresses. There were literally hundreds of styles to choose from in every shade imaginable. They were all gorgeous, but none of them caught my attention. I am hoping I have better luck at the next store.

"Good choice," Nicole agrees. "That dress looked terrific on you."

"I think that is the right one too," I answer sincerely.

"What about you, Nicole?" Jenny nudges her elbow.

"I haven't seen anything that I like," Nicole frowns.

"What about that short green dress?" I remind her. "That was cute and on sale."

"Nah, it's not the right style. I want something different, something that—"

"Something that makes Mike go… *'Hmmm!'*" Jenny teases and Nicole throws her napkin at her, which Jenny easily dodges.

"What about you, Selena?" Nicole blushes.

"I think you should buy the silvery-blue dress," Jenny chimes in before I can answer. "It brings out the color of your eyes. Andrew will love it!"

"Why would that matter?" I reply, avoiding their surprised gazes.

"Aren't you going to homecoming together?" Nicole stops eating.

"Mike said that Andrew said that he was going to ask you to go with him," Jenny's voice is laced with annoyance. "I can't believe it. He's such a liar."

"He's not a liar," I defend Andrew's reputation.

"Then why aren't you two together?" they ask at the same time.

Oh no! This is the moment I have been dreading. The moment I have to admit my stupidity for letting Amy bully me into giving up the solo and Andrew. Not to mention, my lip is tingling where the wasabi was. Quickly, I dip one end of my paper napkin in my cup of water and press it to the spot.

"He asked me," I confess. My voice lowers to barely a whisper. "I said no, and that was the end of that."

Nicole stares at me for a moment before offering her advice.

"Andrew is a great guy," Nicole's voice is filled with passion. "He's smart, funny, and hot as hell."

The burning continues, but I ignore it.

"I know, but—"

"I know more than ten girls who would cut off their right arm to go out with him, and the only girl that he wants doesn't want him," Nicole interrupts; her hackles up. "You're an idiot."

Suddenly, she pauses as she realizes her harshness.

"I'm so sorry," she apologizes, obviously shocked at her own behavior.

"It's alright," I let her off of the hook.

Jenny smiles and takes my hand.

"I love you," Jenny states sweetly. "But you're still an idiot."

"Thanks for being gentle," I reply, not shocked that these words came from her mouth instead of Nicole's, who is usually the voice of reason. Out of nowhere, my upper left thigh starts to itch. Then my right one follows. Soon the itchiness begins to spread down my legs until it reaches my ankles.

What the heck is wrong with me?

"Do you want him or not?" Nicole looks sternly at me, waiting for an answer.

"Okay, Wong, take a step back a moment," Jenny jumps in, looking at me curiously. "Why did you say no to him?"

As subtly as possible, I reach under the table and scratch the tops of my thighs while using my left foot to scratch the right, then switching them.

Am I allergic to sushi?

"Amy told me to leave him alone," I blurt with heated cheeks and more itches.

Nicole stops in mid-bite.

"No way!" she snaps; her temper activating.

"And you listened to that little wench?" Jenny looks at me, unsure of what to say next.

Wanting to get it all out in the open, I take a deep breath.

"She threatened to get my dad fired if I didn't stop seeing Andrew and if I accepted the Chorus solo."

Both girls glare at me, nostrils flaring, and fists clenched.

"Damn!" Jenny swears. "That little—"

"Why didn't you tell us?" Nicole interjects, surprised that I did not share this important fact with them earlier.

"There's nothing you could have done about it," I smile, scratching harder until I want to cry.

"Didn't you say Amy congratulated you about getting the solo?" Nicole sounds more confused than ever.

Tears begin to well, but not because of the Amy situation.

"Selena?" Nicole is looking at me funny, but I ignore her.

"Yeah, after school on Friday," I stop short, remembering Miss Khan's strange reaction when I told her about Amy's threats. "She just walked up to me and apologized. It was strange… just plain strange."

The itchiness is on my neck now.

Dear Father! It burns!

"Well, maybe she's okay with you dating Andrew?" Jenny finally finishes her sundae, pauses to stare at my neck, where I am now scratching.

"I think you should go for it before some other girl decides to make a move on him," Nicole adds, and I nod in acknowledgement.

"Selena?" Jenny says again, this time pointing to my face.

"What?" I snap, now in utter and complete pain.

Jenny's eyes are wide.

"What is wrong with your face?" the auburn teen questions in a tense whisper.

Nicole's mouth is gaping and her eyes are even wider than Jenny's.

"Huh?" is the only sound that escapes me.

They both point at me and immediately I touch my neck. Tiny bumps can be felt below my trembling fingertips. I groan before darting from the table, almost capsizing my chair, and sprint to the nearest washroom. Flinging open the door to the ladies' room, I go straight to the nearest sink. In the mirror, I see what all of the fuss is about. I am decorated with spots and not just any kind of spots: multicolored, shimmering, luminescent *spots!*

What should I do?

From outside the washroom door, I hear footsteps, two separately distinct footsteps, and for some reason the steps are amplified like whoever it is, is wearing microphones on their feet.

Like a terrified animal, I dash into an empty stall, locking myself in.

"Selena?" Nicole's voice sounds first.

"Are you okay, sweetie?" Jenny is next.

"Selena," Nicole's voice loudens. "Don't make me kick this door in!"

I roll my eyes and giggle.

"Please don't do that," I plead, my blood pressure rising at being found in this condition.

"Can you please come out of there?" Nicole begs. "You know how I feel about public restrooms."

I do. Being a germophobe, she is intolerable sometimes.

"I've got spots," I groan unhappily.

"We know," they both say in unison.

"You're probably just allergic to something in the sushi," Jenny educates.

My eyebrows arch.

"You think so?" I exhale, feeling calmer.

"I do," Jenny states firmly. "My cousin Clementine once ate a salmon roll with wasabi not realizing she was allergic and she blew up like a pufferfish."

"My Dad ate eel once, and he broke out in a puffy red rash," Nicole informs. "It was even on his butt."

I actually laugh at that.

"Really?" I ask as the itchiness disappears and my skin feels normal again.

"Really!" Nicole giggles at her poor father's expense. "My mother had to put calamine lotion on it."

We all laugh, right there in the ladies' washroom.

"C'mon on out, heifer," Jenny sighs. "I've got to buy that dress."

"Okay." I take one last breath to steady myself as I unlatch the stall door and step out with my eyes closed.

"See," Nicole says, touching my face lightly. "All gone."

My eyes spring open as I touch my cheeks, my fingers frantically feeling over my now smooth face.

"The spots are gone!" I exclaim excitedly.

"Hooray!" Jenny exclaims sarcastically. "You're back to being drop-dead gorgeous. Can we go now?"

I hug her, then Nicole, then both of them together.

"Yeah, I'm ready," I grin, knowing that I have such great friends.

♪♪♪

We walk around the mall for another hour as Jenny purchases her black cocktail dress; Nicole buys a pair of red pumps. I get some make-up, but still cannot find any dresses that I like. Before we know it, David and Ando are picking us up in front of the mall entrance. My stepfather even offers to drop Jenny and Nicole to their perspective homes. Their guardians agree that would be very helpful and greatly appreciated.

We spend a few minutes at each house. At Jenny's home, her grandmother offers us tea and freshly baked oatmeal cookies. Nicole's mom feeds us freshly fried shrimp chips and pineapple soda. They were all so incredibly welcoming.

Right before we leave, I pull Nicole off to the side before getting back into the Jeep.

"I thought you said your mom looks old?" I glance back at Mrs. Wong, who waves at us from the front doorway. "Your Mom is beautiful."

"Do you really think so?" she mumbles.

"Yes, you moron," I give her a quick hug. "Bye Mrs. Wong, thanks for the snacks!"

Bashfully, she nods and goes back inside to finish her chores.

"See you at the dance?" Nicole questions, making sure that I am still attending and have not changed my mind.

"Maybe," I tease, hoping to get her goat.

In true Nicole form, she playfully sticks her tongue out at me.

So far, this has been a great start to what hopefully will be a memorable night.

♪♪♪

With just hours before the homecoming dance begins, I still have nothing to wear. Frantically, I dial Mom's cell phone on my way back to David's apartment, desperate and panic filled.

"Calm down, Selena," Mom tries to soothe me over the phone. "I'll bring something over."

"Thank you so much," a sigh of relief escapes me. "That would be great!"

"Was Mom able to help?" David asks.

"As a matter of fact, she was very helpful." I reach over the seat and give him a hug while he is driving, causing the car to swerve into the next lane.

"Selena!" David cries out, but quickly gets it under control, shooting me a disapproving frown.

I sit quietly for a moment to allow the adrenalin of the moment to settle.

"She's going to bring something over to the apartment," I begin again.

"That's great!" He tries without success to hide his enthusiasm. "Good thing she was a former model."

"I hope she has something that doesn't look too mom-like," I grimace.

"Believe me; I'm sure she has something that will do. She's definitely coming to the apartment?" David sighs, sounding more excited about seeing Mom than me finding something to wear.

CHAPTER TWENTY

To my surprise, Mom is already waiting in the brightly lit parking lot of David's apartment complex, holding several garment bags. Ando rushes out of the car to meet her, running as fast as his little legs can carry him.

"Mommy! Mommy!" He throws his arms around her waist, squeezing her as tightly as he can. I notice the stream of tears rolling down his cheeks. "I'm so glad to see you!"

"You've grown since last weekend," she laughs, squeezing him back.

David approaches slowly.

"Hi, Marina," he smiles nervously.

"Hello." Mom glances at him wearily.

Nervously, he shuffles his feet like a little boy drawing circles on the ground.

"How are you?" he finally asks.

"Good," she abruptly lies. "How are things going with you? How are things at work?"

"It's good." He stares too long at her face, which makes her cheeks redden.

"Okay, you two," I interrupt the ineptness. "I don't mean to interrupt your social awkwardness, but I have a dance to get ready for and time is running out. So, could we please continue this later?"

Swiftly, we walk to David's unit while my parents make small talk. I unlock the door with the spare key my stepdad had made for me, and Mom enters the apartment cautiously as if she was entering a dragon's lair. Slowly, she examines the room.

"You haven't done much to the apartment. It's so—"

"Empty," David finishes her sentence with a chuckle.

Mom smiles and blushes at the same time.

"You should buy some real furniture," she comments on the seventies-style, green furniture he is currently using. Next, she boldly walks over to the kitchen and proceeds to open the fridge. She is also surprised at how empty it is.

"If you need help getting settled, I can—" she begins.

"That's alright," David interrupts again. "I won't be here very long."

He winks at Ando and me.

As I stand watching my parents talking and smiling, the memory of what happened at the mall comes flooding back. Should I tell them about breaking out in spots after eating a ton of sushi? If I mention it, they might change their minds and forbid me to go to the dance. No way am I letting that happen. I decide to keep the information to myself.

My mother, clearing her throat, breaks my mental musings as she refocuses on my wardrobe dilemma.

"C'mon then," she announces. "Let's see what I've got in my formal wear arsenal."

♪♪♪

The Grand Ballroom at the Buccaneer Bay Resort is the most beautiful place I have ever seen. The fifty-foot ceilings are adorned with crystal chandeliers that glimmer like stars; softly illuminating hand-carved mahogany staircases embellished with carved native flowers and tropical birds. Off to the side, glass elevators that sparkle when the light hits them hover magically over koi ponds fitted with cascading waterfalls and floating water lilies. In multiple areas hang huge brass cages with multicolored parrots, toucans, and songbirds; their chirps and whistles fill the space with natural music. White marbled tile-accents dot the hardwoods, and throughout the entire room, there are intricately carved furnishings that take your breath away. Even the floors seem to glow.

Almost immediately, I notice Nicole gliding towards me.

"Oh-my-gosh! You look absolutely flawless," I gush, admiring her beauty as she air-kisses me so not to smear her lipstick.

She exudes grace.

"Wow!" I gasp even louder. "Where did you get your dress?"

Nicole's cheeks turn bright pink.

"It's my mom's from back in the day," she beams. "Do you really like it?"

Leisurely, she spins so I can see her outfit. It is a long, fitted, red, silk, Chinese gown decorated with hand-embroidered gold lotus flowers. Her hair is up in a bun and secured by two gold hair clips in the shape of chopsticks. Makeup applied lightly, but enough to accentuate her beautiful Asian features.

"I love it!" I giggle with delight. "Vintage is always in style."

"And look at you!" she gushes, making me anxious.

Purposely, she walks around me, like my own personal fashion consultant.

"I almost didn't recognize you," Nicole pokes. "Let me really take a good look."

I smack her arm playfully.

"My mom let me borrow one of her couture gowns," I smile proudly.

"I'm so jealous," she jokes, knowing that she is just as stunning.

I am so happy that I want to sing for joy, but I suppress it.

"It looks expensive," Nicole adds under her breath as she touches the delicate fabric.

"It's Dolce and Gabbana," I whisper back, uncomfortable at the price tag associated with the one-of-a-kind garment. "My mother said she might disown me if anything happens to it."

My friend's perfectly sculpted eyebrows arch.

"I totally agree with her," she snickers, like the cartoon character *Snagglepuss*.

It truly is a stunning frock; sky blue, floor-length dress with a striking, silver lace overlay mimicking the movement of the ocean that shimmers when I walk. My only accessories are a pearl choker with matching earrings and bracelet that my aunts found in the hull of a Spanish galleon several hundred years before I was born. On my feet, silver high-heels finish the look. I couldn't have imagined a more gorgeous outfit.

Nicole touches my face.

"Did you do your own makeup?"

"No, my mom did," I snicker. "Who better to apply makeup than an ex-model?"

I have to admit, my mother did an amazing job with my makeup. She used shades of browns with a hint of blue to deemphasize my eyes, allowing them to appear less intense; to my lips she used a soft shade of coral lipstick. On my cheekbones, she dabbed blush in a deeper shade of coral; she even straightened my curly locks into layers of smooth strands.

"Your mom did a remarkable job," Nicole hugs me gently so as not to wrinkle our outfits.

Distracted by our conversation, Jenny is able to creep up behind us, looking nothing like her normal self. Richard stands beside her, obviously honored to be her escort.

What a transformation!

"Oh! My! Gravy!" Nicole and I both squeal excitedly.

She is breathtaking!

"Jenny?" Nicole and I answer as one as we stare in disbelief.

"I know, you don't have to say it," Jenny poses. "I look gorgeous."

She really truly does!

Jenny's simple black cocktail dress accentuates every curve of her slender, 5'9" frame; a frame which is normally covered by clothes one size larger, being a reserved teen and all. Her makeup is simple as well and just enough to cover her freckles. Around her neck she wears a silver chain that holds an emerald and silver shamrock-shaped charm, and glistening on her ears are small silver hoops.

Even Richard, the class clown, looks charming in his classic two-button black suit with an emerald-colored tie to match Jenny's shamrock.

"Richard," I tease. "You look very handsome."

Very out of character, he blushes.

"You guys look great too," he gushes sweetly. "But not as beautiful as my date."

I think that is the nicest thing I have ever heard Richard say.

"If you ladies would excuse us, we'll see you inside," the young man informs.

We hear music blaring as the double-doors open. A song by a popular group is on, and the few people who have arrived are all dancing. Jenny gives us a wink as the two disappear into the Grand Ballroom.

"Where is Mike?" Nicole sounds nervous. "Suppose he changed his mind? Suppose he decided to stand me up?"

"Nicole—"

"I can't believe he would do that to me after all of these years of friendship," she continues ranting.

"Nicole—"

"Men are pigs! No, they're rats! Wait… they're lower than rats! They're pond scum."

"Nicole!" I grab her by the shoulders to calm her down. "Mike is standing over by the koi pond, checking you out."

Frantically, she looks around, searching for her date. A huge grin spreads across her face as she sees him slowly sauntering over; in his hands is a clear, square plastic container. As he gets closer, it is obvious that it contains a white lotus blossom corsage.

Nicole's face lights up, not only because of the stunning flower but also because of the dashing teen wearing a dark grey pinstripe suit with a coordinating red tie. The pinstripes make him look extra tall. I have to admit it again, if I had not seen Andrew first, I would have definitely fallen for Mike. It is funny how the universe works.

"You look a-amazing, Nicole," he stutters, grinning. "So do you, Selena."

"Michael Taylor, Junior—*Love God* indeed," I poke.

"Is that for me?" Nicole asks, eyeing the lovely corsage.

Mike nods his head, but says nothing. With shaky fingers, he opens the container, removing the corsage and hands me the empty vessel. Carefully, he takes her hand in his and places the lotus blossom on her delicate wrist. Nicole takes his much larger hand and leads him to the ballroom.

"See you inside, Selena," Mike finally speaks, his voice sounding a little shaky. "Don't be too long, okay?"

"I'll be in soon," I give a playful wink.

♪♪♪

On pins and needles, I stand outside of the ballroom, contemplating my next move.

Should I stay or should I leave? I admonish myself. *I'm always the third wheel; I should have just stayed home. At least I could have gone swimming with Ligeia and Leukosia. That sounds pretty good right about now.*

Fifteen minutes pass before I muster enough nerve to enter the ballroom. Inside, it feels like you are in an underwater cave with sparkling fabric stalagmites hanging from the ceiling. Shimmering buttresses of blues, pale greens, and luminescent silver cascade overhead like the waves of the ocean. On the surrounding walls, patterns of light imitate the movement of moonlight dancing across a watery surface; causing the room to come alive with color.

It is breathtaking!

On both sides of the enormous space there are buffet tables laden with hors d'oeuvres of every kind, from deviled eggs and finger sandwiches to potato latkes with Creme Fraiche decorated with dollops of imported Beluga Caviar. Freshly baked fruit-filled pastries on platters with delicate meringues and miniature tarts cover another table toward the back of the room.

However, the most astonishing sight of all is the students; freed from their uniforms and clothed in the most beautiful and elegant of garbs: young women in satin and chiffon, young men in suits and ties.

All regal…

All extraordinary…

All of them getting along and having a wonderful time.

I spot Nicole and Mike first, standing near the appetizer tables. Mike carries two plates with an assortment of delicacies, with Nicole next to him collecting a variety of finger foods. They actually make a cute couple.

Jenny and Richard are sitting at a table near the dance floor, eating, drinking, and talking. Leaning in like she is divulging a secret, Jenny whispers in his ear, then Richard leaves the table and heads toward the bar area, probably to get her another drink. I cannot help but smile. Never in my wildest dreams would I have put those two together.

Holding back my disappointment at being jilted, I join them at the shared table. Both guys stand as I approach.

"Selena, we were wondering where you had disappeared to." Mike kisses me on the forehead. "Have I told you how beautiful you look tonight?"

"Yes, you have, thanks," I grin.

"Really, really great—" Richard adds, but is cut short as Jenny gives him an elbow to the ribcage, and true to his nature of being a clown, he pretends to double over in pain.

Looking around at all of the happy-go-lucky students dancing and having a good time makes me feel ill. Suddenly, all I can think of is escaping. Everything feels so alien. So loud. So bright. I feel a panic attack barreling down on me like a seven-ton truck.

"I need some air, you guys," I inform, placing one hand over my stomach to lay emphasis on my point.

"Do you need us to go with?" Jenny reaches for her black evening bag.

I try to give a genuine smile, but I cannot muster one.

"I'll be fine," I blatantly lie. "Be back in a few minutes."

♪♪♪

I have never walked so quickly in my life. As elegantly as I can in high heels, I weave between groups of chatting teen couples, laughing and pointing at students attending the dance stag. All around me, I pass athletes who are basically there for the food, teachers forced to chaperone, not to mention the prissy princess-types reapplying make-up on the stairs as if they are about to step out onto the red carpet. Me, I am just trying to get outside before I toss my cookies and embarrass myself. I am already the new kid; I definitely do not want to be the dweeb who threw up at homecoming on top of that.

Some things you just cannot come back from.

Luckily, I reach the balcony on the second floor without incident. Here I relish the fresh air accompanied by the muffled music coming up from the ballroom below without the droves of people and the prying eyes. Wholeheartedly, I appreciate the solitude that this space offers.

Inhaling deeply, the night's air fills me with contentment; the scent of hibiscus, along with the moonlight which gives the water below a soft radiance, eases my jitters.

"I knew I'd find you here." Andrew's voice startles me, making me jump.

"What are you doing out here?" I snap and then soften. "I mean, where's your date?"

He grins like Ando sometimes does; all teeth and narrowed eyes.

"I don't have a date," he admits humbly as he moves the hair out of his eyes. The sky-blue tie around his neck makes his emerald irises appear even more vibrant.

"Really?" I glance down, feigning irritation, holding back a grin as I admire my high heels and painted toenails that match my dress. "I didn't peg you for a solo act."

He chuckles with that raspy lilt to his voice that I like so much, but even that irritates me.

Feeling his gaze, I look up to see him studying me from the top of my head to the bottom of my shoes. The action makes me blush, but knowing he can make me so flustered bothers me even more.

"You are the most beautiful girl here," he compliments and I know he is being sincere. His admission makes me smile even though I do not want to.

"You are very handsome too," I manage to say without turning colors. "I love your tuxedo."

"Thanks, my dad let me borrow it. Why did I say that? Would it have killed me to let you think I had bought it?" He keeps speaking, unable to stop. "I'm such an idiot! No wonder you don't wanna go out with me. You're the only girl to ever make me this nervous. When I'm around you, I stick my foot in my mouth constantly."

His revelation stuns me into silence.

"Do you know that I actually practiced what I was going to say to you?" he confesses. "I can't believe I just admitted that to—"

"Stop," I whisper with a huge grin and he quiets. "You are the most incredible person I've ever met."

"Would you like to dance?" he manages to ask.

"Here?"

"Why not?" He grins roguishly.

"I don't think that's a good idea—"

"Damn it, woman!" he chuckles, pulling me close. "Dance with me."

The cologne he is wearing puts a spell on my senses, and I obediently wrap my arms around his neck.

"Just dance with me," he hums along to the ballad drifting up to where we dance.

"I'm sorry," I sniffle.

"For what?" Andrew shakes his head. "Being mean to me?"

"Yes," I murmur, completely ashamed.

"I'll forgive you if you keep dancing," he whispers back, his nose nestled in my hair. I realize he is inhaling my hair conditioner.

That knowledge makes me giggle.

"You're laughing at me."

He holds me tighter, but it does not hurt.

"Am I?" I joke, holding back a full-out laugh.

"Thank you," he says, maneuvering my chin with his hand so we are now eye to eye.

"For what?" I gulp, feeling his warm breath against my cheek.

"For just being you," he compliments with a sincerity that overwhelms my soul.

To my surprise, his head begins to lower as his lips graze mine. It is like a dream. A beautiful, incredible, romantic dream, right out of a fairytale, with the lapping waves in the distance and the music surrounding us.

It is better than anything...*ever*.

"Is it okay if I kiss you?" he asks with a smile.

"You better," I admonish, closing my eyes in anticipation.

Slowly, his head lowers and my entire body tenses as he—

"What the hell is going on?!" Amy's voice breaks the bubble around our perfect moment. *"Get your hands off of him, you bitch!"*

CHAPTER TWENTY-ONE

"A my!" I step away from Andrew, not sure what else to do.

"*You're a backstabbing whore!*" she shouts, taking a step toward me. Instinctively, I stand my ground, fists clenched tightly, just like David taught me. Andrew steps between us; his face has the same shocked look that mine does.

"Go away, Amy!" His words are stern and harsh. "I'm not your boyfriend, and regardless of what you think, I'll never be!"

"*She's* the reason why we're not together!" The teen hisses and takes two steps in my direction. This time, she is close enough for me to see her eyes. Just like before, when she had spoken with Miss Khan, her eyes are dark, full, and extremely scary.

"What's the matter with you?" I snap, taking another step back.

"You are!" she growls and lunges as I side-step, but she grabs my shoulders and our momentum sends us both over the balcony railing. Instinctively, I grab it and cling to it like a spider monkey for dear life; Amy gripping my bare ankles in terror.

Without thinking, Andrew immediately grabs my wrists and pulls with all of his might. Unfortunately, because of both of our weight plus the fact that the hem of Amy's gown is securely skewered to a projecting piece of iron, it is impossible for him to pull us up.

"Amy!" I shout. "Hold on! Andrew, get help!"

He nods, then runs to find help.

My brain is filtering through all of the possibilities of how this scenario could possibly end, and all of my versions end with death. That is definitely unacceptable.

Dear God! Don't let go!

"Selena! Help me!" Amy screams with desperation and terror as she tightens her grip on my legs.

"Help's on the way!" I insist, giving hope to us both. My mind is racing a million miles an hour as we continue to dangle.

Where is Andrew?

Suddenly, a thought comes to mind.

"Amy, I'm going to let go!"

"What?!" she bellows, already in tears. *"Are you freaking crazy? We'll drown!"*

"I won't let anything happen to you; I promise!"

"What are you going to do?" she whimpers on a strangled cry.

"I'm going to let go of the railing and we're both going to jump!"

"You are crazy!" she begins to truly cry.

"Listen to me, please," I beg. "I won't let anything happen to you."

Amy's hands are beginning to sweat; I can actually smell the saltiness of it. Her fingers loosen as they begin to slide down a little more with her body weight. The unnatural cloudiness in her eyes is gone, and although I do not know what is happening, at the moment I do not care.

Her hands slip again. The action makes both of us screech.

"I don't want to die, Selena! Don't let me die!"

"I won't!" I promise. "I want you to close your eyes."

Her eyes are wide with fright.

"The fall will kill us even if we miss the rocks!" she exclaims through falling tears.

Without speaking, I try to pull us back over the railing, ripping my mother's gown in the process. Well…maybe if I die, it is better than facing my mom. I cannot rationalize things right now. Somehow, I remember my aunts and who I am. I am the descendant of ancient bad-asses and their blood courses through my veins. Their courage pumps through me with every beat of my heart. Their power is mine.

"On the count of three, I'm going to let go," I warn, voice shaking uncontrollably. "Do you hear me, Amy?"

Looking down, Amy's eyes are closed and she is now bawling hysterically.

"Okay," she whimpers.

Taking a deep breath, I pray to whatever god is watching this messed up scene to protect me or at least let me into the afterlife just in case this does not go well.

"Are you ready?" I ask as calmly as possible.

She opens her eyes again and looks at me like I am stupid. *"Hell no!"*

I try my best to ignore her, concentrating on the task at hand.

"One…" I begin, "… two …" -*I'm so not ready*- "… th-three!"

Against our better judgement, we let go, and as we plummet, Amy flails and screams all the way down with eyes tightly shut.

Immediately, a millennia's worth of instinct and inbred experience takes over as I feel my breathing shift from lungs to gills. Holding my breath, I suppress the urge to scream when the webbing between my toes and fingers violently burst through my skin; instead, I simply try to focus on the rapidly approaching sea.

Everything seems to be moving in slow motion, even the air rushing over my excessively sensitive Sireny skin feels as if I am being slowly stabbed by thousands of tiny pins. Out of nowhere, the once tiny pinpricks now change into sharp piercing slashes that cut through my flesh like I am being filleted from the inside out. Utterly terrified, my concentration wanes, making me scream both in shock and pain at what is happening to me. As I glance down at myself, there, before my eyes, hard scales of shimmering blues, golds and greens are spreading across the surface of my appendages; shielding my human epidermis in preparation for the impact which is about to happen.

I guess I was not having an allergic reaction after all! I really am a fish!

The fall feels like an eternity: all in slow motion…all in high-definition.

I cannot breathe now as my lungs hibernate and my gills frantically search for oxygen, but to my relief, the surface is right below our feet. Instinctively, I grab Amy and curl into a ball like one of those pill bugs, avoiding danger.

Unbeknownst to me, my scales have accidentally torn her delicate skin and her arms and legs are all covered in thin scrapes, but I cannot worry about that right now. It is only then that the realization of my actions truly hits me as mind-numbing pain accompanied by the deafening sound as we crash through the water's surface, as fragile flesh meets the unforgiving fists of the sea.

Thank you, Father! I can breathe again! But unfortunately, Amy cannot.

Needing to shield her, I hug her form tightly to me, trying to fight the current with the extra weight while avoiding the knife-like edges of the rocks protecting the island. The sea is choppy and wild tonight, and I can feel my limbs getting heavier as my body tires. A scant trace of copper—not more than a wisp—assaults my nostrils and it is then that I realize I must have bumped into a protruding edge. As I watch, a gush of blood spews out of the large tear in my dress as we begin to float in a haze of red. That's when the pain hits me right below my ribcage, wracking every nerve ending in my side.

Please…don't let there be sharks!

My eyesight is a little blurry now due to the sudden blood loss and intense pain, but somehow my enhanced Siren-senses kick into overdrive. I am able to see microscopic sea life floating among the clumps of seaweed, hear the undertow as it pulls at our bodies, and even taste the extra brininess of the sea. If I was not so terrified, I would be totally elated to have these gifts. Unfortunately, I cannot focus on them even if my life depended on it, and right now, it does.

Then it happens…the one thing that I have dreaded through this entire ordeal: Amy opens her eyes.

With terror-filled eyes, she begins to hit me with all of her might as she kicks and swings her arms. Several times she even bites me, but fortunately, my scales are strong enough to protect me from her teeth.

Willing all of my remaining strength, I paddle toward the surface with Amy in tow. We break the barrier, allowing Amy to take a long and much needed breath. Using her temporary stillness to our advantage, I swim toward the marina lights; their illumination showing us the way to shore, but before we can make it, Amy turns on me again. This time her blow is to my temple, which makes me lose my grip on her. Dazed and unable to focus, I lose sight of her as she slips below the churning sea.

No, this can't be happening! Not after all that! I can't—

"Selena!" I hear David's voice bellow from the distance, accompanied by the low droning of a small outboard motor.

"Selena...Amy!" another voice calls out from the darkness.

Dear father! Is that Andrew?

Suddenly, there is a harsh light in my eyes. As it illuminates the area around me, I see Amy as she bursts through the surface, then vanishes once more like a bobber on a fishing line. Quickly, I swim to her, diving and wrapping an arm around her; pinning her arms firmly to her sides.

"They're over there!" Andrew shouts.

"I see them!" David shouts back as he speeds towards us in a small motorboat, and as he gets near us, he dives in, securing Amy and Andrew hauls her onboard.

"Selena!" I hear him calling for me, but I cannot answer due to exhaustion; all around is red coppery liquid swirling around me, blinding me.

Blood brings sharks, doesn't it? The thought teases me, but I am too tired to care. *Let them eat me. All of the little scavengers in the sea need to eat too, don't they?*

As I float down into the unseen depths, I hear that song: that old familiar tune that calls me to it. In the distance, I spot two blurry shapes racing toward me: one shape shines despite the darkness, the other seems to blend in a bit more, and although I cannot make out the figures clearly, I can see four shining orbs of aquamarine. Carefully, gentle hands lift me up toward the surface and the next thing I remember is opening my eyes. Staring down at me is David; hair drenched, breaths coming in short shallow pants, and his face covered with scratches.

"Hi, Daddy," I whisper, giving him a thankful smile.

"Hello, my baby," he responds, smiling back.

I close my eyes again and open them slowly. At last, they start to focus, but I wish they had not. I really do wish I was dead at the bottom of the Caribbean. Above me, wide-eyed and staring, are Nicole, Jenny, Mike, and Andrew.

♪♪♪

"David! I thought I'd lost you," Mom gasps, unable to stop hugging him and kissing his cheeks as they sit in the back of the ambulance talking with the police. Ligeia and Leukosia watch from a safe distance in the harbor, and although I cannot see them, I can feel their presence. Pre-programmed over millennia ago, we are drawn together to complete the missing parts of a whole.

"I guess he is acceptable for a *Human*," they chime simultaneously inside my head. I notice that David is grinning and his cheeks are turning color, and he seems unsure of what to say to the authorities. Apparently, he can hear them inside his mind, too.

"Do you think Amy will say something to the police?" Andrew asks as we all watch the lights of the ambulance carrying Amy disappear in the distance.

"Even if she did, who would believe her?" Mike answers, trying to reassure.

Unable to stop, Nicole hugs me for the third time in five minutes.

"Lucky thing your aunts and David were there to save you," Nicole adds.

"You saw my aunts?" I gulp, surprised they are not screaming or sprinting towards the hills.

They nod simultaneously.

"Why aren't you two freaking out?" I blurt exactly what I am thinking, which I seldom do.

"Would that make you feel better?" Jenny jabs, making me smile.

"Yes…maybe…I don't know," my frustration grows. "I thought Nicole might."

Nicole takes a deep breath as she sits next to me.

"When I was little, my grandfather would always take me to his favorite fishing spot, not too far from here," she points toward the huge stalagmite mass about two miles out in the harbor. "Grandpa had been fishing there since he was a child. He'd always tell stories of these gorgeous women with long flowing hair, who'd sun on the rocks, singing lovely songs that always made him cry."

The teen smiles at the memory.

"Of course, I never believed him," she whispers, so only Jenny and I can hear. "I just liked the idea."

"That's understandable," I state supportively.

"One morning, just as the sun was rising," Nicole continues. "We anchored our small fishing boat in the same area and casted our lines. Shortly after, I felt a strong tug at the end of my line. I called to my grandfather to help pull up my catch, but

388

he couldn't get to me fast enough. I ended up in the sea being pulled down by a massive swordfish…"

Her words trail off as she recounts the incident.

"What happened next?" I gulp, feeling my pulse quicken.

"I was holding my breath, trying to let go of the pole, but the fishing line had gotten wrapped around my legs."

"Holy crap, Nicole!" I gasp as I take her hand in mine; enjoying the heat she gives off, for my hands are still freezing.

"Finish the story," Jenny urges; eyes wide with suspense.

Obliging our friend, Nicole clears her throat before continuing, "Needless to say, I started panicking and taking in water. I knew I was going to die…right then…right there."

"Holy moly!" Jenny whispers, grabbing Nicole's other hand.

"Then I saw her long blonde hair with streaks of gold intertwined," Nicole smiles, her eyes welling with tears. "Her eyes were as aquamarine as the sea on a summer's day…aquamarine eyes just like *yours*."

Nicole touches my face with a shaking hand.

"My Aunt Leukosia saved your life?" I query, full of awe.

She only nods.

"What are they?" Jenny stares at me. "What are you?"

Jabbing her with my finger, I remind her that we are not alone.

"I'll tell you later."

Jenny looks out toward the sea, mouth hanging open in disbelief.

"Will they kill and eat us if we tell anyone?" Jenny wonders out loud, completely serious.

"No, you look like you'd be too tough to eat," I tease, looking her up and down.

Jenny laughs sarcastically, then becomes serious again.

"You're joking, right?" she interrogates with raised brows.

I nod.

"Mostly."

CHAPTER TWENTY-TWO

Every seat in the auditorium is filled. The Winter Concert is about to begin and my stomach keeps doing somersaults. Horrified, I take another cleansing breath, trying to gain my composure, but it does not help.

"Are you nervous?" Jenny peers around the curtains, hiding the entire Chorus class on stage.

"I think I'm going to throw-up," I gag, trying not to lose my dinner.

"You'll be fine," Nicole convinces, unsuccessfully. "Just picture everyone in the audience in their underwear."

I stare at her with a disgusted glare that makes her snicker.

"Then I really will be sick."

"We've heard you practicing for the last couple of weeks, and you sound amazing!" Nicole hugs me as she rolls her eyes. "Stop overreacting."

"I can't breathe," I gasp like a fish out of water.

Quickly, she grabs a tissue from her pocket and hands it to me.

"Pull yourself together," Nicole commands, her forehead furrowed deep in contemplation. "You're a gosh darn Siren, for goodness' sake!"

I frown at her cavalier attitude. This concert can go wrong in so many ways. The best I can hope for is that no one gets killed.

"That's why I'm so worried," I whisper as my lower intestines do a belly-flop.

Immediately, her features soften as she pulls several more tissues from the pocket of her Chorus dress. All of the female students look professional in their simple high-necked gowns, while their male counterparts appear debonair in matching black tuxes. If I was not so terrified, I would be grinning right now.

"Wipe off your forehead and just calm down," she orders in her motherly way. "The aria is perfect and you're perfect singing it."

I glance at her, trying to focus, but my eyes are blurry and unable to.

"Suppose something *Sireny* happens?"

"What do you mean?" Jenny's brow furrows with concern.

"I've never sung in front of so many people," I admit, lowering my voice to barely a whisper.

"And…?" Jenny states flatly.

"And suppose everyone in the audience loses their minds…or worse!"

"Think positively," Nicole scowls.

"I am thinking positively!" I huff on a loud exhale.

"Selena," Jenny interrupts. "You have the voice of an angel."

"What could go wrong?" Nicole adds optimistically.

"It's time, students," Miss Khan claps her hands to get our attention. "Take your places, please."

All of the students obediently race to their spots, some smiling with eagerness, others looking just as nauseous as me.

"Remember to enunciate… breathe from your diaphragm… Richard!" her attention shifts as she reprimands him. "Do I have to give you detention?!"

"No, ma'am," Richard instantly stops poking Jenny with his finger.

"Alright everyone," she gives an ecstatic smile. "Break a leg."

"Oh, my gravy," I mumble, trying again to control the pterodactyls dive-bombing my stomach.

Don't be sick! Don't be sick!

"Selena, you are going to ace this!" the energetic music teacher states in her soothing voice,

Solemnly, and with great effort, I nod in agreement, all the while singing the aria in my head. From the corner of my eye, I notice Mike making a funny face at me while Richard winks playfully, making me laugh. Just as distracting, Andrew waves from the bass section as the heavy red velvet curtain begins to rise.

"You've got this!" he mouths with an enthusiastic thumbs-up. I return a genuine smile that I can feel it in my toes.

I can do this! I know I can! and with that sentiment, I take another deep breath as the fabric barrier reaches its apex and the house lights fade just as the bright spotlights illuminate the stage and all of its performers.

Then my eyes focus directly on the hundreds of pairs of eyes watching us from off-stage; glistening and peering as tiny beads of perspiration stealthily glide over my heated face. My palms begin to sweat too, making me wipe them on the sides of my dress, and in my throat, I also feel the grapefruit-sized lump forming.

Will this nightmare ever end?

As I stand as still as possible, the musicians in the orchestra pit begin to play. Their metallic notes rise in an intimate allegro similar to tiny skylarks rising above the constructs of metal and concrete as they breach the heavens. Clashes of wood against animal skins stretched tight against frames of intricate machines are all aglow from overhead spotlights, even in the dark bowels of the pit. Strings strum as agile fingers pluck, creating a complex musical rendition, while mouths blow air into trumpets, flutes, and clarinets along with the one lone tuba droning in the background. All around me, the music slips and slides and wriggles and twists, contorts and meanders like a mountain stream slithers around a rocky path, until it joins the river, then next the sea.

Ahh! The sea! I longingly lament. *How I wish to be in the sea surrounded by the peaceful depths; surrounded by the currents that cause the coral beds to sway and prance as they brush against them.*

Just as we practiced, the other singers join the fray. Our voices lift up into the high ceilings of the auditorium where they entwine in a samba that fills my soul, releasing that inner need I want to control, but cannot. I close my eyes and wait for my cue, and then I open my mouth and sing.

There I am, high above the Earth with my wings outstretched, just like my aunts once did, as the moon shines on each slender feather. I feel its caress drift across my body. I understand my place in this world. In my vision, I sing to the purple mountains that almost touch the heavens, and whisper to the winds that race through the leafy branches that grace them. I chirp a gentle lullaby to each gosling sleeping in their homes of twigs and stems. I speak to every thistle and call to every dew-covered flower curled up beneath the starry skies, and they answer me.

I am not sure how much time has passed before the song disappears into the night, but when I finally open my misty eyes, every male in the room, big and small, tall and short, thin and heavy-set, old and young, are all gathered around the stage;

pushing against one another like a mosh-pit at some heavy metal concert.

Loud, bone-shattering screams fill the cavernous room. Masculine shouts accompanied by terrified feminine pleas rise up as people are being trampled, as the tidal wave of bodies rushes the stage. Chorus members join the chaos from down below, as the males in my class fight one another to get to where I stand. The girls, on the other hand, are being pushed off of the risers; their bodies thumping against the wooden stage planks as the battle forges on. Their deafening cries batter my ears, and my head begins to throb. All around me, people are screaming for help.

"Stop!" my voice booms like thunder as it climbs above the commotion, frightening me.

Everyone cowers and becomes silent.

"Move away from the stage!" I order without thought.

Slowly, but surely, the crowds of bruised bodies begin to recede, just like the ocean during low tide. I glance around the area, only to notice all of the female onlookers are staring at me, bewildered, wide-eyed and with even wider mouths. Then I see my mother and Ando standing, their aquamarine eyes locked on mine.

'*Selena,*' I hear Mom's voice inside of my head. '*Do what I do.*'

At that moment, my mother opens her mouth, releasing a string of cries and bellows, followed by a delicate stanza of melodious whimpers similar to doves cooing. She nods and I join in; mimicking her sounds quite proficiently. Next, my brother adds his small, childish voice until we blend and harmonize; repeating until everyone has returned to their seats, both men and women alike. Even the students on stage are docile and back in their previous locations.

All smiling…

All clapping…

All oblivious to the events that had preceded…all except for Miss Khan, her mother and Amy.

♪♪♪

"Selena," Nicole hugs me for the third time. "Your solo was magnificent!"

"It was?" I ask, filled with trepidation, hoping that whatever my mom, brother, and I did is still intact.

"Absolutely!" Jenny chimes in with a hearty snort.

"You nailed it!" Mike adds in his baritone.

Andrew is glowing.

"I'm speechless," he glowers with a blush.

"None of you remember anything strange happening during the concert?" I whisper.

They all shake their heads.

"Remind me to fill you all in later," I smirk.

As we chat, Amy appears at my side with hands on her hips, wearing a frown of epic proportion.

"What the hell was that?" she sneers, mouth curling up at each end into a snarl.

"Huh?" is all I can get out.

"What did you do?!" she accuses as we come toe to toe.

"I didn't do any—"

"I saw what happened!" She interrupts before I can finish my sentence.

"Saw what?" I rebut, trying to appear innocent.

"I know what you are!" she snarls, looking at me from head to toe.

"And what might that be?" Mike pipes up, his ire growing.

Jenny steps between us, pushing us gently away from each other.

"Okay, ladies," she commands like a referee. "Neutral corners please."

Amy pushes her hand away, but does not step forward again. I am pretty sure she is afraid of Jenny.

"You're a demon!" her voice rises and everyone turns to stare at her.

Andrew steps up to my defense.

"Amy," he soothes in his most gentle tone. "You're still recovering from the fall...remember the fall?"

"I'm fine!" she spits, blue eyes full of rage combined with fear.

"You're not making any sense," I respond, my temper flaring as well.

"Your little spell doesn't work on me," she states proudly. "I know the truth."

"Spell?" Andrew repeats. "Amy, you hit your head on a rock when you fell. The doctor at the hospital said you had a concussion. You were out of school for over a week."

"She is a monster!" Amy scowls, pointing a boney finger at me.

"You have lost your ever-loving mind," Richard chuckles.

"No," Amy shakes her head in denial. "I saw her...*It!*"

She looks more confused now.

"You were hallucinating," I respond, feeling a bit guilty.

"And tonight… " her words fade into a whisper.

"What about tonight?" Andrew asks, expression full of concern for the obviously distraught teenager.

"There was a riot," Amy begins to whimper then to weep. "She did something to the crowd…then she and her mother and brother…made them stop."

Miss Khan rushes to our group, face lined with uneasiness.

"Amy," our teacher touches her arm. "Let's find your dad."

Surprisingly, Amy pulls away from her too.

"And you!" she begins to sob uncontrollably. "I remember…I remember what you did to me!"

Everyone stares at Miss Khan with bewilderment and shock, but she remains as cool as a cucumber.

"Let's find your father," she repeats even softer than before, then leads Amy away toward her father, who is waiting near the bottom of the stage.

CHAPTER TWENTY-THREE

"**I** don't understand what's happening?" I ask my mother while we sit at the rocky shoreline watching Ando and the aunts frolicking in the waves. "Why does Amy remember what happened?"

Mom appears to be mulling over my question.

"When you and Amy fell, how did you survive the rocks?" she probes, looking up at the cloudless sky.

Embarrassed to admit what had happened that night, I stay quiet.

"Did you happen to sprout…*scales?*" she smiles ruefully.

My eyes open wide.

"How did you know that?" I question, cheeks turning bright red.

Mom laughs before revealing, "Our scales can be summoned with practice. They offer our bodies extra protection. During imminent danger or high-stress situations, they have a tendency to appear on their own."

"Terrific," I groan sadly.

"Amy saw you change, didn't she?"

I nod.

"I see." Mom frowns, but does not get upset.

"Our mind-control-thingy didn't work on her," I add, ready to divulge everything.

"Did she get cut by your scales?" Mom asks and I nod, and then she gives a low whistle. "The substance in our scales is made to protect us, too. It's sort of Siren medicine. It can be used on animals to heal them as well. Maybe when she got scratched by them, its healing properties intermingled with her blood, and now she is temporarily immune to our powers."

She shrugs indifferently.

"I'll ask the aunts," she says, more to herself than to me. "The effects will probably fade with time, I hope."

"She also remembers the concert," I reveal quietly so no one else hears.

Mom sighs before interjecting, "That may be a problem."

"What about Dorinda and Miss Khan?" I remind. "They were immune too."

"One thing at a time, my dear," Mom exhales her frustration. "One thing at a time."

♪♪♪

Just like every evening this week, the sea seems chilly, melancholy, and unnaturally still. There are no birds flying in from offshore. The palm fronds are hanging motionless. Even the lapping waves are barely audible.

Aunt Ligeia is listless and despondent, and has flown into fits of uncontrollable tears several times this week for no reason at all, as well as disappeared for days at a time. Aunt Leukosia, on the other hand, has only left the mangrove grove once to explore around the chain of islands, which is completely out of character for her. I do not recall hearing them sing this entire week, either.

"What's wrong?" I ask Ligeia as we lay on one of the stalagmite rocks in the harbor where Nicole's grandfather took her fishing as a little girl. "Why don't you sing anymore?"

"We are tired," they say together, and the sound of their unhappiness almost breaks my heart.

"Do you sleep?" I ask, curiosity taking hold.

"We do not need to sleep," again they speak as one, "but we have on occasion."

"You're scaring me," I whimper, feeling a tear escape. "You're not acting like yourselves."

"We miss the sea," they admit soulfully.

"But you're in the sea," I remind. "All of the time."

"We have not cared for the animals in a very long time," they announce in stereo.

"Then take care of them," I blurt, not understanding.

"We are two," they murmur, glancing in the direction of open water. "We are alone."

"Mom swims with you," I remind. "So do Ando and I."

"You belong to the sea," they both say with a hopeful lilt.

"I can't leave," I convey, feeling guilty.

"Come with me," they sing as one. *"Into the sea...in the ocean's waves we will play."*

"You want me to be the third?" I acknowledge at last.

They both nod.

"We once were Three," they sing. The sound breaks my heart.

"I know," my voice cracks with sadness.

"Parthenope," they say her name like a prayer, a soft prayer pregnant with longing.

Understanding hits me as I sit up.

"My grandmother?" I whisper. "You need my grandmother to be complete?"

They both nod and repeat, "We need to be *Three*."

♪♪♪

"Please, take care of them," Mom says to David, who is obviously distraught.

"Marina, don't leave," David holds her tightly. "We're a family, no matter what."

Tears stream down my mother's suntanned face, and her vivid eyes begin to glisten under their influence.

"I have no choice," she comments sadly. "My aunts need me right now."

"But we need you too," I remind, choking back my sobs. "We're your family. How do you expect us to live without you... here... every day? What makes you think that this is okay?"

"Selena, there must be a balance for the world to continue. Without me, Ligeia and Leukosia will cease their search for the third. I must do this in order to release you from your destiny.

The only honorable thing to do is take my rightful place among them...for now."

Ando suddenly breaks his silence.

"Mommy, don't leave me," he hugs her waist; moist circles appear on her green top.

Determined to keep her word, Mom smooths his hair, then kneels to look him in the eyes.

"Fernando, I won't be gone forever," she promises.

"I don't believe you," Ando murmurs.

Holding on to her composure, Mom closes her eyes, trying to find the right words.

"Remember when you were little, and you had gotten that really high fever?" she quizzes and my brother nods. "The doctor said that you had caught a virus, and it was making you sick, so we gave you antibiotics to make you feel better."

He nods again and wipes away his tears.

"Ligeia and Leukosia are sick," Mom informs meekly. "Actually, they are dying, and the only medicine that can save them is me."

My sobs are coming in uncontrollable waves now, hard and angry.

"Then let them die!" I blurt, not caring who hears. "Everything in nature dies; even the ancient gods knew when they were no longer a part of the world. Why shouldn't they suffer the same fate?"

Mom grabs my shoulder and holds me still; her eyes darken to sapphire, warning me that I have gone too far.

"Don't you ever say that again!" she hisses like a feral feline. "Do you understand?"

"Yes," I whimper, averting my gaze.

"Apologize!" my mother barks. "Now!"

"I'm sorry, Ligeia, Leukosia," I shamefully beg for forgiveness, knowing that I had no business saying what I had. "I didn't mean it."

They both nod, absolving me of my grievous mistake.

"*I kopéla échei díkio,*" Leukosia states in Greek, then clarifies in English which stuns me: "The girl is right, Marina."

Ligeia looks sadly from the water's edge, her features lined from hours of contemplation.

"There may be a solution," the Siren remarks flatly.

"What solution?" David asks, unafraid of her wrath, and she smiles at his newfound courage.

"Six months at sea with us… six months here with you all," Ligeia recommends.

Leukosia's eyes gleam as she nods in agreement.

"Like Persephone," Mom beams.

"Yes, Marina, just like Persephone," Leukosia clarifies. "You would straddle both the mortal world and ours, and you would be able to fulfill both of your destinies."

"Mom," I speak up. "I understand now about family and the obligations we have to them. In the few short weeks that I've spent with Ligeia and Leukosia, I am able to see the beauty of both worlds."

Mom studies me curiously.

"What are you hinting at?" she probes.

"You and Dad sacrifice so much for all of us, let me sacrifice something also," I state as I turn to my aunts. "Tia Ligeia, may I join you and learn about our lineage? After all, I am a part of you as well."

David steps forward, uneasy about the direction I am heading.

"Selena, what are you saying?"

"Let me go with them for three months during the summer," I offer. "That way, Mom only has to be away from you for three months."

"What about your life here?" David questions.

"I'd still have a life here," I grin.

He cringes.

"I don't know about this—"

"Selena would join us during her summer vacation and Marina could be with us during the winter," Ligeia recommends. "Ando could spend a week with us during the winter with Marina and a week with us during the summer with his sister. After all, he is a part of us, too."

My brother is smiling from ear to ear.

"Yes!" he beams. "Please, Mommy, let me come too!"

David is shaking his head, trying to make heads or tails of the entire supernatural predicament. After several silent minutes, he sits down on the rocks and rubs his temples. My mother sits beside him and rests her head on his shoulder.

"This is so unfair to you," Mom whispers. "I won't go if you—"

"No," David interrupts. "You need to go. I understand your loyalty to them; that's one of the things I love most about you."

"David could join you just like Theo joined Parthenope," Leukosia chimes into the conversation. "Maybe for a day at a time until you get accustomed to it. You all can join us…as a family.

David's face lights up.

"I'm a marine biologist, after all," he chuckles. "I would love studying the sea from a more up-close-and-personal approach."

I roll my eyes and grin at my nerdy science geek of a stepfather.

"How long do the children have off during their winter break?" Leukosia continues.

"Two weeks," Mom answers excitedly.

"And during the spring?" the aunt continues.

"A week," I inform, trying unsuccessfully to hold back my enthusiasm.

"Then it is settled," Ligeia proclaims, without further negotiations. "The Human will join his family, for it is his heritage now too."

They both smile at David, who is now blushing.

"Maybe he can grow a beard like Theo?" Leukosia inquires.

"Yes...a beard will cover up those homely features of his," Ligeia winks teasingly.

Glancing over my shoulder, I see it; the emerging glow of the sun as it begins to break through the darkness. Sluggishly, the pale light creeps over the Earth, sending night shadows fleeing back to their realm. Soon, we will witness the birth of a new day.

"Say goodbye to your family, Marina; it is time for us to go," Leukosia urges and points to the fast-approaching dawn. "Quickly!"

Mom turns to Ando first.

"Be good for Daddy, and remember to be respectful and obedient," she reminds, her eyes welling.

"I'll be good, I promise," Ando hugs her tightly as she covers his face with kisses.

"And no more sneaking off at night, okay?" her eyes flare.

My brother nods, blushing and fidgeting his feet and next, she turns to me.

"Help Dad with the chores and don't fall behind on your homework. Also, give Andrew another chance. It's obvious how he feels about you... how they all feel about you. Trust Nicole,

Jenny, and Mike; they are good people and even better friends, and most of all, don't turn your back on Amy. I don't trust her."

At her comment, my eyes narrow.

"I thought you wiped away her memories of what happened?" A new surge of panic begins to grow.

"Some people are strong-willed, like your father," Mom makes a face at David. "I don't think we've heard the last from her or her dad. Be careful."

I hug her, breathing in the scent of her hair; trying to retain its floral lilac fragrance in my memory.

"I'll be careful and I'll look after them," I smile and then Mom kisses me on both cheeks.

Lastly, Mom turns to David: the love of her life.

"And you…" we all hear the anguish in her voice. "What do I do without you?"

David swallows hard against his closing throat.

"Just don't be away for too long, *mi carina*," he purrs with a sultry Latin lilt; grabbing her up and kissing her passionately. The rest of us turn respectfully away as they share their last moment together.

"I'll be waiting for you," he reminds, lovingly touching her cheek with his palm.

Finally, my parents' part; their breaths come in short bursts. Shamelessly, Mom turns away and begins to disrobe while Ando and I cover our eyes. We hear a loud splash as she dives headfirst into the gently churning Caribbean. With a heavy heart, she waves at us, then disappears beneath the glassy surface.

Ligeia and Leukosia swim toward us, allowing our palms to touch. Ligeia motions for David to come closer to the edge, and cautiously he walks toward her. Carefully, she opens her hand, extending her palm towards him. David mirrors her actions, and they press their hands together in a gesture of forgiveness and acceptance. Leukosia smiles and repeats the same ritual and then blows him a kiss.

She's such a flirt!

In the blink of an eye, they are gone as well, leaving behind a trail of bubbles. Ando holds my hand as we silently walk back towards the carved stone steps. Feeling that emptiness once again, I wipe away the tears that have started anew. Quickly, I walk up the steep flight of steps, trying not to look back, but once at the top, I take one final glance.

It does not take long for the sun to begin peeking over the color-streaked horizon; crimson and gold identical to Ligeia's hair. The raven-colored canvas begins to give way to a warm yellow, and I begin to grasp the significance of the transformation.

In ancient times, nighttime was guided by the light of the moon goddess, Selene, but during the day, *The Three* would take her place. Even now, The Sirens still fulfill their duties. My mother, whose onyx tresses resemble the abyss of night, controls the mood of the seas. The crimson and striking gold represents the passion and fire of the transition between night and day, which Ligeia embodies so well, while the soft yellow that comes right before the entrance of the day exemplifies Leukosia's gentle nature and kindness which is freely given to all creatures.

Suddenly, I realize that all elements are balanced once again.

CHAPTER TWENTY-FOUR

It has been several months since Mom departed with the aunts on their own personal vision quest. The day after she left, our father gave up his apartment and moved back home to where he belongs. The family misses her, of course, but we know that wherever she is, she is well-protected and well-loved.

David and Ando have felt her absence the most, I think. They keep each other busy doing 'guy things' that usually deal with maintaining the vehicles or watching sports on television. Personally, I think they just use the sporting events as an excuse to stuff themselves with junk food and to be loud.

I, on the other hand, have become my stepfather's unofficial research assistant at Ocean World. So far, all I am allowed to do is log data into charts and feed the creatures in the tidal pools, but I do not mind the simple tasks. Although I do not get paid, it gives Dad and I time to spend together. Ando normally follows Dr. Khan around since she enjoys his company and insightful commentary.

The only thing I do not like about spending so much time at Ocean World is sometimes I run into Amy and her father. Most of the time, she ignores me, which is fine, but on a few occasions, I have had to make uncomfortable chitchat. One day in particular, I caught her staring at me like she was mentally dissecting me. It was unnerving to say the least.

Other than that, the rest of the school year has been calm, cool, and collected. Besides having a few little spats with Andrew over nonsensical things, everything has been wonderful. Sadly, I did withdraw from the Chorus class in order to avoid any complications due to Sireny side effects. Miss Khan was disappointed, but lets me visit her anytime I feel like it.

All in all, life is perfect.

♪♪♪

At last, the day we have been looking forward to since mid-December has arrived. Mom and the aunts will be here shortly to pick us up for our summer adventure. Everyone is excited to experience the oceans up close and personal, especially Dad, who has been talking almost nonstop about our upcoming trip since last week.

Right now, I am attempting to finish packing while my brother runs between his room and mine like a bunny hopped-up on sugar.

"Ando, hurry up!" I yell, trying to find my scrunchie. Finally, my little brother appears in the doorway holding his teddy bear and a couple of *Spiderman* comics.

"What about these?" Ando asks breathlessly. "Can I bring these?"

"Are you dense?" I reply meanly. "Where we're going, you can't bring your teddy because it will get ruined."

He crosses his eyes at me, then runs back to his room. Impatiently, I glance at the new waterproof watch that David bought for me; actually, he bought us all new watches for the trip. My head is spinning.

What do you pack for a trip like this?

In the middle of my internal banter, the phone rings, startling me.

"Hello!" I bark as I pace my room, confused about every aspect of my life so far.

"Hey, gorgeous," Andrew's voice comes through the receiver, deep and soothing, making me smile. "How's the packing going?"

"Terrible," I answer. "I don't know what I'm doing."

"Close your eyes," he laughs, then instructs me in a calm tone.

"I don't have time to—"

"I said…close those hypnotic eyes of yours."

Reluctantly, I close them.

"Okay, oh great Swami, they are closed and just to let you know…I feel ridiculous."

Still standing with my eyes tightly closed, I hear familiar giggling in the background. Immediately, I look up to see Nicole, Jenny, Mike, and Andrew wedged in the doorway of my room. Nicole and Jenny run up to me, throwing their arms around me, squeezing until I think I am going to faint. Mike lifts me up and kisses my cheek. Andrew, on the other hand, stays where he is and just smiles at me. His dimples make him look adorably innocent.

Mike looks at his watch.

"It's almost time for you to go," he says in that deep timbre of his.

Lost in our own thoughts, we walk silently downstairs. My father is waiting on the front porch holding his keys, and hands them to Andrew, who takes them without speaking. David pats him on the back as he gives a reassuring smile. The girls are holding Ando's hands, reluctant to let them go. Quietly and with solemn steps, they follow us across the front yard, around the side of the house, and down the narrow winding steps to the shoreline below.

It is a clear night. The purple heavens are adorned with shimmering jewel-like stars; a chilly, salt-kissed breeze blows in from the north.

"It's midnight," David informs. "It is time to do your magic."

Knowingly, I nod.

Just as I had seen my mother do, I take a seat cross-legged on the rocky ground. Ando joins me and we clasp hands. He smiles at me, letting me know that he is ready. Filled with expectation, I close my eyes and remember the day we arrived on the island.

I recall how the majestic mountains worshipped the sky; how the gentle Caribbean breeze boldly caressed my form, and the sounds of the waves beating against the land created its own ancient opus. Lastly, I remember Andrew and the new friends that I have made.

My soul begins to ache with both joy and sadness, and it takes all of these memories to create my Siren's Song.

Determined to get it right, I open my mouth and filter all of those emotions inward from my extremities, up through my heart and lungs, into my diaphragm, then finally out in an orchestra of sound. The melody comes to me from a distance, like an orchestra playing somewhere beyond the sea. Slowly, I open my eyes and see the girls holding Andrew and Mike away from the water, but I am compelled to continue my wordless aria.

Suddenly, the clouds begin to roll in from the sea and the wind begins to blow harder. I listen closely, trying to hear over the rising volume of the pounding waves. A few feet out in the sea, a golden-blonde head pops out of the water; followed by a crimson one, then lastly, a third head adorned with jet black curls cascading downward like tentacles.

Of course, Tia Leukosia speaks first.

"You are late," she chastises with a blinding smile.

Compelled to check, everyone glances at their watches.

"By only a minute," I say matter-of-factly, sticking out my tongue, which makes her chuckle.

"Just like your stubborn Yaya Parthenope," Ligeia winks playfully. She looks around at the motley group of students and says, "Oh, how wonderful! You are now sharing our moment with... *Humans?*"

Leukosia frowns at her sister's sarcasm, but then gives her opinion.

"Humans are notoriously gossipy!" Leukosia glances at the members of the group. "Suppose they tell our secret?"

"Well, the front-page article I put in the local newspaper won't be out for another few hours," Jenny mocks.

Ligeia, in true Ligeia-form, growls her disapproval and Mike takes a step backward; the girls contemplate doing the same. Andrew, however, steps forward, kneels at the edge of the rocks and holds his hand, palm open, toward Ligeia, just like I taught him. Speedily, Ligeia swims forward and touches her palm to his, making him jump. Leukosia delicately laughs, the melodious tones tickle our ears.

"Andrew the Noble...a fitting name," Mom says approvingly. "I hope these are the only other people who know about our double lives?"

She winks at the group.

"They are," I smile encouragingly.

My mother sticks her tongue out at me.

"Say goodbye to your friends, Selena." Leukosia hurries along the procession. "We have to catch the Antilles Current before it dies down."

Dad pauses with his head cocked to the side as he dares to interrogate.

"Won't the Antilles Current take us northward toward the United States?"

Ligeia rolls her eyes with an unnerved sigh.

"The fastest route to your destination is not always a straight line. Sometimes you must go the long way around to travel the shortest distance."

"Huh?" he frowns, confused.

"Off the coast of Virginia, we will catch the Gulf Stream, which will catapult us to the Mediterranean," she explains dryly, leaving Dad to scratch his head.

"Where are you heading?" Jenny dares to ask.

"To an island off the coast of Naples called Capri," Ligeia answers. "It is time that Ando and Selena see where it all began."

David clears his throat.

"And David, of course," *The Three* answer in unison.

"Come on, young ones," Ligeia almost sounds motherly. "It is time."

Not wanting to make us late, Nicole runs to me and gives me another tight hug.

"I already miss you," she admits sadly.

Mike is next. He hugs me tightly; his swim team jacket has the soothing scent of mozzarella and tomato sauce.

"Take care of yourself," he orders as he kisses my cheek.

Jenny playfully punches me in the arm; it hurts a little.

"Bring me back some souvenirs," she whispers in my ear.

Nicole pulls her away.

Andrew, on the other hand, does not move.

"I guess this is it," I announce nervously.

"I guess it is," he replies as he traces the ground with his size twelve-foot.

With heavy feet and an even heavier heart, I walk to him, wrapping my arms around his waist. As is his custom, he rests his chin on my shoulder and I hear as he inhales deeply. This always makes me smile. The sound of his heart beating makes a song of its own... sad and soulful. That is all it takes for tears to begin to well and clouding my vision.

"Oh geez, go ahead and kiss her already!" Jenny commands boldly.

Then, just like in the movies, Andrew pulls my body against his, and I feel his heat against me and close my eyes, and then we kiss. His lips are soft and full like delicate pillows as our mouths intertwine in a long-anticipated dance; slow, fast, then slow once more. I feel my knees buckle as my head suddenly begins to swim and I lose my balance, but to my surprise, Andrew holds us both steadily on solid ground.

The sound of David clearing his throat brings us both back to the present, and slowly, I take it all in.

Andrew looks a little dizzy and I am not surprised when Mom and Dad avert their gaze and attempt to be cool about my first real kiss. Being a boy who thinks girls are yucky, Ando wears a totally disgusted expression. Mike, on the other hand, is giving us two thumbs-up, while the girls are both grinning from ear to ear. Surprisingly, the aunts look rather intrigued by the process and are giggling and clacking at each other. To end our embarrassment, he kisses my left cheek and then my right and then my lips one last time.

"I'll wait for you," he declares reassuringly.

"You won't have to wait too long," I realize my arms are still around his waist. "We'll be back in three months."

"C'mon, let's go," Mom says firmly.

"Turn around," David instructs in his fatherly tone.

All three turn their backs as we get undressed. Only Mike turns back around to sneak a peek.

"You're wearing a wet suit?" he gasps with mock disappointment.

"Duh! I'm not going naked, you pervert!" I exclaim, making a face as he frowns. David and Ando are also wearing new wet suits. We figured—being novice Sirens and all—that some decorum should be shown. I wave, then jump in feet first, letting the sea engulf me. Ando does the same, followed closely by David, who lowers himself in carefully so not to damage his SCUBA gear. It is then I notice Ando is carrying a waterproof, blue and red *Spiderman* backpack.

"What is that?" I scoff with amusement.

"It's my necessities," Ando answers.

Mom stares at us both.

"Ando, what is in that bag?" she inquires.

"Double-stuffed Chocolate Oreos, Doritos, goldfish-shaped crackers, and some juice boxes," he replies. "I'm not eating fish and seaweed for the next two weeks."

The aunts grin at his determination.

"Alfredo is in it too," he grins impishly.

Ignoring him, I dive under. Ligeia takes my hand and guides me through the sea. Happily, I glance backward at Mom, who is swimming beside David; they are holding hands too. Ando is holding Leukosia around the neck, enjoying an underwater piggyback ride. Somehow, this all feels right; surrounded by everyone I love together as a family. For the very first time in months, I feel complete. I could not ask for anything more.

My name is Selena Antonius Thermopolis Marquez, and this is the beginning of *my* Siren Song.

THE END

(Not!)

ABOUT THE AUTHOR

Alisa K. Michaels, an American author and schoolteacher, lives with her husband in the South-Eastern United States. Michaels is a Rollins College Alumna having degrees both in English and Secondary Education.

She brings to her authorship her experiences growing up on a beautiful, tropical island paradise in the U.S. Virgin Islands before coming to the mainland in her youth. She draws from those experiences to create her fantastical vision.

Alisa K. Michaels is a proud mother of three grown daughters, and a closet monster named *Bucky*.

COMING SOON BY ALISA K. MICHAELS!

Aria

Book Two of The Siren Series